*"Before
thinking*

Terri confi...

"Seducing me would be like inviting a starving man to a banquet." Jeremy traced the soft fullness of her mouth with his thumb, yearning to kiss her.

"It's been six months since I've been held. That's what I miss most. When I'm around you, I think about how good it would feel to have you holding me tight."

"We shouldn't be having this conversation," Jeremy groaned. "It's not going to clear the air."

"Why does the air need to be cleared? What's wrong with our being attracted to each other?" Terri asked.

Her mouth was just inches away. Maybe if his life had depended on it, he could have kept himself from kissing her. "We're wrong for each other," he said, closing the distance.

Dear Reader,

September celebrates the onset of fall with a refreshing Special Edition lineup!

We begin this month with our THAT SPECIAL WOMAN! title. *The Secret Wife* by bestselling author Susan Mallery is book two in her TRIPLE TROUBLE miniseries and tells an uplifting tale about an estranged couple who renew their love. Look for the final installment of this engaging series in October.

Travel to the mountains of Wyoming with *Pale Rider* by Myrna Temte—a story about a lonesome cowboy who must show the ropes to a beautiful city girl, who captures his heart. Can she convince this hardened recluse that she loves him inside and out?

The sweet scent of romance catches these next heroes off guard in stories by two of our extraspecial writers! First, veteran author Carole Halston spins a delightful tale about a dad who's in the market for marriage but not love in *Mrs. Right*—book three of our FROM BUD TO BLOSSOM promotion series. And look what happens when a hard-driven city slicker slows down long enough to be charmed by a headstrong country gal in *All It Takes Is Family*, the next installment in Sharon De Vita's SILVER CREEK COUNTY series.

Finally, we round off the month with a story about the extraordinary measures a devoted dad will take for his infant son in *Bride for Hire* by *New York Times* bestselling author Patricia Hagan. And keep an eye out for *Beauty and the Groom*—a passionate reunion story by Lorraine Carroll.

I hope you enjoy each and every story to come!

Sincerely,

Tara Gavin,
Senior Editor

Please address questions and book requests to:
Silhouette Reader Service
U.S.: 3010 Walden Ave., P.O. Box 1325, Buffalo, NY 14269
Canadian: P.O. Box 609, Fort Erie, Ont. L2A 5X3

CAROLE HALSTON

MRS. RIGHT

Silhouette ®

SPECIAL ▼ EDITION ®

Published by Silhouette Books
America's Publisher of Contemporary Romance

If you purchased this book without a cover you should be aware
that this book is stolen property. It was reported as "unsold and
destroyed" to the publisher, and neither the author nor the
publisher has received any payment for this "stripped book."

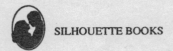

SILHOUETTE BOOKS

ISBN 0-373-24125-9

MRS. RIGHT

Copyright © 1997 by Carole Halston

All rights reserved. Except for use in any review, the reproduction
or utilization of this work in whole or in part in any form by any
electronic, mechanical or other means, now known or hereafter
invented, including xerography, photocopying and recording, or in
any information storage or retrieval system, is forbidden without
the written permission of the editorial office, Silhouette Books,
300 East 42nd Street, New York, NY 10017 U.S.A.

All characters in this book have no existence outside the imagination of
the author and have no relation whatsoever to anyone bearing the same
name or names. They are not even distantly inspired by any individual
known or unknown to the author, and all incidents are pure invention.

This edition published by arrangement with Harlequin Books S.A.

® and TM are trademarks of Harlequin Books S.A., used under license.
Trademarks indicated with ® are registered in the United States Patent
and Trademark Office, the Canadian Trade Marks Office and in other
countries.

Printed in U.S.A.

Books by Carole Halston

Silhouette Special Edition

Keys to Daniel's House #8
Collision Course #41
The Marriage Bonus #86
Summer Course in Love #115
A Hard Bargain #139
*Something Lost,
   Something Gained* #163
A Common Heritage #211
The Black Knight #223
Almost Heaven #253
Surprise Offense #291
Matched Pair #328
Honeymoon for One #356
The Baby Trap #388
High Bid #423
Intensive Care #461
Compromising Positions #500
Ben's Touch #543
Unfinished Business #567
Courage to Love #642
Yours, Mine and...Ours #682
The Pride of St. Charles Avenue #800
More Than He Bargained For #829
Bachelor Dad #915
A Self-Made Man #950
The Wrong Man...the Right Time #1089
Mrs. Right #1125

Silhouette Romance

Stand-In Bride #62
Love Legacy #83
Undercover Girl #152
Sunset in Paradise #208

Silhouette Books

To Mother with Love 1992
"Neighborly Affair"

CAROLE HALSTON

is a native of south Louisiana, where she lives with her husband, Monty, and two lazy, overweight cats named Pat and Mike in a rural area on the north shore of Lake Pontchartrain, near New Orleans. Her favorite pastime is reading, but she also gardens and plays tennis and is an amateur potter, a hobby that grew out of taking pottery lessons as research for a romance novel. She and Monty enjoy the excuse to travel to the various locations she uses as settings for her stories.

Dear Reader,

I hope that reading *Mrs. Right* leaves you with the same warm glow in your heart that I felt when I typed the words "The end." Never has bringing two characters together been more rewarding. Terri and Jeremy both are such likable, fine people, desperately in need of the healing power of the deep, abiding love between a man and a woman.

They're ready to settle for less—for affection and companionship. In Jeremy's case, he has known the eternal love between soul mates during a happy marriage to an adored wife. Somehow he has survived the tragedy of losing her, but he doesn't ever want to be so vulnerable again. In his mind "Mrs. Right" is a compatible helpmate and maternal stepmother for his two young children. Gorgeous, sexy Terri quickens his pulse, but he can't imagine her in the role of small-town matron.

Very soon in the story Terri knows for certain that she wants to be Jeremy's Mrs. Right, because he is exactly what she is looking for—a decent, faithful family man. Terri doesn't trust romantic love or expect to fall hard for a guy the way she'd unwisely fallen for her ex-husband.

Of course, she does fall hard for Jeremy and he falls for her. Terri is truly his Mrs. Right, the woman he loves deeply and passionately and who loves him in return. What a pleasure it was for me as an author to bring Jeremy and Terri together and guide them through the miracle of finding the perfect mate.

Carole Halston

Chapter One

Terri Sommers knew she was being oversensitive, but the word *bridesmaid* came to her ears from every direction as she sat, a space on either side of her, waiting for the wedding to begin. The major topic of conversation among the early arrivals at the church, decked out in their Sunday-go-to-meeting clothes, seemed to revolve around the question pricking like a thorn in her mind: Who had Pat Tyler asked to be her bridesmaids?

Or bride's attendants. Pat was twenty-nine. All Pat's old girlfriends were married or—as in Terri's case—had been married. If Pat hadn't been so universally well liked by all generations in Marion County, Arkansas, the old saying *Always a bridesmaid and never a bride* would have long since been applied to her.

In Terri's case, the saying would go, *Once a bride but never a bridesmaid.* How many times had she *not* been included in a female friend's wedding? Enough times that it shouldn't hurt so much. Especially since Terri understood the reason. Back in college it had been spelled out to her by an outspoken roommate who had gotten married and excluded Terri, too. "Once you walk down the aisle, no one's going to look at *me*," Lindsey had blurted out earnestly. "All eyes are going to be on Miss Arkansas. I'm not saying you'd deliberately upstage me. It's something you can't help."

"Maybe I shouldn't come to the wedding at all," Terri had suggested, unable to hide her wounded feelings.

"I want you to be there. In your best sackcloth dress."

In the end, Terri had gone. She'd worn a beige outfit. To her embarrassment, the photographer had followed her around at the reception, snapping pictures. Her friendship with Lindsey hadn't survived.

Today Terri wore a beige linen dress. Her only jewelry was a strand of pearls. She'd arrived early at the church and stationed herself on a pew near the aisle. Now she sat with a pleasant expression fixed on her face, ignoring the frequent admiring glances at her and hearing the word *bridesmaid* uttered repeatedly, until the voices formed a mocking chant, *Bridesmaid, bridesmaid, bridesmaid....*

She wanted to jump up and announce at large, *It really doesn't matter.* But it did matter. When Terri had heard the news that Pat Tyler was getting married and having a church wedding, she'd thought that Pat just might ask her to be one of her bridal attendants. Cute, tomboyish Pat had always been too popular, too brimming with personality, to be jealous of Terri, who'd progressed from child pageant princess to teenage beauty queen to contender for the Miss America title.

Back when they were in the elementary grades, Pat had invited Terri to her birthday parties when other little girls hadn't. During their high-school years, she'd included Terri in pajama parties, sat by her in class, greeted her in the hallway when the other girls were giving Terri the cold shoulder. Pat had never spoken the first catty remark to her or whispered behind her back. She was the one person among Terri's classmates who seemed to realize that Terri wasn't conceited about her looks, that she wasn't standoff-ish, but just shy and not confident enough to be outgoing and friendly.

Pat hadn't changed. When she was planning her wedding, she wouldn't have ruled Terri out because she was afraid of being upstaged. The explanation was simply that they hadn't kept in touch the past few years. Other women friends were higher on the list.

Goodness knows Terri had no burning desire to parade down a church aisle, holding a bouquet of flowers. With her background, she was overqualified for the role of bridesmaid. It would be like a concert pianist playing "Chopsticks" at a recital.

Plus she was too cynical about love and marriage to throw herself wholeheartedly into the whole wedding ritual. In modern times the symbolism had become empty and outdated. The white bridal gown stood for innocence and purity. More often than not these days, bride and groom had been living together. The wedding rings signified eternal love. Everyone knew the chances were good that the average young woman and young man would wear more than one gold band in their lifetimes. They would mouth the same vows again to different partners, promise to love and cherish someone else in sickness and health as long as they lived.

Terri was definitely better off being among the crush of wedding guests in the church rather than standing up front at the altar in full view. With no one noticing her, she wouldn't have to work so hard at concealing her pessimism, which was mixed with the pain of remembering her own marriage ceremony.

Still, she would have traded any one of her titles, including Miss Arkansas, for being one of Pat Tyler's attendants.

"Excuse me, are you saving this place?"

A pleasant male voice interrupted Terri's thoughts. She

glanced up and recognized the attractive sandy-haired, blue-eyed man standing in the aisle, waiting with a hopeful air for her answer. He owned a gas station in Yellville. Terri had encountered him a couple of months ago when she'd stopped to fill up her car shortly after moving back to her hometown in the Arkansas Ozarks.

"No, I'm not," she answered with a polite smile.

"Would you mind if I sat down by you?"

"Please feel free." Terri scooted over a few inches farther.

"There's plenty enough room," he protested, sitting next to her. "Are you sure you wouldn't rather take this spot by the aisle?"

"This spot is fine, thanks. I can see well from here." And not be conspicuously visible herself.

"By the way, I'm Jeremy Wells. You probably don't remember, but you bought gas at my service station here in town a while back." The ruddy color beneath his tan deepened at the reminder, and his tone was oddly embarrassed.

"I do remember," Terri said. She extended her hand. "It's nice to meet you, Jeremy. I'm Terri Sommers."

He clasped her hand in a gentle grip. Terri could feel calluses on his palm. Somehow the handshake was comforting, and she left her hand nestled in his a few extra seconds before she pulled away.

"You haven't been back since," he said. "I figured I'd probably offended you."

"Offended me? Because you weren't interested in hiring me as your station attendant?" Terri had noticed the Help Wanted sign in the window and inquired about the pay, knowing that she couldn't live forever on the money in her bank account. Eventually she would need to get a job. The less glamorous, the better.

Jeremy shook his head, his expression sheepish. "Because I gawked at you as if I'd never seen a beautiful woman before."

"As I recall, you were a gentleman. Actually, I've filled up my gas tank at your station a couple of times since then. You happened not to be there."

"I'm sorry I missed you." He sounded genuinely regretful.

I hope you'll come by again soon when I am there. Terri was expecting words to that effect, but surprisingly, he didn't say them. Perhaps more surprising was her slight disappointment. She hadn't thought she would welcome the attention of any man for a long time. But she liked Jeremy Wells.

Her own impressions of him reinforced the favorable remarks she'd heard around town during the weeks after she'd seen him that day at his gas station. He seemed like the decent, rock-solid family man he'd been described as. Apparently he'd adored the wife who'd died tragically more than two years ago, leaving him the sole parent of their little daughter and son. Despite his grief, he'd carried on, continuing to run his business successfully and do a good job of bringing up his children.

Jeremy Wells possessed none of the glib charm of Terri's ex-husband, Christopher Sommers. That was a big point in the station owner's favor. An even bigger point was the fact that after this length of time, he continued to wear his wedding ring. Terri had spotted the broad gold band on his left hand. It suggested that he was reluctant to let even death free him from his role of husband to the woman he'd loved devotedly.

Devoted. Faithful. Steady. Those were the character traits Terri would be looking for if she ever remarried. Traits that handsome, witty, urbane Christopher had lacked.

"If it's not being too inquisitive, have you come back to Yellville with the intention of making your home here?" Jeremy was asking. He added with a rueful smile of confession, "I happen to know the bare facts of your background because I was curious and made some inquiries about you after you came into the station. According to my source, a mutual friend of ours, when you left Marion County, you went off to the University of Arkansas at Fayetteville and from there to Little Rock, where you did TV commercials and magazine ads until you married.''

Terri nodded to indicate that his information was accurate. ''Who's the mutual friend?''

''Pat Tyler.''

Momentarily she'd forgotten about being left out of Pat's wedding. Now the sense of rejection swept back, stronger than before. It was an effort for her not to let a downhearted note creep in as she responded.

''Pat's a terrific person. I hope this ex-marine from Chicago she's marrying appreciates her.''

''Clint worships the ground she walks on. And vice versa. It was love at first sight for both of them.'' He smiled, looking amused and reminiscent. ''I don't know whether Pat has told you the story, but they met at my gas station on the very same day she and I caved under the pressure from the matchmakers in Marion County and agreed to start dating each other.''

''As a matter of fact, I haven't talked to Pat since I got back to town,'' Terri admitted. ''I was going to call her after I was settled. Then I heard she was getting married and knew she'd be busy planning a church wedding.''

''My daughter's responsible for Pat having a church wedding. Otherwise, she and Clint would have had the minister marry them without the fuss and expense.'' He went on when Terri silently encouraged him to continue. ''Mandy's biggest goal in life is being a flower girl. She cornered Pat one night when I'd invited her to supper at my house to get to know my children. Out of my hearing, Mandy swung a deal to be in Pat's wedding if and when she married, whoever the groom turned out to be.''

''So Pat is living up to her promise.''

''Right. And my daughter is in seventh heaven. Get ready for the flower girl performance of the century.''

''I can't wait.'' Terri was glad he'd sat down beside her

and given this insight into her old girlfriend's wedding. She felt enormously better, imagining little Mandy's excitement and putting the slight to herself in the background. "Is your son in the wedding, too?"

He showed surprise at the question that revealed she knew he had a second child. "As a matter of fact, he's the ring bearer. Poor little guy didn't sleep well last night for worrying about discharging his responsibility."

The blend of dry humor and fatherly affection in Jeremy's face and voice made him even more likable and appealing to Terri.

"How old is he?"

"Jerry's eight. Mandy's five." He shifted in his seat. "Sorry, I didn't mean to bore you with talk about my kids."

"I'm not bored," Terri replied. "I hope you'll introduce me to Jerry and Mandy at the reception."

"Sure thing."

His agreement came readily enough, but she could sense that he thought she was merely being polite. Terri could have told him that she'd intended to bypass the reception altogether and now was actually looking forward to it.

"Who are the adults taking part in Pat's wedding?" she asked.

"There aren't many. Old Homer Perkins, a lifetime friend of her dad's, is giving her away. Homer's daughter, Ethel, who has a fine singing voice, is singing a solo. The church organist, the minister. That's about it. Pat ruled out having bridesmaids because she's been a bridesmaid in so many friends' weddings that she couldn't possibly have included everyone, and she didn't want hurt feelings. As it happened, none of Clint's marine buddies could have made the wedding anyway."

Pat hadn't excluded Terri. None of her old girlfriends had been asked to be a bridal attendant.

The realization awoke a deep gladness that spread through Terri. For the first time in six months, since she'd learned about Christopher's affair and had faced up to the failure of her marriage, she felt almost lighthearted.

"I hate to interrupt, but could Fred and I squeeze past, Jeremy?" requested a stout woman standing in the aisle. "There's just barely enough room for the two of us on your pew."

Jeremy's glance along the pew was skeptical, but he rose to his feet courteously. "How are you, Melba? Fred."

Melba answered for both of them. "We're fine. I knew we should've come early, but Fred came dragging in late from his fishing trip."

Terri turned sideways, tucking her feet safely out of the way while the middle-aged couple pushed their way past. By the time they were seated farther down, everyone had been forced to slide either to the right or left and sit closer together. Jeremy's shoulder pressed against Terri's, and their thighs would have touched if he hadn't angled his knees toward the aisle.

"This is uncomfortable for you, being packed in like sardines," he said. "I should go stand in the back and make more room."

People had been streaming into the church during the past five or ten minutes, and all the pews were full.

"It's not that uncomfortable," she objected. "The wedding's about to begin, and the ceremony probably won't last long." In truth, Terri didn't find the physical proximity to him in the least unpleasant. She was getting a whiff of his shaving lotion and liked the masculine, woodsy scent. His shoulder felt solid and warm.

"You know, you're really a nice person." He had the good grace to look embarrassed as soon as he realized what he'd said. Obviously it was an unexpected discovery for her to be "a nice person."

"Thank you," Terri replied simply. "So are you."

The organist began to play, and the music hushed the many conversations in the church or at least reduced them to whispers. The sense of expectation that was already present swelled and became almost tangible. Smiles broke out on every face, including Terri's, as Mandy Wells made her entrance, wearing a frilly pastel-blue dress and carrying a basket of pink rose petals. Black curls bouncing and big brown eyes shining, she took mincing steps down the aisle, pausing to scatter the petals a few at a time.

"She's adorable," Terri breathed to Jeremy, who was beaming with fatherly pride. "She must resemble her mother."

Immediately Terri regretted the comment, which she hadn't intended to be thoughtless and cruel. Jeremy's grin faded. "Yes. I wish Susan could see her today...."

His tone was so bleak and sad that Terri's heart ached for him. "Perhaps she can," she murmured, touching his arm to offer him comfort. If only Christopher could have loved her the way Jeremy had loved his wife, Terri thought with a deep wistfulness that claimed part of the ache in her heart for herself. To this day Christopher declared his undying love, and she didn't doubt its existence, but it was a shallow, faithless emotion.

Mandy passed their pew, favoring her father with a smile and a dainty wave. With the poise of a little princess, she continued down the aisle, plainly reveling in being the center of attention. Reaching the raised platform at the front of the church, she sprinkled the remainder of the contents of her basket, turned and curtsied toward the rear, where Pat Tyler appeared on the arm of an elderly man half a foot shorter than her. He was dapper in his brown vested suit, his chest puffed out like a pouter pigeon.

Jeremy chuckled and said in a low voice to Terri, "I hope old Homer doesn't pop with his own self-importance. He's tickled pink to be in Pat's wedding."

Terri whispered back, "I could tell she didn't have to twist his arm. Pat looks lovely." The word *radiant* usually used to describe brides, truly applied to Terri's old girlfriend, who wore a calf-length white dress and a short veil.

"I see Clint won the hairstyle debate."

Evidently the groom had insisted that Pat forgo the req-
uisite trip to the beauty parlor for an elaborate hairdo. Her
glossy dark-brown hair was pulled back and caught in a
jaunty ponytail.

Terri smiled at the sight, delighted and filled again with
the sense of gladness that had flooded her when Jeremy had
revealed there wouldn't be any bridesmaids. The world was
a happier place somehow because Pat's wedding was so
right in every way. Trust her to plan her big day to make
as many people happy as possible and not to be in the least
concerned about impressing anyone.

The occasion Terri had dreaded and meant only to en-
dure had turned out to be uplifting at a time in her life
when she badly needed a boost of spirits. One of the nicest
parts was having Jeremy Wells sit next to her.

The groom had entered from a side door, and waited for
Pat at the foot of the aisle. It was easy to imagine him in
full-dress marine uniform. Even in a suit he was tall and
imposing as well as ruggedly good-looking, with dark-
brown hair and dark eyes. His expression was almost sol-
emn as he gazed at Pat approaching him, and somehow that
was right, too. A vision of Christopher in his morning coat
waiting for her with a confident smile appeared before Terri's eyes. She cleared away the memory with a little shake
of her head.

Pat had reached the foot of the aisle, where she embraced
Homer and he patted her on the back and addressed her
soon-to-be husband audibly. "You be good to her now or
you'll answer to me and everybody else in this here
church." There was a general round of applause in response and then titters of amusement as Homer whisked
out his handkerchief and wiped his brow on the way to
taking a seat on the front pew.

All traces of merriment disappeared during the song sung
by a rawboned woman with an untrained, but beautiful,
contralto voice. After the last note had died away, sniffles

and throat clearing could be heard. Terri's own throat had tightened with her emotion.

In the reverent hush that followed, the minister began the marriage ceremony. Terri sucked in a deep breath and focused with determination on the present. Recollections of herself as a bride would only make bitterness well up, and she didn't want to experience negative feelings now when Pat was embarking upon matrimony, undoubtedly with the highest hopes.

Beside her, Jeremy sat absolutely still. Glancing over, Terri saw that his hands were linked tightly, so tightly that his knuckles showed white. She raised her gaze to his face and had to stifle a sound of sympathy at the sight of the naked anguish in his expression. He was thinking about his wedding, she surmised, remembering the occasion when he and his bride, Susan, had spoken these same vows, never once suspecting that tragedy lay in their future.

Reaching over, Terri laid her hand on his briefly. He reacted with a reflex startled movement, like someone awakened from a trance or a nightmare, and looked over at her. "Are you okay?" she whispered.

Jeremy nodded and whispered back, "I'm fine. Thanks."

For long seconds they held eye contact. Terri read fervent gratitude mixed with frank male admiration, then guilt before he averted his head. Why guilt? she wondered, and was able to guess at the answer, watching him stroke the wide gold band on his left ring finger. Jeremy's faithfulness to Susan was so ingrained that he felt guilty responding to another woman.

The urge was strong once again to reach over and squeeze his hand. This time, though, it wasn't a totally unselfish urge. Terri would have been satisfying her own desire to touch him, to convey messages other than compassion. She restrained herself, clasping her hands firmly together.

It would be wise to take things slowly and get better acquainted with Jeremy Wells. Before she told him in any

kind of language, *I like you and find you very attractive,*
she needed to give him time to learn to like her in addition
to finding her physically attractive. For Terri wanted Jeremy to like her. Not just be dazzled by her looks.

"I now pronounce you man and wife," the minister declared, and addressed the groom, giving him permission to
kiss his bride.

The brief kiss was tender and possessive, yet sparked
with passion. Watching, Terri felt a wave of longing.

She missed the physical intimacy of marriage. She
missed being held and kissed. She missed making love. Not
just the sexual pleasure, but the emotional closeness, which
had soothed a great need in Terri to love and be loved
unconditionally. For the person she was inside.

*"What if I developed some sort of hormone imbalance
and put on a lot of weight? Or got disfigured in an accident? Would you divorce me?"* she had asked Christopher
one night on their honeymoon. Lying in his arms, she'd felt
confident enough to reveal her insecurity.

*"No, darling, I'd send you to the best medical expert in
the country or hire the top plastic surgeon in the world to
make you beautiful again,"* he'd answered without pause.

She'd bitten her lip hard against the ache of disappointment and hadn't persisted in the conversation. Words didn't
carry real assurance anyway, Terri knew. Actions did. In
time Christopher's actions had told her plainly that she was
one of the beautiful possessions that marked his success
and propped up his ego. He would no more have stayed
married to her if she'd gotten overweight or disfigured than
he would have driven his luxury cars with a scrape or a
dent.

"Are *you* okay?" Jeremy asked. His hand rested on her
back, communicating the concern in his low-pitched voice.

Terri had risen to her feet along with everyone else as
bride and groom turned to face the wedding guests and
headed arm in arm up the aisle. "Not really," she said with
bleak honesty.

"Is there anything I can do?"

Hold me. The unspoken reply unleashed a surge of yearning. It would be wonderful to be held close in Jeremy Wells's strong, but gentle, embrace. "I'll be fine, thanks. Look, here come your children." She focused on his blond, blue-eyed son and little brunette daughter, who completed the small wedding procession. The sight of them walking side by side brought a smile to Terri's lips. "You must be a very proud parent," she commented.

"I'm afraid I'm one of those typical fathers who bore people to death with stories about their kids."

His tone held a quiet resignation that Terri found puzzling.

I doubt I would be bored, she wanted to say to him, but she kept the words back, along with the thought that "typical" didn't strike her as a description that applied to Jeremy Wells.

The reception was in the meeting hall of a local civic organization. The hall was festooned with white crepe paper and decorated with papier-mâché doves liberally sprinkled with silver glitter. On a raised platform at one end, a bluegrass band played and sang a lively, toe-tapping number. The small dance floor already had several couples doing an energetic two-step when Terri entered.

She'd gotten separated from Jeremy outside the church when he joined his children and the three of them had been surrounded by a crowd of townspeople. Rather than push and shove her way to his side, Terri had stood back a few moments and then headed to her car. On the way she'd encountered several couples who were old high-school classmates. In response to their lukewarm greetings, she'd stopped to exchange pleasantries, all the while ignoring the gazes of the men drifting down her figure and pretending not to notice the barbed looks their wives directed at them.

It was all such old hat for Terri, so tiresome. She'd had enough complimentary attention from males and jealousy from females to last her a lifetime. *Please, God, don't let*

the bridegroom leer at me, she thought as she stood in line
to congratulate Pat and meet her new husband.

The prayer was granted, much to Terri's gratitude. When
Pat introduced her to Clint Adams, Terri might have been
twice her age and ugly as sin for all the interest he showed
in her as a woman.

With a glass of punch in her hand, Terri stationed herself
where she could keep a watch out for the personable gas
station owner and his children. They soon came through
the door. When Jeremy caught sight of her, she smiled and
waved. He waved back and herded young Jerry and little
Mandy toward her, not stopping to chat with those who
would have stopped him.

During those moments while she waited, all Terri's earlier positive reactions to Jeremy grew stronger. If she hadn't
known he was a widower, she'd have sized him up as a
husband and father in his early thirties. In guessing his
profession, she would have ruled out attorney or office ex-
ecutive, jobs that required him to dress every day in a suit
and tie. He was comfortable enough in his navy blazer and
gray slacks, which nicely emphasized a broad-shouldered,
solid build, but she could easily imagine him shedding the
clothes as soon as he got home and donning khaki slacks
and a short-sleeved shirt.

Without any knowledge of his source of livelihood, Terri
was sure she would have assumed he was successful, a
good provider. He had the bearing of a man with self-
esteem as opposed to ego. His summer tan was the kind
that came from mowing the lawn and taking his family on
outdoor excursions. He might drink a cold beer in front of
the TV while he was watching a football game or enjoy a
glass a wine with dinner out at a restaurant, but he wouldn't
be a habitual drinker any more than he would be hooked
on nicotine.

An engaging grin, clean-cut fair good looks, friendliness
tempered with a slight reserve that might be shyness all
added to Jeremy Wells's appeal. His brand of attractiveness

was totally different from Christopher's. Briefly Terri visualized her ex-husband, and felt the familiar pain like tentacles squeezing her heart.

She wasn't entirely over Christopher yet.

But then, Jeremy wasn't over his wife, either. In a way they were in the same boat, both needing to heal. Maybe she could help him and vice versa.

Chapter Two

"Daddy, I'm thirsty. Can I have some punch?" Mandy was asking as she and her father and brother came up to Terri.

"Sure, angel. After you say hello to Ms. Sommers." His reply was patient and loving, but firm. "Hi," he said to Terri. "I was hoping you hadn't decided to skip the reception."

"No, I wanted to meet Mandy and Jerry and tell them what a good job they did as flower girl and ring bearer in the wedding."

The little girl wriggled with delight at the praise, while young Jerry turned red with boyish embarrassment. Blond-haired and blue-eyed, with fair skin tanned to a golden brown from playing outdoors, he strongly resembled his dad.

Jeremy introduced his namesake first. Terri offered her hand to the eight-year-old boy as though he were an adult. He clasped it, blushing a deeper shade of crimson, and blurted, "You're as pretty as Dad said. No wonder you got named Miss Arkansas."

Some of the warm pleasure Terri was experiencing from the rough abrasion of his boy's callused hand faded. Apparently Jeremy had described her to his children en route to the church, and the emphasis, as usual, had been on her looks, not on how likable she was. "I'll return the compliment. You're as handsome up close as you are from a distance."

Mandy burst into giggles. "Jerry's not *handsome!* He's only a *boy!*"

Her brother scowled at her, but whatever scathing retort was on the tip of his tongue, he muttered it silently. An approving glance passed from father to son for the latter's restraint in a social situation.

"This is my daughter, Mandy, who doesn't like to be left out of any conversation," Jeremy said, ruffling her black curls.

"Daddy! You knocked my bow crooked!" cried the little girl in a tone of genuine dismay. She gazed up imploringly at Terri as though instinctively turning to her to remedy the damage.

"Let me straighten it for you," Terri said. "Jerry, would you hold my glass of punch, please?" After handing the punch to him, she squatted in front of Mandy and repinned the pale-blue satin bow. She took her time about the task because it was so thoroughly enjoyable; it awakened Terri's maternal nature. Mandy's hair was like silk, and her big brown eyes were fixed trustingly on Terri's face. The urge was strong to envelop her small body in a hug when she had finished, but she said simply, "There."

"Thank you," Mandy said sweetly. She reached and touched Terri's cheek with her fingertips. "You have pretty skin. And your eyes are the same color green as my grandma Ames's ring."

"The stone is jade," Jeremy put in.

Mandy's hand lifted to Terri's red-gold hair. "One of my dolls has beautiful hair like yours."

"No way," Jerry interjected scornfully to dispute the comparison. "Your doll's hair doesn't shine the way Ms. Sommers's does. Hers looks like it's on fire."

"Your brother's right, angel," Jeremy declared. "None of your dolls has hair quite that gorgeous."

"But I bet she loves them just as much anyway. My favorite doll when I was Mandy's age was partially bald." Smothering a sigh, Terri stood up, ringed by her admirers. "Now that we've gotten acquainted, doesn't anyone else want punch?" she asked, accepting her glass back from Jerry.

"I do," Mandy piped up right on cue. "I'm thirsty."

Her brother accompanied her to the nearest punch bowl, with their father staying behind to keep Terri company. She wasn't surprised that he didn't caution his children to locate a serving station where the recipe didn't include the addition of champagne or some other alcoholic beverage. Marion County was a dry county, and wedding receptions without alcohol were the norm.

From the laughter and buzz of conversation that blended with the music of the bluegrass band as the hall filled up, no one minded. A commotion on the dance floor drew Terri's and Jeremy's attention. He grinned, observing, "Old Homer's about to cut a rug with Pat."

"She looks so happy, doesn't she?"

"About the only thing that could make her happier would be having her parents here today. As you probably know, her mother passed away five or six years ago and her dad's been dead a little over a year." Jeremy's gaze had switched back to Terri.

"Yes, I do know. I guess the downside of having wonderful parents is losing them." All Terri could do was "guess," since she would never know from personal experience.

"Pat told me you were raised by your grandmother."

"Yes, my mother died in childbirth, and I never knew my father. He left Arkansas after my mother's funeral and never reestablished any contact. Apparently he'd been very closemouthed about his background. My grandmother couldn't tell me much of anything about him, not even what state he was from. Other than her description of him, I have no idea what he looked like, since I don't even have a picture."

"Something tragic must have happened to him, or once he recovered from his grief he would have come back," Jeremy said with certainty. "A father just doesn't abandon a child for twenty-odd years."

"Not a father like you. Or like Mr. Tyler, Pat's dad." Terri smiled a self-derogatory smile of confession. "I envied Pat when we were growing up because she was so popular, but I envied her most for having a daddy who would scoop her up in his arms, regardless of how smeared with dirt she was."

"Knowing Pat, I'll bet that was pretty often."

"It was. I remember one time in particular at the county fair. We were both probably about four. She did a belly flop in a big mud puddle and splashed muddy water on my pageant dress. My grandmother was fit to be tied. She hustled me off to the bathroom to clean me up before the pageant began. Mr. Tyler didn't even scold Pat. He swung her up on his shoulders in her filthy overalls. I won the pageant, by the way," Terri added, embarrassed by the revealing wistfulness in her voice. "My grandmother bought me cotton candy afterward. Don't get the wrong impression that I was mistreated as a child."

"People don't usually come back to hometowns where they were miserable children," Jeremy remarked.

"I hadn't planned to move back or I wouldn't have sold my grandmother's house when she died. That was shortsighted, but then, I hadn't figured on getting divorced."

"Then you *are* divorced, not just separated from your husband."

"I'm divorced," she confirmed. "After a four-month separation period. It took forever to get a court date scheduled because my ex-husband's an attorney and pulled strings to delay our appearance before a judge."

"Pat had told me you married a successful attorney." He hesitated before adding, "Being a man, I'm not surprised he wanted a reconciliation."

"Still wants a reconciliation. Christopher hasn't given up," Terri admitted frankly.

"Is that why you moved away from Little Rock?"

She nodded. "I wanted to get far enough away that he couldn't show up on my doorstep with a bouquet of roses."

"Why—" He broke off, making a face of apology for his inquisitiveness.

"Why did I divorce him? Because I discovered he played around on me."

"Played around? You have to be kidding." Sheer disbelief shone in his eyes. He'd been scrupulously keeping his gaze from dropping below the level of Terri's short string of pearls, but now he let it drop lower to the swell of her breasts and skim down farther over her slender, but lush, figure. "Sorry," he said, and she knew he was apologizing for the appreciative male inspection as well as his incredulous reaction. "I know this is a painful subject for you."

"Very. I don't usually go into this detail when I'm explaining my marital status." The reason she'd confided in him must be fairly obvious: she liked him and hoped to see more of him. Before he would ask her out, he would want to know that she was completely unattached and open to dating.

"Don't worry. I'll certainly keep what you've told me in confidence."

"Here, Dad. I brought you some punch."

Young Jerry's announcement interrupted the conversation. The children had returned.

"Thanks, son."

Mandy bore her almost empty glass in both hands, extended in front of her. "Look, Daddy. Look, Ms. Sommers. I didn't spill any punch on my dress."

"No, she spilled it on everybody she bumped into," Jerry said, rolling his eyes.

"They bumped into me!" The little girl carefully brought her glass to her lips and drained it. Then she eyed it with dismay. "I'm still thirsty."

"You can have mine, angel."

"Drink yours, Dad," Jerry instructed in a disgusted tone. "I'll go get her a refill." With another roll of his eyes, he took the glass from his sister and headed off again.

"He's being good to me because of you, Ms. Sommers," Mandy explained.

"Oh?"

A wise nod sent her black curls dancing. "He wants you to think he's a nice boy. And he isn't always. Sometimes he calls me names like 'Squirt.'"

"Hey, you're talking about your brother behind his back," Jeremy chided. "Aren't you on your best behavior, too, because you want Ms. Sommers to think you're a nice little girl?"

Mandy squirmed, put on the spot, and sneaked a hopeful glance at Terri that melted her heart. "I do think you're a sweet little girl," Terri said. "And I think Jerry's a very nice boy. It's no wonder your father is proud of you both."

"We're proud of him, too. Mrs. Grambly says he's a fine man and would make some lucky woman a wonderful husband."

"Mrs. Grambly is the woman who does housework for me. And a bigger fan than I realized," Jeremy put in quickly before Terri could respond. His sheepish look was easy to interpret. "Let's talk about something Ms. Sommers would find more interesting. She was on TV when she competed in the Miss America Pageant. Maybe she'll tell us what that was like."

"You were on TV, Ms. Sommers?" Mandy exclaimed.

Jerry walked up in time to overhear her. "No kidding, Ms. Sommers? What program?"

The spotlight was back on Terri, with Jeremy's son and daughter regarding her with the awe they might have shown a TV celebrity. Jeremy was every bit as attentive himself.

Fortunately, Mandy's attention span was short, and Terri didn't have to expound at any length on her on-camera experiences. In addition to the Miss America telecast, these included interviews during her stint as Miss Arkansas and commercials for cable stations in Little Rock between the time she'd left college and had married Christopher.

The cake-cutting ceremony took place. Although Terri didn't really want cake, she ate the piece that Jerry brought her. At one point she also accompanied Mandy to the rest room at the little girl's request. Bride and groom departed, and the guests began to leave, too.

Despite the moments that she'd felt as if she were under a microscope, an exotic human butterfly, Terri had enjoyed the reception. Enjoyed the company of Jeremy Wells and his delightful children. If he'd invited her to accompany them home for a visit or join them later for supper, she would have promptly accepted.

But no invitation was forthcoming. Father and son and daughter said their goodbyes with seeming regret that the time together was over but also with acceptance that good things end. They treated her like a glamorous personality they'd been privileged to meet.

"Maybe when school starts, you could come and talk to our class, Ms. Sommers," Jerry said. "Tell us about being on TV and almost winning Miss America."

"You could come talk to my class, too," Mandy chimed in. "I'll be in kindergarten."

"For the record, I didn't 'almost' win the title of Miss America," Terri replied. "I was eliminated after the first round. But I'd be happy to visit your classes next fall. Hopefully we'll see each other again before then." She let her smiling glance include Jeremy.

He didn't use the opening. "If you have car trouble or any other problem I can help you with, feel free to call on me," he said with the utmost sincerity. "Take care."

"You, too," she responded, and kept the smile plastered on her face as she waved and turned to walk away. Without looking back, she knew the three pairs of eyes were watching her. Admiringly.

"Daddy, are you going to take Ms. Sommers out on a date, like you did Miss Tyler?" Mandy inquired in the van.

"Don't be *stupid*." Jerry spoke up with scornful emphasis before Jeremy could answer. "Ms. Sommers isn't going to date Dad. She was Miss Arkansas and might have been Miss America if those dumb judges hadn't picked somebody else. I'll bet the one they picked wasn't nearly as pretty as her."

"It's hard to imagine anyone being any prettier, isn't it, son? Of course, there are other categories in the competition, like talent." What had been Terri's talent? Singing? Dancing? Acting?

"You aren't going to ask her on a date, are you, Dad?" For all his certainty that Terri was out of reach for his father, Jerry still wanted it from Jeremy's lips that she wasn't a potential replacement for his deceased mother. During the brief period that spring when Jeremy had taken Pat Tyler out on a few dates, his son had strongly objected, to the point of turning into a rude as well as unhappy boy.

Jeremy had tried to explain to him that his dad wouldn't ever love another woman the way he'd loved Susan, but he needed a wife, a companion, a helpmate, as much as Jerry and Mandy needed a loving stepmother. Jerry had argued strenuously that he and Mandy didn't need a stepmother. According to him, Mrs. Grambly, together with Jeremy, took care of their needs.

"Are you going to ask her out, Dad?" Jerry persisted.

"Probably not, son."

"Because she'd turn you down?"

"I'm not as positive as you seem to be that Ms. Sommers would turn me down. Not for the first date, anyway. But I have several factors to consider. The main ones are you and your sister. Any woman I date has to be a prospective wife and stepmother, not just someone for me to have fun with."

"You don't think Ms. Sommers would want to marry you and be our stepmother," Jerry concluded with a cheerfulness his father didn't share.

"Ms. Sommers has just ended a marriage. I doubt she'll be ready to consider remarrying for some time." There were other reservations he didn't spell out for his son. Terri had acknowledged that her husband hadn't wanted the divorce and was bent on winning her back. It wouldn't be the first time a divorced couple got back together. Even if Sommers's efforts proved to be futile, her stay in Yellville was surely temporary. By her own admission she'd fled Little Rock to escape her ex-husband's attentions and probably to heal her wounds. Eventually she would be drawn back to big-city life.

No, Terri Sommers wasn't a good prospect for the wife Jeremy needed. The stepmother Jerry and Mandy needed.

"I like Ms. Sommers a whole lot." Mandy invited herself into the conversation.

"Me, too," Jerry concurred. "I like it when she smiles at me."

Not half as much as your dad likes it when she smiles at him, Jeremy thought. Just looking at her was sheer pleasure. And her husky, sexy voice did things to him. Would she be interested in dating him?

There wasn't any point in wondering other than torturing himself.

At his house Jeremy went into his bedroom to change clothes. Standing inside the large walk-in closet, he hung his navy jacket on a hanger. A full six inches separated it from his camel-hair jacket. There was twice as much hanging space as he needed, since the closet had been designed for two people. Mrs. Grambly, bless her kind heart, had spread his wardrobe out after Susan's clothing had been removed, leaving empty drawers and racks and shelves.

That was two years and three months ago, and Jeremy still got a bleak, lonely feeling when he slid open the double pocket doors and didn't see Susan's dresses and other hanging outfits and shoes and handbags. Today was no exception, but, unbuttoning his shirt, he found himself thinking, *This closet probably wouldn't be big enough for my clothes and Terri's.*

No doubt she had a huge wardrobe that included a whole selection of evening gowns and cocktail dresses. Pat had said Terri's husband was a partner in a high-powered law firm, that he was ten or twelve years older than her and socially prominent in Little Rock.

"It won't be a problem you'll ever have to worry about," Jeremy said. His voice sounded glum to his own ears.

Wearing a cotton knit shirt open at the neck and a pair of jeans, and carrying socks and athletic shoes, he sat down on the edge of the queen-size bed in which he had slept alone since Susan's death. Her face smiled at him from photographs on the dresser and from the enlarged snapshot on his bedside table. Jeremy picked up the framed snapshot and gazed into his wife's expressive brown eyes, reading her emotions the day he'd taken the picture. Happiness. Love. Good humor. Susan had always been on the verge of laughing.

Of course there was no hint of reproach in her gaze because he'd enjoyed the company of another woman this afternoon. Just as there was no encouragement, no approval. Jeremy could no longer look to his dead wife for support, for advice. He was on his own. But he knew that she'd been a levelheaded, practical person, far less sentimental than he was. If she had died of a lingering illness, like cancer, she would have urged him to remarry. Instead she'd died instantly and unexpectedly when an aneurysm burst in her brain. There hadn't been any chance to discuss a future without her.

It would never be as happy a future now as it would have been with her. Jeremy accepted that fact. Susan had been the love of his life, and he would never adore another wife the way he'd adored her. But he would settle for affection. For companionship.

For compatible sex. Not only was Jeremy lonely, but he was tired of sleeping alone.

Jeremy recognized that he was one of those men who thrived on married life. He needed—he wanted—a wife. For him, dating was finding a wife. A stepmother for his kids.

So why had he sat next to Terri Sommers in the church today? Jeremy asked himself as he returned Susan's picture to the bedside table. Why had he hotfooted it to the reception, all eagerness, and stuck close to her, like a high-school boy with a crush on the homecoming queen?

Because he was a normal man as well as a father. If dating wasn't finding a wife, he would be on the phone in the next five minutes, getting Terri's number from information and calling her to ask her to go out with him. Just the thought of hearing her sexy voice made Jeremy's pulses quicken. It also awoke a sharp ache of dissatisfaction in his groin.

"Daddy, are you ready to go to the ballpark?" Mandy inquired at his bedroom door.

"As soon as I put my shoes on, I'll be ready, angel," Jeremy replied, back in tune with reality. "You and Jerry wait for me outside." Hurriedly he pulled on his socks.

As he tied his shoelaces, Jeremy's hands suddenly stilled, and he gazed for long seconds at his wedding band. Slowly he finished tying the laces, stood up and even more slowly grasped the ring and drew it off. For a moment he held the circle of gold in the palm of his right hand, his fingers closed tight around it. Then he walked over to the dresser and placed the ring inside the handsome walnut jewelry box that had been an anniversary present from Susan.

Jeremy's left hand felt naked. He glanced at it, noting the wide strip of white on his ring finger that contrasted with his tanned skin. Jamming the hand into his jeans pocket, he went to take his children to the ballpark.

Have you come back to Yellville with the intention of making your home here?

The question Jeremy had posed to her in the church played in Terri's mind as she drove through downtown Yellville on the way to her rented cottage in a modest neighborhood. All neighborhoods in Yellville, population roughly two thousand, could be generally described as modest, and downtown consisted of only a few square blocks of businesses located in primarily plain, one-story buildings. Even the historic courthouse lacked the ornamentation of courthouses in many small towns.

Did she plan to make her home permanently in Yellville? No, probably not. She'd fled Little Rock to put enough distance between her and Christopher, as she'd explained to Jeremy. Also, she'd wanted to get away somewhere and avoid constantly running into social acquaintances and well-intentioned friends. Avoid the attentions of men, both single and married, who'd treated the news of her separation from Christopher as an announcement that she was available.

In a sense, Terri was holed up in her hometown in the Ozarks, where her presence might create a few waves of curiosity but life would go on as normal around her.

Or at least that had been the situation in a nutshell before she'd attended Pat's wedding today, before she'd sat beside Jeremy on a pew and met his children. Why hadn't he expressed any interest in seeing her again? He'd certainly given every indication of being attracted to her and of enjoying her company at the reception, just as she'd enjoyed his company and Jerry's and Mandy's, as well.

Surely it had been apparent to him that her sole reason for lingering was to be with the three of them.

Maybe he would call her. If he didn't, Terri might just have to be more forward than she'd been today. She'd never asked a man out on a date, but there was a first time for everything.

She liked Jeremy Wells and wanted to get to know him better. She wanted to see more of his delightful children.

The gas gauge in Terri's car indicated an almost full tank. Yesterday, Friday, she'd filled up at a gas station in Mountain Home, a town located approximately twenty miles away with modern shopping facilities. The next time she needed to buy gas, she would make it her business to refuel at Jeremy's gas station.

When he was there.

Arriving at her cottage, Terri found a card from a florist in Mountain Home on the front door. More flowers from Christopher, she reflected, turning the card over and seeing a scrawled message from the deliveryman. By the time she'd deciphered it, her next-door neighbor had emerged from the house on the right-hand side, holding a big bouquet of deep-pink roses.

"I was hoping you'd get back before we left for the ballpark," Zelda Williams said. She was a short, plump woman in her sixties. "Frank's softball team has a game."

Terri had gotten acquainted with her neighbors on both sides and knew that Frank, Zelda's husband, coached Little League softball. The couple had moved to Yellville five years ago from Ohio, choosing to retire in the Ozarks.

"Thanks, Zelda." Terri took the vase of roses without enthusiasm.

"My pleasure. I told Frank, 'I would hate to give this bouquet up, but Terri will probably take it to the nursing home before the flowers wilt. I can enjoy it there, along with everyone else.' Your bouquets really brighten up the place," she added.

Zelda had mentioned during a prior conversation that she did volunteer work at the local nursing home. It hadn't occurred to Terri, though, that her neighbor was privy to the fact that she routinely delivered Christopher's flowers to the home—minus the card.

"I'm glad," Terri said.

If it wasn't for stirring up curiosity, she would remove the wand with the card and hand the roses back to Zelda to enjoy at her house until she went to the nursing home, at which time she could take them. Instead Terri decided she would take them herself a little later, after she'd changed.

"Well, I'd better run. Coach Frank's waiting on me."

"Thanks again." Terri unlocked her door and was about to step inside, when she stopped suddenly and called, "Oh, Zelda."

The other woman had already reached her yard. She turned around, a questioning expression on her face.

"What age group does Frank coach?" Terri asked.

"Ten-year-olds."

"I met a little boy today who's eight. Jerry Wells. He mentioned that he plays softball. The thought occurred just now that he might be on Frank's team."

"No, his dad coaches his team."

A horn honked, and Zelda waved and hurried on before Terri could question her further and find out whether all the teams had games scheduled tonight at the ballpark.

Maybe Jerry had a game, and that was the reason Jeremy hadn't invited her to visit them at their house and/or join them for a family supper that night. Possibly he'd assumed she wouldn't be interested in going out to the ballpark and cheering Jerry on. If so, he was wrong, even though sitting in bleachers with moms and dads of youngsters would be a novel experience for Terri. She hadn't gotten much of an opportunity to be a stepmom to Christopher's two children, Caitlin and Chris Junior.

After she'd gone inside the cottage and set down the bouquet of roses, Terri briefly considered the idea of going over to the ballpark on the chance of watching Jerry Wells play ball. The chance of having little Mandy come and sit beside her.

The chance of observing Jeremy in action as a coach.

There was nothing preventing her. Nothing except the old, ingrained shyness and fear of not fitting in, which her poise concealed so perfectly. She cringed at the thought of all the curious stares when she showed up. The lukewarm friendliness.

No, Terri needed an invitation to join any gathering in her hometown. Or at least she needed to be secure in the knowledge that her presence would be welcomed by someone there. Jeremy and his children might not be at the park.

Even if they were, she wasn't one hundred percent sure the three of them had fallen for her the way she'd fallen for them.

After she'd returned from delivering the roses to the nursing home, Terri phoned Christopher. He picked up on the second ring. His "Hello" managed to convey his polished manners and the male charm he exuded. She'd once been so susceptible to that charm, which he'd used to sweep her off her feet when she was twenty-three and he was thirty-five and recently divorced from his first wife.

"Hi, Christopher. I thought this might be a good time to catch you, before you went out for the evening. Please stop sending me flowers."

"Terri, *darling,* how wonderful to hear your voice. I was thinking about you when the phone rang. But then, I think about you constantly. Sweetheart, come on home. You've punished me enough. The affair with Gina meant nothing. *Nothing,* I swear. She was never any threat to you. You were my wife."

As opposed to his mistress.

"We've had this conversation a dozen times. I'm *not* punishing you. I divorced you because our expectations of marriage are different."

"But you've won, sweetheart."

"Won?" Terri asked, puzzled.

"Didn't you read the card with the roses?"

"No," she admitted. "I knew they were from you." And she was still vulnerable to his declarations of undying love, even knowing he'd been unfaithful to her, and not just with Gina. There'd been other affairs, too, she'd learned.

"I'll marry you this time without a prenuptial agreement. With the stipulation that you don't file for divorce for a five-year period. That's fair, don't you agree?"

Terri was too taken aback to answer immediately. "Christopher, you don't actually think that I divorced you as a ploy? To negotiate a better prenuptial agreement?"

His sigh came over the line, followed by a strained chuckle. "Okay, no stipulation. You drive a hard bargain, darling. I'm leaving myself wide open. You can take me to the cleaners, just as my first wife did, if I don't toe the line. That's got to tell you I'll do anything to get you back."

"I don't want a husband who has to be made to 'toe the line.' I want a man who's faithful to me because he takes his wedding vows as seriously as I do. A man I can trust." A picture rose in her mind of Jeremy Wells sitting next to her in church that day, stroking his wedding band, which he'd continued to wear after his wife had died.

"You haven't met someone, have you?" he asked, his voice hardening with suspicion.

"Actually, I have met someone who impresses me as being a very fine person. If he turns out to be interested in me, I'll date him."

"Of course he's interested in you. Does the sun rise in the east? What does the guy do for a living in Yellville, for God's sake?"

"He owns a gas station. He's a father with two children. A widower."

Christopher cursed softly. His voice held a resigned note as he pleaded, "Come back to me, Terri, and we'll talk about a baby, if being a mother is really that important to you."

"A baby isn't a bargaining chip!" Terri protested. "If you'd been faithful, I would have stuck with our marriage even though you didn't want us to have a child. It was partly my fault that I became your wife without ever discussing the subject of a family. I shouldn't have assumed that Caitlin and Chris would eventually have a half brother or sister." She sucked in a deep breath before she went on in a calmer voice, "The only reason I called, Christopher, was to ask you not to keep sending flowers. Please accept the fact that our marriage had problems that can't be solved. You'll be fine. You'll remarry and be happy."

"Those problems are only in your mind, Terri. At least move back to Little Rock so that I can see you. I'll pay your rent. Pay all your expenses, for that matter. Whatever my faults, I'm not a tightwad."

"You were always extremely generous, and you have many good traits. But I'm not moving back to Little Rock, and if I did, I wouldn't let you support me. Goodbye, Christopher. I'm going to hang up."

"It was heaven hearing your voice. Goodbye, darling," he got in quickly.

With a sigh of defeat, Terri cradled the phone. The call hadn't accomplished anything. He would continue to send flowers, continue what amounted to a second court-ship.

Why couldn't he see that the breakup of their marriage, though painful, was best for her *and* him in the long run? Even if he'd remained constant, she would ultimately have had to contend with not being fulfilled. The endless round of dinners out at fine restaurants, cocktail parties and gala fund-raising events with evenings at the theater and tennis and golf sandwiched in—it wasn't enough, not even with all the committee work for worthwhile causes.

Terri wanted something more out of life. More that was meaningful. And less that was superficial.

She wanted what Jeremy's wife had had—a home, children, a husband who was a family man.

Chapter Three

Jeremy didn't call.

On Thursday Terri drove to his gas station to buy gas. Pulling in off the street, she noticed a sign in the plate glass window that read Help Wanted—Attendant. She also glimpsed Jeremy inside.

Apparently he saw her, too, because he quickly emerged from the building and strode toward her car as she got out. His royal-blue short-sleeved knit shirt, unbuttoned at the throat and tucked into khaki slacks, turned his eyes a deeper shade of blue. He was as clean-cut and fit, as good-looking, as Terri remembered, his sandy hair made more blond by the contrast to his tanned skin.

"Hello, there," he said, smiling at her. "You're definitely my prettiest customer today."

His gaze had taken in her jeans and sleeveless blouse, but hadn't lingered on her breasts and hips.

Terri smiled back at him, reacting with pleasure to his

voice as she had to his wholesome masculinity. "Hi. I can get used to this red-carpet treatment."

"Regular?"

He was unscrewing the gas cap, obviously intending to pump her fuel.

"Either regular or the higher octane. I usually alternate."

"Not a bad idea. But your car engine probably runs fine on regular." He plunged the pump nozzle into the tank opening.

"Well, then I'll use regular and save myself some money."

"If you like, you can go inside," Jeremy offered. "Gasoline fumes aren't all that pleasant to inhale."

Terri wasn't minding the pungent scent of gasoline. "Out in the open like this, the fumes don't bother me much. How are Jerry and Mandy?"

"They're fine."

"They're such well-mannered children. I thoroughly enjoyed both of them last Saturday." And the company of their father.

"Don't be misled into thinking they're always that well mannered. They're normal kids. It's a rare day that I don't have to referee a dispute." He gave his head a good-natured shake.

"Are they at home with Mrs. Grambly today?"

Her question drew a surprised look from him. "Say, you have a good memory for names, don't you?"

"Not always. Mrs. Grambly's name came up quite a few times." Besides that, she remembered all the conversation with him and his children because she'd been totally focused on them.

"She's an important person in our household." A worried expression crossed his face. "I certainly hope nothing serious is wrong—" He broke off, not finishing the sentence. "To answer your question, Jerry and Mandy are at home with Mrs. Grambly this morning."

"What did you start to say?" Terri asked.

He looked at her as though doubtful that she could really be interested in what he'd been about to say. "Mrs. Grambly's daughter who lives in Texas has been having some health problems. She's going into the hospital next week for tests. If something serious is wrong, Mrs. Grambly will go and stay with her and look after the daughter's three children."

"Leaving you in the lurch."

"As should be the case. Family comes first."

His slight shrug called attention to shoulders that were broad and solid. As solid as his sense of values. Terri recalled the warm, secure sensation of sitting close beside him on the pew, their shoulders touching.

A click from the gas nozzle indicated that her tank was full. Jeremy replaced the nozzle in the pump housing with a vigorous masculine motion. "I'll check your oil," he said. "How about popping open the hood?"

"Thank you. I would appreciate that." Terri complied with his direction. "Don't be afraid you're setting a bad precedent," she remarked, watching him as he pulled out a long metal rod from the car engine. "I certainly won't expect this kind of service every time I come to buy gas."

"I don't mind giving service to customers when I'm here, but for a gas station this size, I can't justify a full-service row of pumps," he replied. "It's not cost effective these days, when the majority of people are accustomed to pumping their own gas for the sake of economy."

"I know I am," Terri said, hiding her disappointment that he hadn't used her opening to tell her she was a special customer and he'd be happy to give her special attention anytime.

"Really?" He slid the rod into place and glanced up at her dubiously. "I guess I assumed you weren't."

Which explained his rushing outside to wait on her.

"Do I seem inept?"

"No, not inept. Just too, well..." He faltered, looking

for the right word. "Beautiful to have to fill your own gas tank."

"I'm as self-sufficient as the next woman."

Jeremy was checking belts. "No offense intended. I'm sure I also factored in the information that your ex-husband is a successful attorney and you haven't had to worry about saving a few cents a gallon."

"No, I haven't," Terri admitted. "In fact, my ex-husband hates the whole concept of self-service. He'll go for miles out of his way to find a full-service island."

"Everything's fine under the hood." He closed it and let his hands rest on the white painted surface. Terri noticed for the first time that he'd removed his wedding ring since Saturday. Did the reason have anything to do with her? She hoped the answer was yes.

"What kind of car does he drive?" Jeremy put a slight emphasis on *he*.

Terri answered, giving the make and model of Christopher's current luxury automobile.

"Nice," he said.

She could sense he was holding back a comment. "But what?"

"More stereotyping. High-powered attorney with a beautiful wife he loves to show off. I would have expected him to buy you an automobile in the same class as his." He patted the hood of her car before he drew his hands away.

"He did." She named the sports car version of the same expensive make of car that Christopher drove. "From the last account, it's still parked in the four-car garage of our house. *His* house," she corrected herself.

"Waiting for you to return and claim it when you move back in?"

"That's the general idea. This car belonged to my great-aunt Evelyn. She can no longer drive, and she gave it to me. I believe I may have mentioned Saturday that she lives in a nursing home now."

"You did mention that."

Two other vehicles had pulled into the station, and the drivers were getting out, slamming doors. Terri retrieved her purse to go inside and pay him, wanting to continue the conversation.

They walked together toward the building, the one-inch heels of her sandals clicking on the concrete pavement. Saturday she'd worn high-heeled pumps, and the difference in her height and Jeremy's hadn't been as pronounced as it was today. Terri judged him to be a shade over six feet tall, to her five foot seven. She'd always favored tall men, but if Jeremy had been shorter, she didn't think it would have made a difference.

True, she found him physically attractive, but his big drawing points were his likable personality and his character. Did she have any drawing points with him, other than her looks? He was free with compliments about her beauty, but once again he wasn't making any overtures to indicate he wanted to ask her out.

"I see you've put up another Help Wanted sign," she said.

"Yes, I'm shorthanded again. The woman I hired a couple of months ago quit."

"She didn't like the job?"

"She liked it fine, but she patched things up with her husband, and he's working down in Florida."

They'd reached the plate glass door. Jeremy opened it for Terri to enter ahead of him. The phone was ringing. "Excuse me," he said, walking quickly behind the counter with the cash register to pick up the receiver.

Terri got out her credit card and waited while he conducted a short exchange with his caller, someone named Bob who was obviously a friend.

"Sorry for keeping you waiting," Jeremy apologized after he'd hung up.

"I'm not in a hurry."

"Your gas is $13.60." He took her credit card and began processing the payment into the cash register.

"I see you have one of those cash registers that does all

the work," Terri observed. "Scans the credit card and prints out the receipt for the card owner to sign."

"It practically eliminates human error. My son can operate it as well as any adult."

"Probably better than some adults. Jerry impressed me as being a brighter-than-average eight-year-old."

The register had ejected duplicate slips of Terri's gas purchase. "Have you dealt with children?" Jeremy asked as he laid the slips on the counter, aligning them one on top of the other.

"Very little," she admitted, taking the pen he handed her. "Christopher has a son and a daughter. They were eight and six when I married him, but his ex-wife had custody. His agreement with her was that he'd see his children without me around. Dana didn't want Caitlin and Chris Junior to get to know me as a stepmother."

"And your husband actually went along with her?"

"I think the arrangement suited him fine. It meant the children didn't come and stay for entire weekends at our house. He took them out somewhere for a few hours every other Saturday and entertained them. Mostly he took them shopping and spent money on them. Christopher isn't the kind of father you are." Terri signed her name on the top slip, amending her last sentence in her mind, to *Christopher isn't the kind of man you are.*

"In case you're wondering, the arrangement didn't suit me fine," she went on as she laid the pen down. "I wanted very much to be a stepmother." Wanted even more to be a mother.

"You and he didn't discuss all this before you married?"

"No, I just assumed his children would consider our home their second home. Just as I took it for granted that he would want a second family with me."

"He didn't."

"No."

"How old are Caitlin and Chris Junior now?"

"Fourteen and twelve. Christopher and I were married six years. I was twenty-three and he was thirty-five."

The drivers of the two other vehicles, both male, entered to pay for their gas. Terri stuck her credit card receipt into her purse and moved to one side. While she waited, she glanced around, taking a casual inventory of the merchandise and ignoring the admiring looks in her direction. Jeremy's gas station wasn't one of those new superstations with a large convenience store, but there were several aisles with candy and gum and chips and other snacks, plus a selection of motor oil and transmission fluid, a rack of magazines and a variety of additional items travelers might find of use.

Presumably the station attendant job included restocking shelves when he or she wasn't busy at the cash register. It was a bright, cheerful environment, with everything neat and clean.

Both customers exited, but in the meanwhile another vehicle had pulled into the station. In a matter of minutes, that driver would come inside to pay. And Terri's car was blocking one of Jeremy's pumps.

"Could I ask you a personal question?" she blurted, unwilling to leave without finding out where she stood with him.

"Sure."

"Are you dating someone?"

"No. Since my wife died, I've had a total of four dates, depending on your definition of a date. All with Pat Tyler. My kids were present on two of the occasions," he added.

"Then you're unattached."

"Completely." He sighed. "I should be dating since I want very much to remarry. I need a wife, and Jerry and Mandy need a stepmother.

Suddenly, Terri understood all too well. She swallowed hard. "And you don't see me as a good prospect."

"Unfortunately not. Would I like to date you if you would agree to go out with me? Of course I would. I could enjoy just looking at you, hearing your voice. But I can't picture you living in Yellville permanently. Or picture me uprooting my kids and raising them in a city environment. As for imagining being married to you..." He busied himself behind the counter, avoiding her gaze. "Frankly, that comes under the heading of male fantasy."

"Eventually I want to remarry, too. The kind of man I'll be looking for this time around will be a family man." Like him.

"I envy the guy," Jeremy said. "And wish you a lot of happiness."

The door opened, and the driver of the vehicle outside entered, greeting Jeremy by name. A disheartened Terri deliberated whether to wait out the latest interruption or just leave. She decided on the latter. After all, what was there left to say? In the most tactful way, Jeremy had made his position plain. He had no intention of dating her, because, based on a superficial acquaintance, he'd ruled her out as the type of woman who would make him a good wife and make his children a good stepmother.

The snap judgment hurt. But Terri wasn't going to change his estimation of her character by telling him she thought he was wrong. Jeremy had to discover for himself by getting to know her that she had more to offer than just the pleasure of looking at her.

To get to know her, he needed to date her.

Terri drew on her considerable experience in dealing with rejection as she put on a smile and made a graceful departure, waving to Jeremy as she went out the door. His expression and his voice conveyed regret as he bade her goodbye.

By the time she'd gotten into her car and started it, the customer was exiting. Terri glanced up and saw that Jeremy was gazing out at her. She also noticed the Help Wanted sign again. "No, he *doesn't* necessarily have to date me," she said in a tone full of resolve. "If Muhammad won't give the mountain a chance..."

After parking in a spot where she wouldn't block access to the gas pumps, Terri headed back inside the station. "While the coast is clear, I want to apply for the job as attendant," she explained before Jeremy had a chance to speak. "I was looking around earlier and thinking to myself that working here would be pleasant. If you're worried about training me and having me quit in a couple of months, like your last attendant, I'm willing to commit for at least a six-month period, which will take us through January, since it's the first week in August. The tourist season will be over by then."

He'd come from behind the counter. "You don't want a job as gas station attendant, Terri. There are more interesting ways for you to occupy yourself, even in Yellville."

"The object isn't 'occupying myself.' At the present time I have no income except interest on savings. It's not enough to pay my living expenses, so I'm dipping into principal."

"Surely you're getting alimony."

"Not a cent. I signed a prenuptial agreement freeing Christopher of any responsibility for supporting me in the event of separation or divorce."

Jeremy frowned. "He hasn't offered you any support voluntarily?"

"Only in the form of bribes to persuade me to move back to Little Rock. So I can use the salary you'll pay me."

"Terri, you're too...too—"

She cut him off. "Please don't tell I'm too 'beautiful' to work as your station attendant, Jeremy. Think of all those sexist ads for auto parts with female models in bikinis. In case you're in doubt, I'm also bright enough and competent enough. Honest and reliable, too."

"Of course I'm not in doubt, not in those areas." He sighed. "And business would probably pick up. Until all the wives and girlfriends put a stop to their husbands and boyfriends buying gas here."

"At any point where my employment causes you to lose

business, I'll train a replacement and quit," Terri replied. "That is, if I'm hired."

Jeremy lifted his shoulders in a shrug of defeat. "I'll take down the sign. When can you start?"

"If this outfit is okay as working attire, I can start immediately." She glanced down at herself. Jeremy's gaze ran over her, too.

"Your outfit's fine." He hesitated. "My female attendants usually wear a sort of jacket over their clothes. I had it made up by a uniform company. There's a stack of them in the storeroom. They're more practical than fashionable. And it's not a condition of the job that you wear one." He plainly questioned the notion of her choosing to wear the garment.

"Show me where they are."

Without any ado, Terri took the top jacket, slipped it on and snapped it down the front. It was red, with dark-blue lettering that spelled out the name of the station. To say it wasn't fashionable was the understatement of the century, but the dowdier the better.

Looking good had absolutely nothing to do with what Terri was setting out to prove.

"You don't have to stay and supervise, Jeremy, unless you're uneasy about leaving me to handle things by myself."

"No, I'm not uneasy," Jeremy denied. He glanced at his watch. "I should go."

Actually, it was past time to go home, and he had no legitimate reason to be running late. He was just having trouble making himself leave his place of business. Supervising had nothing to do with it. He'd stuck around purely and simply for the pleasure of gazing at Terri, of talking to her, of overhearing her exchanges with customers. Pleasure mixed with a certain amount of torment.

Even in the loose uniform jacket, she was incredibly gorgeous and sexy. Her voice, with its husky quality, caused a quiver inside Jeremy's belly. He longed to take the same liberty his small daughter had taken on Saturday and raise his hand to Terri's face, touch her creamy, smooth-textured skin. To curb the urge he'd kept flexing his hands, until Terri had finally noticed and asked whether his hands were bothering him.

You're bothering me, he'd wanted to say.

If she got bored with the job within a week, as he expected, Jeremy wouldn't hold her to the promise of sticking with it for six months. What kind of whim was behind her taking it, anyway? Was this a way of embarrassing her ex-husband, of making him feel cheap because he wasn't giving her any spousal support?

She hadn't applied for the job until after tactfully questioning Jeremy about his intentions regarding dating her. He'd laid his cards on the table and gotten no argument over the basic premise that she wasn't interested in settling down in Yellville and being a wife and stepmother. Nor had she tempted him to postpone looking for a wife while she was in town and at loose ends.

If she had, would Jeremy have stuck to his guns? He couldn't honestly say. But he did know he'd been more than a little disappointed over her easy acceptance of his rationale.

Terri gave every indication that she found him likable and pleasant to be around, but she wasn't suffering from the case of attraction that had Jeremy in its grips.

"Well, I'm off," he announced, and started for the door, his insight making him no less reluctant to go.

"Have a good evening. And say hi to Jerry and Mandy for me."

On the last word, the phone started to ring. Jeremy stopped. "That's probably one of them now. I'll wait and see."

Terri shook her head after she'd answered the call, stating the name of his gas station. She covered the mouthpiece. "Bob Peterson."

Jeremy hit his forehead with his palm as he uttered, "Damn! I completely forgot about calling him back." He returned to the counter, his hand extended for the phone.

"Who's the female with the sexy voice?" the man on the other end of the line asked before Jeremy could get in his apology.

"My new attendant I hired today. Look, Bob, could I put you off again until this evening? I was on my way home to relieve Mrs. Grambly."

"We won't be home tonight, and Shirley has phoned me twice today to ask if you're on for Saturday night. She's dying for you to meet Jennifer Larkins. Whether you two strike a spark or not, it should be a nice, relaxed evening at our house. I'll throw some steaks on the grill. Shirley's planning to serve her twice-baked potatoes that you like so much. What else do you have going Saturday night?"

Jeremy eased out a sigh. "Nothing much. Okay. If I can get a sitter lined up."

"Come at seven."

"Am I bringing Jennifer?"

"No, she's driving herself." Bob chuckled and confessed, "Shirley had to twist her arm, too."

Jeremy had carried on the conversation standing in front of the counter. He gave the phone back to Terri after Bob had hung up.

"I couldn't help overhearing," she said. "What night did you need a sitter?"

"Saturday. Bob and his wife, Shirley, have invited me and Jennifer Larkins, a new schoolteacher in town, to dinner at their house. A matchmaking attempt on their part."

"You've met her?"

"No."

"So that's why you don't seem very enthusiastic. Blind dates are awkward."

Jeremy nodded, feeling slightly dishonest. He could have told her that spending the major portion of the day with her hadn't helped to kindle enthusiasm for the idea of dating any other woman. "I'd better go," he said, heading for the door again.

"Yes, you had," she agreed. "By the way, I don't have plans for Saturday night. I'd love to be your sitter, free of charge."

"Even this late in the week, I can probably hire a high-school girl who lives in the neighborhood."

"Please don't. I'll look forward to seeing Jerry and Mandy again. With your permission, I'll suggest taking them to Mountain Home for pizza."

"They would really enjoy that, I'm sure."

And their father will be envious as hell, Jeremy thought as he strode with long steps out to his van.

Chapter Four

Terri wasn't expecting the Wells residence to be an architect-designed house. She experienced a moment's disappointment at the first sight of the handsome brick exterior softened by an abundance of tall, graceful windows. Then she noticed how the informal landscaping created a homey air. But it was the unmistakable evidence that children played in the yard that brought a relieved smile to her face—a colorful kite lodged in the branches of a tree, a pink bicycle parked near the garage, a soccer ball half-hidden under a shrub.

Jeremy's house was a home for a family, not a small-town showplace on a lesser scale than Christopher's elegant five-bedroom house on an estate-size lot.

The front door swung open before she could ring the doorbell. Mandy and Jerry Wells greeted her in chorus, excitement in their young voices.

"Hi, Ms. Sommers!"

Evidently they'd been keeping a watch out.

Behind them stood Jeremy. He looked showered and shaved and handsome in a short-sleeved plaid shirt and navy blue slacks. Terri's pulse quickened with female appreciation. The thought that his date, Jennifer Larkins, would react similarly dimmed some of the warm pleasure at the reception by father and son and daughter.

"You can leave now, Daddy," Mandy said. The little girl had nestled her hand inside Terri's.

"Yeah, Dad. Go out on your date with that schoolteacher." Jerry added his permission, but in a glum tone.

"Jerry doesn't like Daddy to go on dates," Mandy explained cheerfully. "But I don't mind at all. Come on, Ms. Sommers, I want to show you my room. I've already given my daddy a good-night hug and kiss." She tugged at Terri's hand.

"Have a good time," Terri said to Jeremy as she followed along. "And you don't have a curfew."

"I won't be any later than eleven or eleven-thirty. Thanks a lot, Terri," he added, sounding almost as glum as his son.

Being the kind of father he was, Jeremy would be bothered greatly by his son's strong opposition to his going out on a date. At the root of that opposition, of course, was Jerry's resistance to the idea of another woman replacing his mom, Terri reflected with a pang of sympathy for both father and son.

The route to Mandy's bedroom provided glimpses into a living room and dining room that were as cozy and inviting as they were attractively furnished and decorated. Susan Wells had created the kind of home environment Terri admired, combining comfort and aesthetics. Jeremy's wife had apparently been superwife, supermom and superhomemaker, all rolled into one.

A hard act to follow for his next wife.

"Jerry's room is across from mine. My daddy's room is down there." Mandy pointed out the locations before leading Terri into her own dainty pink-and-white bedroom.

"How pretty!" Terri exclaimed in appreciation.

"Thank you. If you want, you can sit on my bed, and I'll tell you the names of my dolls."

But Terri's eyes had sought out a five-by-seven framed photograph of a pretty brunette on the top of a chest of drawers. "This must be your mother," she said, walking over for a closer look.

"Her name was Susan. Mrs. Grambly says I'm going to be my mommy's spitting image when I grow up."

"Mrs. Grambly's right. I'll bet you inherited your mommy's personality, too." The camera had captured Susan's vivacious, happy nature. No wonder Jeremy had adored his wife. Terri knew just from gazing a few seconds at her picture that she would have liked Susan Wells and wanted her for a friend.

"Would you like to see more pictures of my mommy?" Mandy inquired. "Some of them are with her and my daddy, like their wedding picture. He just moved them from his room into the guest bedroom. Come on. I'll show you." The little girl took a step, beckoning for Terri to follow her.

"Why don't you show me your dolls, instead?" Terri quickly suggested. "Which one has hair like mine?" It was easier to sidetrack the little girl than to try to explain that Mandy's father might not want his employee and volunteer sitter roaming throughout his entire house.

"Oh, that's Sarah."

The revelation that Jeremy had "just moved" the photographs of his deceased wife out of his bedroom occupied part of Terri's thoughts as she perched on Mandy's bed and responded to the introduction to each doll. His taking that action was significant, like his finally removing his wedding ring. Both actions indicated he was serious about remarrying. In that frame of mind, he would spend the evening with Jennifer Larkins, the schoolteacher, a woman his friends, the Petersons, obviously liked and approved of.

Tonight might be the beginning of a meaningful relationship for Jeremy that would lead to the marriage he wanted. It was selfish and wrong of Terri to have her fingers mentally crossed that Jennifer *didn't* turn out to be the perfect candidate for the second Mrs. Jeremy Wells.

But would another six months make that much difference? Before he got involved with another woman, Terri wanted a chance to prove to Jeremy that he'd misjudged her. It was important that he come to like her for herself, value her as an employee, credit her with having some depth as a person.

During that time period Terri might set her sights on being Jeremy's Mrs. Right. After a few more months, she could judge better whether she would be happy settling down permanently in her hometown.

Jeremy was exactly the kind of man she wanted in a husband. The fact that he had two wonderful children was a big plus.

"Dad left to go to Mr. and Mrs. Peterson's house." Jerry made the morose announcement from the door of Mandy's bedroom. "I don't know why he didn't just call them up and say he wasn't coming. He admitted he'd rather go and have pizza with us, instead."

Did *us* include her? Terri wondered as she gave the correct reply of an adult, "You can't cancel a dinner engagement at the last minute without a legitimate reason, Jerry. It's not polite or fair to your host and hostess."

"That's what Dad said." He sighed. "I hope that school-teacher is fat and ugly and has bad breath like Miss Appleton, who teaches third grade."

"That's kind of a mean thing to hope, isn't it?" The words of admonition were for herself as well as Jeremy's young son.

"Jerry didn't even like Miss Tyler when he thought Daddy might marry her," Mandy spoke up.

"I did so like her."

"Then why were you rude?"

"You're too little and dumb to understand. All you could

think about was being a flower girl if she and Dad got married.''

"Did you hear him calling me 'dumb,' Ms. Sommers?" Mandy demanded. "I told you he wasn't always a nice boy."

"I would be interested in your answer, Jerry," Terri said gently. "Why were you rude to Miss Tyler, when you actually liked her?"

"Because Mandy and I don't need a stepmother. Mrs. Grambly takes good care of us when Dad's working."

"What about your dad's needs? He married your mother because he wanted a companion, someone to share his life with."

"He still has Mandy and me. We do things with him." Jerry dug in his pocket and pulled out paper money. "Dad gave me this money to pay for supper."

In other words, end of discussion.

Terri didn't persist, reflecting that perhaps she'd given the young boy some food for thought. "Supper is my treat," she said. "Why don't you put the money somewhere safe and give it back to your dad tomorrow morning?"

He nodded, immediately agreeable. "Sure, Ms. Sommers. I'll put it in my room."

"Then let's head for Mountain Home and find a pizza restaurant."

The suggestion met with eager responses. Jerry's downcast air disappeared, and he seemed to have pushed the whole troubling matter of his father's date to the back of his mind.

"Can I ride in the front seat by you, Ms. Sommers?" Mandy asked sweetly when the three of them trooped outside to Terri's car.

"She's trying to pull a fast one, Ms. Sommers," Jerry was quick to put in, glaring at his sister. "Dad settled the argument before you got to our house. She gets to ride in the front seat on the way to Mountain Home, and I sit up front with you on the way back home. If it's all right." He shrugged. "Unless you would rather Mandy sit by you."

Terri smiled at him. "I'll enjoy having the two of you take turns in the front seat."

He smiled back shyly, blushing to the roots of his blond hair. "It's good in one way that Dad's not coming along, because Mandy and me both would be stuck in the back seat."

"If Daddy was with us, we would go in our van and he would drive, like when we went to Miss Tyler's house and picked her up and she sat by him." Mandy joined the conversation.

"That was different," Jerry objected, frowning at his sister. "Dad was dating Miss Tyler. He's not dating Ms. Sommers."

Thus a foursome including her wasn't objectionable.

Jeremy's son didn't see Terri as a potential romantic interest for his father. That was why it was okay to like her, okay to vie for the opportunity to sit in the front passenger seat.

Her popularity with the eight-year-old boy would fizzle in a second if he realized how much she would like to be Jennifer Larkins's competition. The insight made Terri feel deceitful and put a damper on her pleasure in her role of sitter.

"How's your steak, Jer?" Bob Peterson inquired.

"Perfect," Jeremy hastened to assure his friend and host, a big hearty man with prematurely gray hair. "Cooked just the way I like it. The twice-baked potato is delicious, too, Shirley. A great meal. Good company, too," he added, raising his glass of wine.

It was all true, but Jeremy spoke out of appreciation and politeness. He would gladly have traded the succulent rib eye on his plate for a piece of pizza in a noisy family restaurant with Terri sitting next to him and his kids facing them across the table. His only consolation for missing out on having supper with her tonight was the thought of returning home and finding her there. A thought that speeded up his pulse and awoke impatience that he tried to combat with common sense.

Nothing had changed since he'd stated the situation to Terri on Thursday, when he'd hired her: There was absolutely no point in getting involved with her. She wasn't interested in settling down in Yellville, Arkansas, away from big-city social life and shopping and the life-style she would no doubt return to soon.

"You'll have to give me your potato recipe," Jennifer Larkins said to Shirley from her place at the dining-room table directly across from him. A brunette about Jeremy's age, with blue eyes and a sturdy build, she'd turned out to be as attractive and pleasant as Bob had promised.

"I'll be happy to," Shirley replied, looking pleased. She was small boned and plump, her ash-blond hair styled in a pixie cut. "Do you like to cook?"

"When I have someone to cook for, I do. I grew up in a family with four kids and find it hard to make small meals. I'll have to invite the three of you over to my place soon." She brightened, putting down her fork. "Or better yet, we could include Heather and Bobby." The Petersons' two children, aged four and nine, were absent tonight, staying overnight at friends' houses. "And Jerry and Mandy." Jennifer looked over at Jeremy as she included his offspring in the guest list.

"You must like cooking for a crowd!" Shirley exclaimed.

"Especially a crowd that includes kids. It gives me an excuse to serve grilled hamburgers and hot dogs and side dishes of potato salad and macaroni and cheese—food kids enjoy."

"Food adults enjoy, too," Bob put in. "How about tomorrow afternoon?" The suggestion was obviously facetious, but Jennifer's expression indicated she was taking it seriously.

"Tomorrow afternoon? Sure. Why not?"

"You don't want to feed seven people on such short notice!" protested Shirley. "Bob was joking."

"Would you believe I have a big batch of homemade chili in the freezer? And enough beef patties and packages of wieners for a small army? A quick trip to the supermarket tomorrow either before or after church to buy the buns and I'll be all set to fire up my grill. It'll be fun. We can play croquet in my backyard." She looked from one to the other, her enthusiasm evident.

"I can't speak for Jeremy, but the Peterson family accepts," Bob declared.

"Do you and the kids have plans, Jeremy?" Shirley inquired.

"None that come to mind." All three of them eyed him expectantly, waiting for a more definite response to the invitation that he shouldn't have been reluctant to accept. A casual Sunday-afternoon cookout at Jennifer's place in the presence of his kids and good friends was made to order for getting better acquainted with her. He *should* want to get better acquainted with her. "What time?" he asked lamely.

"About three o'clock?" Jennifer suggested. "Does that suit everyone?"

"Suits us to a tee," Bob said after a questioning glance at Shirley.

"Same here," Jeremy said, doing his best not to sound resigned.

Following the meal, the two women shooed the men into the living room, refusing the offer of help in clearing the table.

Bob took the opportunity to quiz Jeremy, pitching his voice low enough that it wouldn't carry. "Don't you like her, Jer? She's down-to-earth, a real person. And nice looking, too."

"Jennifer's very likable, Bob."

"She's crazy about kids. Loves the outdoors. Likes

small-town life. That's why she took the teaching job here. When Shirley and I met her, we couldn't wait to get you two together.''

"And I'm appreciative," Jeremy stated with sincerity.

"But we should let you carry the ball from here. Right?"

"Or not carry it, as the case may be."

Bob nodded. "You and Jennifer need to go out on a few dates without other people around. It's how you click one on one that'll be the deciding factor. I understand that. But take some well-intentioned advice. Don't drag your feet, or some other guy might snatch her out from under your nose, the way that ex-marine snatched Pat Tyler."

"Luckily for Pat. Her ex-marine has made her a much happier woman than she would ever have been married to me."

"I was sorry Shirley and I had to miss the wedding. We heard that Mandy stole the show."

Much to Jeremy's relief, the conversation veered away from the subject of a possible relationship between him and Jennifer Larkins.

Bob's mention of Pat Tyler helped to define for Jeremy his lack of interest in dating Jennifer. From the outset, he'd liked and admired Pat a lot as a person, but had never felt the first urge to get her alone, to monopolize her company and satisfy a keen curiosity about all her thoughts and feelings. The spark of physical attraction had been totally absent.

The same was true with Jennifer.

And all those missing elements were present in triple strength when he just visualized Terri, who was the wrong woman for him.

At ten o'clock Terri clicked off the TV with the remote. "Time for bed," she said. "If your dad comes home and finds you up, he'll give me a flunking grade as a sitter."

Mandy was curled up beside her on the sofa, while Jerry lay on his stomach on the carpet, near her feet. They'd watched the last hour of a movie after returning from Mountain Home. Both children had already seen it, but they'd gotten thoroughly engrossed in the plot, and so had she. The whole evening had been hugely enjoyable, except for those lapses when she'd found herself wondering how Jeremy's evening was going and had to struggle with herself not to hope he was bored stiff with Jennifer Larkins.

"Will you come into my room and read me a story to make me sleepy, Ms. Sommers?" the little girl asked, yawning as she obediently climbed down from the sofa. "And tuck me into bed, the way Daddy does?"

"I would love to, dear," Terri said, melting at the request. She smiled encouragingly at Jerry, who'd pushed himself to his feet with the nimble ease of an eight-year-old boy. From his expression he had something to ask of her, too, but felt shy about stating it. "You're probably too grown-up for your dad to tuck you in."

He shrugged and nodded. "He usually just sticks his head in the door and says good-night. Sometimes he sits on the edge of my bed and we talk a little while about stuff."

"Maybe I could look in later and tell you good-night. If you're not already asleep."

"Sure, that would be okay," he agreed at once.

His body language as he picked up a throw cushion he'd been cradling earlier and sailed it to an armchair told Terri that her suggestion was a lot more than okay with him.

"Come on, Ms. Sommers," Mandy urged, reaching for her hand. "You can talk to me while I put on my nightie."

This is what I've missed, what I want so very much, Terri thought, her heart overflowing with affection for both children.

The little girl barely managed to stay awake until Terri had read the final page of the picture book they'd selected together. Her long dark lashes kept dropping. "I'm sleepy now," she confided drowsily when Terri had closed the book. "Thank you for reading to me, Ms. Sommers."

"I probably enjoyed it more than you did, sweetie. Good night." Terri bent and kissed her soft pink cheek. Mandy's small arms closed tightly around her neck. The childish hug touched off emotions of aching tenderness inside Terri's chest and awoke a kind of happiness she'd never known before. "Sweet dreams," she whispered, her lips curved in a smile.

The smile didn't fade when the embrace went lax, and she gently lowered the sleeping child's arms. For a few seconds longer, she sat there, content to watch over Mandy while she slept, innocence and trust mirrored in the precious little girl's face. Only the thought of young Jerry, waiting for her to tell him good-night, brought Terri to her feet.

Some impulse made her glance toward the chest of drawers, where the glow from a pretty china lamp with a Cinderella figurine shone on the photograph of Susan Wells. The same impulse made Terri walk over closer. She wasn't a superstitious person and knew that a photograph was simply a photograph, but the warmth in Susan's smile seemed to beam approval.

Leaving Mandy's door ajar a few inches, Terri crossed the hallway to Jerry's room and tapped on the door frame before she looked inside. He was lying in bed, his blond hair tousled and golden against a bright-blue pillowcase that matched his sheets and coordinated with a blue comforter decorated with baseball players in red and yellow and green. A glance around was enough confirmation that loving attention had gone into creating a special environment for a boy, the same attention that had made Mandy's bedroom fit for a little princess.

"I like your room," Terri said. "It's so full of energy, the way you are." His furniture was painted in primary colors and large, framed sports posters covered the walls, along with team pennants and sports memorabilia.

"Thanks. My mom fixed it up for me."

"I figured as much."

"That's her picture."

Terri's gaze followed his to a framed photograph of Susan on his chest of drawers. Instead of a five-by-seven, it was an eight-by-ten. "She was pretty. I can tell from her picture that she was also a very happy person."

He nodded. "She was always smiling and laughed a lot. I don't know why God had to let her die."

"It's sometimes hard to understand why certain things happen. You were fortunate, though, to have known your mother. For the rest of your life, you'll have wonderful memories. I never knew my mother at all."

"You didn't?"

"No, she died when I was just an infant."

"So your dad raised you, too?"

"No, I never knew him, either. He went away. I was raised by my grandmother."

Terri had taken a step inside the room. Jerry scooted farther over on his bed, making room for her to sit. Accepting the unspoken invitation, she went and sat on the edge of the bed.

"Was she good to you?" he asked.

"Very good to me. So was my great-aunt, my grandmother's sister. I wasn't a deprived child, but my childhood was quite a bit different from yours and Mandy's."

"You said your dad went away. Where did he go?"

"I really can't answer that. He left without saying where he was going, and we never had any word from him."

"Maybe he got amnesia."

"Or maybe he was killed in an accident. There are numerous possibilities."

"At least I know what happened to my mom," Jerry reflected. "And my dad would never let anybody else raise me and Mandy."

"No, he wouldn't. You and Mandy are your dad's number-one priority. Not only does he take his responsibilities as a parent seriously, but he enjoys being your dad. That's what is so nice." Terri patted his hand on the sheet. "Now, I'd better tell you good-night and let you go to sleep."

"Thanks for taking us to eat pizza. It was real fun having you be our sitter tonight."

"I certainly had fun. You and Mandy are delightful company."

"Dad hires a sitter for us when he has meetings with the Lions Club and the Jaycees." He scowled, his gaze going to his mother's photograph again. "And he might be going on more dates with that schoolteacher."

"I'll make sure he knows I'm available when he needs a sitter." Terri patted his hand again and squeezed it, touched by his indirect statement that he hoped she would be their sitter on future occasions. "Good night."

"Good night."

The urge to express the maternal affection she felt for him was too strong to suppress. Terri leaned over and kissed him on his forehead before she rose to her feet. His expression and the blush on his cheeks told her he hadn't minded in the least. At the door she clicked off the light switch. "Sleep well," she said.

"Ms. Sommers?"

"What, dear?"

"I'm sure glad you and Dad aren't dating."

The fact that they weren't made it all right for him to open his boyish affections to her.

I'm not glad, Jerry, especially not after tonight, Terri thought. It bothered her that she hadn't corrected his wrong assumption that she and Jeremy never would date.

But then, it might not be a wrong assumption. Tonight, while Jeremy's children were tapping into the surplus of maternal love in her heart, he might have been getting acquainted with their future stepmother.

Please let that not be the case. Try as she might, Terri couldn't keep the selfish prayer from forming.

"You can close my door, Ms. Sommers." Jerry yawned

as he issued the instructions. "Play the TV if you want. It won't keep me awake."

Terri suspected he was fast asleep by the time she stepped out into the hallway. A glance inside Mandy's room revealed that the little girl lay exactly in the same position, the contented smile still on her sweet face. Playing the TV low wasn't likely to disturb her deep slumber, either.

After she'd returned to the living room, though, Terri didn't reach for the remote control, but instead curled up on the sofa and savored the quietness in the house, which wasn't an empty quietness, but rather a temporary ceasing of the busy activity of a family. It occurred to her that she'd never felt cozy and comfortable in quite the same way curled up on a sofa in the home she'd shared with Christopher during six years of marriage.

House, not *home,* she corrected herself.

After being here in Jeremy's home, the distinction was clearer than ever before. Terri also knew with more certainty than ever before that she wanted a real home for herself someday. She wanted to be a homemaker. A wife to a family man. A mother.

The woman Jeremy married would instantly have everything Terri wanted. Whether Terri could meet his needs in a wife and those of his children—that was another matter.

If I was surer of myself, I'd go after the Mrs. Jeremy Wells title, she reflected with a sigh as she maneuvered into a lying position.

What would be her plan of action? Obviously she would need to play the physical-attraction angle. Jeremy *was* attracted to her. And she to him. If Terri could get him to date her against his better judgment, hopefully he would soon discover there was much more to her than her looks and figure. In the meanwhile, he wouldn't be dating someone else.

Of course, it might be too late if he'd already fallen for Jennifer Larkins.

Terri sighed again, nestling her cheek into a throw pillow. Whether or not he had, trying to seduce Jeremy wasn't really a viable plan. It might backfire on her. She might end up destroying all his respect for her, not to mention her respect for herself. Terri wasn't a vamp.

No, things would have to take their natural course....

Her eyelashes dropped as she yawned and stretched, abandoning the whole notion. Lulled by the peaceful quiet, Terri didn't fight her drowsiness, since there was time for a catnap before Jeremy got home from his dinner date.

Chapter Five

It was the first time Jeremy had ever been filled with anticipation as he headed home from a date. The kids would be in bed by now. If Terri wasn't in a hurry to leave, she might stay for a few minutes and talk to him.

At the very least, he'd get to see her. That in itself would be a treat.

He certainly hoped Mandy and Jerry had behaved themselves and hadn't given her any trouble. They'd both been tickled over having her as their sitter, even before any mention had been made of a trip to Mountain Home for pizza. Father and son and daughter were all captivated by Terri.

As long as they didn't come to depend on having her in their lives, what was the harm? Jeremy was the one most in danger, since he might fall for her. He just needed to keep a clear perspective.

Terri's presence in Yellville was temporary. It could be likened to a brief visit from a beautiful butterfly or an exotic migratory bird, like the painted bunting Jeremy had spotted this spring in his backyard. Whether or not she reconciled with her successful attorney ex-husband, whom she'd undoubtedly loved and might still love, she would eventually return to Little Rock and the big-city life-style that had suited her since she'd originally left her hometown.

For however long she kept her job as Jeremy's station attendant, he could count himself fortunate to have her as an employee. In two days she'd earned his complete confidence that he could leave the station in her capable hands.

The only problem was forcing himself to leave when she was there.

No doubt about it, Jeremy was under Terri's spell, probably for the duration of her stay in her hometown. Tonight's experience had shown him that he might as well put on hold finding a wife while she was around. It wasn't fair to another woman to ask her out on dates when he couldn't keep his mind off Terri.

That meant not dating anyone for another month or two. Jeremy's scruples about limiting his dating to the serious pursuit of a wife hadn't changed. Those guidelines still excluded Terri, but the knowledge didn't prevent adrenaline from surging through his body and speeding up his heartbeat as he pulled into his double-car garage and entered his house through the laundry room.

Jeremy assumed that Terri would have heard the van engine and the garage door closing. Even if she hadn't, his footsteps across the ceramic tile of the kitchen floor made noise that must have alerted her to his arrival. No sound was coming from the living room. She apparently had turned the TV off if she'd been watching it.

Trying not to look as eager as he felt, Jeremy reached the living-room door. The word *hi* died on his lips as he saw Terri, lying asleep on the sofa. Jeremy gazed at her, his throat suddenly too dry to speak her name and rouse her.

The temptation to walk over closer was too powerful for him to fight. Once he was standing at the sofa, he dropped

to his haunches. "Terri," he said, his voice coming out
hoarse. "Wake up."

She stirred, turning onto her back more and lifting her
breasts against the thin, pale-green material of her blouse.
It was always a struggle for Jeremy not to look at her
breasts. Now there was nothing keeping him from gazing
hungrily at the lush, rounded mounds or from noting the
imprint of her nipples. The urge to touch first one pebbly
peak and then the other with his fingertip almost brought a
groan to his throat.

"Terri. Wake up, honey." The *honey* had slipped out.

She stirred again, moving her shapely jeans-clad legs and
propping one knee against the sofa back so that her thighs
were relaxed apart. Jeremy's hands clenched into fists as
he blocked out the unconscious invitation of her provoca-
tive position.

Concentrating on her face didn't ease the ache in his
groin. Her creamy skin begged to be caressed. Her vibrant
red-gold hair begged to be combed by male fingers brave
enough to weather the pleasure-shock. Her luscious mouth,
slightly parted, begged to be kissed. Oh, to be the prince
waking the sleeping beauty, Jeremy thought, squeezing his
eyes closed to collect himself.

"For God's sake, Terri, you've got to wake up." Grasping her nearest shoulder, he shook it gently.

"Oh, hi, Jeremy," she murmured.

Her long eyelashes lifted and sleepy recognition dawned
in her gorgeous green eyes.

"You're home already."

Her voice was even huskier—and sexier—than normal,
adding its own element of arousal.

"Did my kids wear you out?" His hand still held her
shoulder, and he didn't want to take it away.

"Not at all. They were wonderful company."

"Glad to hear that."

"You'll have to use me as your sitter from now on."

She raised up, giving him little choice other than to release her. He stood and moved aside, allowing her to swing her feet down to the floor.

"How was your evening?" she asked.

"Pleasant enough," he replied, sitting down beside her. "You should wake up fully before you drive home."

"I agree." She patted her mouth as she yawned. "I was dreaming that you had gone with Mandy and Jerry and me to the pizza restaurant tonight."

"Was it a nice dream?" Jeremy draped his arm along the back of the sofa. When she nodded by way of an answer, tendrils of her hair brushed his wrist. His whole body responded to the feathery contact.

"Very nice. Except I felt guilty because you'd broken your date with Jennifer Larkins."

She yawned again and tipped her head back on the cushion, covering Jeremy's wrist and hand with red-gold curls. He took immediate advantage and began playing with them, replying, "It wasn't exactly a date."

"Did you like her?"

"She's extremely nice. Your hair color is natural, isn't it?" Any subject other than her seemed totally irrelevant.

"Yes."

"It's so beautiful." She rolled her head sideways to look at him with her lovely jade green eyes. "You're beautiful," Jeremy said, uttering the compliment he'd kept back countless times during the past two days. "Your hair. Your eyes. Your skin." His free hand came up and he stroked her cheek. His voice reflected his intense pleasure in the satin-smooth texture as he observed, "You're not even wearing makeup, are you?"

"Not a foundation makeup. Though sometimes I do. Your touch is so gentle for a strong man." She caught his hand and held it against her face, then brought his palm to her lips.

Jeremy felt himself go hard as a rock. "Touching you isn't a good idea, not when looking at you just now when you were asleep aroused me." His words of blunt confession were strained.

"Before I dropped off to sleep, I was thinking about seducing you," she confided, releasing his hand and reaching to caress his cheek and jaw.

"Seducing me would be like inviting a starving man to a banquet. It's been more than two years since I made love." Jeremy traced the soft fullness of her mouth with his thumb, the yearning to kiss her feeding on all the other yearnings inside him.

"It's been six long months since I've been held. More than sex, that's what I miss. When I'm around you, I think about how good it would feel to have you hold me tight."

"Don't tell me that." Jeremy groaned, sliding his arms around her. She moved into his embrace, putting her arms up around his neck and hugging him back. Her full, soft breasts were pressed against the wall of his chest. "You're so...luscious," he murmured. "So sexy and yet feminine."

"And you're so strong and masculine without being macho. Yesterday when you were storing those boxes of motor oil, I watched the ripple of muscles in your back."

She used one hand to caress his shoulders and back. The delicious pleasure set off tremors in those same muscles she'd described.

"We shouldn't be having this conversation. It's not going to clear the air."

"Why does the air need to be cleared? What's wrong with our being attracted to each other? We're both unattached."

Jeremy loosened his arms enough to allow her to pull back and look questioningly into his face. Her mouth was just inches away. Maybe if his life had depended on it, he could have kept himself from kissing her. "But wrong for each other," he said, closing the distance.

Sweet desire heated his blood and sent warmth coursing through his entire body when her mouth met his and clung. He moved his head, gently bruising the lush, soft contours of her lips, gently parting them for the deeper intimacy he hungered for. Then his tongue found hers, and hunger exploded inside him.

Jeremy's world was centered right there on the sofa as he kissed her harder, with unrestrained passion. For her to respond as she did awoke fierce male satisfaction that only spawned the need for more intimacy. With one arm still around her, he caressed her back and slid down farther to discover the tempting shape of her hips and sexy bottom.

Heaven help him, she didn't stop him.

I should stop myself, Jeremy thought, drunk on pleasure. His heart was thundering in his chest and his blood singing in his veins. Calling a halt at this point hardly seemed more possible than getting off a roller coaster in the middle of a thrilling ride. Passion was in control.

Using both hands, he squeezed Terri's small waist, then slid his hands up the front of her body to capture her breasts. Her moan of delight was absorbed into their kiss. The image of her lying on the sofa minutes earlier added an erotic stimulation that Jeremy hardly needed. He found her nipples with his fingertips. They formed small hard pebbles between the separating layers of her blouse and bra. Gently he pinched them, causing her to gasp and arch her back.

"Jeremy..." Terri turned her face aside and whispered his name in her husky voice.

"I want you, Terri," he said, his voice low and resonant with his need. Speaking the words aloud seemed to spawn more powerful urges. He kissed her jaw, her cheekbone, bent his head and kissed the lovely arch of her neck. Reveling in her warm, silky skin and drowning in her scent, he nuzzled with his lips and tasted with the tip of his tongue.

She shivered and tilted her head, giving him better access even as she murmured a caution. "Jeremy, your children might wake up and come in here."

Jerry and Mandy asleep in their bedrooms. He hadn't given a thought to them since he'd entered the house. And didn't want to focus on them now. Guilt sliced through the haze of passion like a laser beam. It didn't dissipate the haze, but conscience and reason found their way through the narrow wound, spoiling any chance that Jeremy could resume making love to Terri.

Which was what he wanted to do, more than anything.

Sighing, he reluctantly lowered his hands and slowly straightened. "Forgive me for losing control like that," he said, making a shamed face. "Another minute and I would have been taking your clothes off."

"I was as much at fault as you were. I didn't make any effort to stop you."

She hadn't taken her arms from around his neck. Still fully aroused, Jeremy didn't dare sit that close. He didn't even dare hug her to apologize for his behavior or give her a tender kiss before he pulled away and positioned himself a couple of feet farther along the sofa. "You were half-asleep, and I took advantage of you," he said, expanding on his apology at a safer distance. Safety had never been quite so dull and frustrating before now.

"It was a nice way to wake up—having you hold me and kiss me. There's no reason you shouldn't have. I'm divorced."

"There's a very good reason I shouldn't have." Jeremy doggedly continued the speech he needed to make instead of telling her that *nice* didn't begin to describe how good it had been for him to hold her and kiss her. "As much as I'd like to, I can't have an affair with you, Terri. I'm not the kind of man who has affairs."

"Why do you think I admire you so much? Because you're not the kind of man to jump into bed with women. I'm not thinking in terms of an affair, but a relationship."

"You and me?" He shook his head. "Only in a movie would a match between us ever work. A gas station owner and a Miss America contestant."

"A gas station owner with a college degree and a *former* Miss America contestant who likes him and his two wonderful children. Can't you at least give me a chance to prove there's more to me than a face and a figure?'' she implored earnestly.

"Of course there's more to you. Good grief, I'm not suggesting you're a shallow person.''

"Then let's get to know each other.''

"Don't you see the risk in that for me? Once I see for myself just how much you have to offer a man, it'll be ten times as hard when you up and leave, either to go back to your former husband or just go back to city life. Because you'll soon get bored living in Yellville.''

"You can't be certain of that. If my life was full, I might be happy living here.''

" 'Might' isn't good enough.''

" 'Might' is all any of us have, Jeremy. We're not guaranteed anything. As for risk, I would be taking as much of a risk as you. I might set my heart on being your wife and Mandy and Jerry's stepmother and come up lacking in your eyes. Shouldn't we at least find out if something lasting could develop? We could take things one day at a time, not actually date, until you were ready, but have family outings with Jerry and Mandy. Tomorrow, for example, maybe the four of us could go on a picnic. Or do something else they would enjoy.''

There was no way Jeremy could have refused if he hadn't been locked into a previous commitment. He couldn't even find it in himself to be glad that he was given a reprieve with time enough for his judgment to reassert itself.

"Actually, Jerry and Mandy and I already have plans for tomorrow,'' he said, regret in his voice. "Jennifer invited the three of us and Bob and Shirley Peterson and their two kids over to her house for hamburgers and hot dogs.''

Terri stared at him, disbelief written on her face. "You have a date with Jennifer Larkins and you came home and made out with me on your living-room sofa?'' she demanded.

"It's not really a date."

"Forget everything I said about admiring you! You're just a typical man!" She stood up, her cheeks flushed and her green eyes bright with hurt as well as indignation.

"Terri, please—wait—"

Jeremy followed behind her helplessly as she sailed out of the room after retrieving her handbag, obviously leaving without another word. "Please don't rush off angry. Let me explain," he pleaded. In the foyer he caught up with her and gently grasped her arm in an effort to detain her. "Please stay a minute and let me explain."

"Explain what? That you'd like to take me to bed, but you don't see me as wife material? I get the picture. Good night, Jeremy." She twisted free.

"Terri, I'm sorry. I was a total jerk."

His miserable words were spoken to her back as she departed through the front doorway. Jeremy followed behind all the way to her car in his driveway, pouring out his humble explanation anyway. "I honestly had no desire to accept Jennifer's invitation for myself. But I thought the kids might enjoy the occasion. I'm not the least interested in Jennifer, though I probably should be. Any woman I meet right now is going to look plain and ordinary next to you. I guess I am a typical man where you're concerned, and I'm not proud of the fact that my pulse speeds up when I picture you in my mind."

By this time they'd reached her car and she'd jerked the door open before he could open it for her. "I'm not proud of it, either," she snapped as she slid behind the wheel.

"Terri, honey, you're too upset to drive—" In his concern, he hardly realized he'd used the endearment again.

She slammed the door, cutting him off. The engine roared to life, and she backed out fast and drove off with a screech of her tires.

"Damn it!" Jeremy cursed under his breath, worry about

her safety adding to his seething frustration. In the state she was in, she might turn a corner too fast or step on the brakes too hard and crash into a tree or collide with another automobile. He shouldn't have allowed her to drive, but short of forcibly restraining her, he'd been helpless to stop her.

At this hour he couldn't call a neighbor over to stay at his house while he hopped into the van and went to make sure she got home in one piece. Not unless she didn't answer her phone after ten minutes had passed. Then Jeremy would bother a neighbor, considering the situation an emergency, and he would also call the sheriff's department.

Actually, Jeremy didn't wait ten minutes before he called Terri and got her answering machine. In spite of everything, the recorded sound of her voice raised pleasure in him. "It's me, Jeremy," he said at the beep. "If you're there, please pick up and put my mind at ease that you've gotten home safely." After a pause, he added, "I'll call again in a few minutes."

On his second attempt, he got the machine again, experienced the same reaction to her voice, left the same message.

On his third attempt, she answered, addressing him without saying hello.

"I'm all right, Jeremy." A click cut the connection.

She'd hung up.

Jeremy had been struck by her nasal tone, which suggested she might have been recently crying. The thought of her shedding tears because of him was simply intolerable. "Damn it, *talk* to me, Terri! Call me a 'bastard,'" he muttered in frustration, punching the redial button. But she didn't pick up.

Obviously she didn't care to talk to him, possibly might not care about ever talking to him again.

Jeremy had let her down, destroyed her respect for him. In his own blundering way, he'd placed himself in the same category with her philandering husband. Somehow or other, he *had* to win back her high regard.

The first step was playing straight with Jennifer Larkins, as Jeremy would do by calling her first thing in the morning and canceling on the cookout invitation. From now on, he wouldn't be pushed into another halfhearted date like the one tonight.

All his reservations about dating Terri remained, but no date with her would be halfhearted. That was his problem. Head and heart—the latter supported by the rest of him— were in conflict where she was concerned.

Not just his well-being was at stake, but Jerry's and Mandy's.

Also Terri's. Tonight she'd opened up and given him a glimpse of her vulnerability. It hadn't occurred to him before that ruling out a relationship with her could be construed as any rejection of her essential worth as a person. But apparently she'd made that wrong interpretation.

What a mess he'd made of things. Jeremy intended to tackle that mess head-on and clean it up for all four of them.

Terri was braced for the phone to ring again as she went into the bathroom to splash cool water on her face, then returned to her bedroom to undress and get ready for bed. She expected Jeremy to make another attempt to apologize tonight. By the time she'd slipped on a nightgown, she felt composed enough to carry on a brief conversation with him and ease his conscience if he did call. Earlier she'd been too overwhelmed by hurt and disappointment, along with a host of other emotions.

Among them were jealousy and envy of Jennifer Larkins, who'd obviously met Jeremy's criteria for wife and stepmother.

Terri's flare of temper had died down almost immediately after she'd driven away, leaving him standing in his driveway. In truth, anger had been mainly a defense mechanism, allowing her to keep her pride intact. She hadn't wanted to break down and cry in front of him.

Jeremy hadn't been intentionally cruel or terribly at fault, for that matter. Terri took her fair share of responsibility for what had happened. Being half-awake was no excuse. She'd given full encouragement for him to kiss her and touch her, and her ardent response had further undermined his self-control. A long abstinence from lovemaking had made him hungry for sex, and she'd done nothing to help him remain in control.

It had been heavenly to feel his arms around her, to be encompassed in his strength and his decency. His raw passion had sparked an answering passion in her. The element of finesse, of expertise, that had characterized Christopher as a lover had been missing, although the comparison hadn't risen in her mind at the time. With Jeremy, lovemaking wasn't exercising learned skills and satisfying his ego. It had to do with the honest give-and-take of physical pleasure between him and his sex partner.

In his moral code—and in Terri's—a sex partner was a marriage partner.

He must be feeling so guilty about tonight, she reflected, glancing at the phone on her bedside table as she turned down the sheet.

Right on cue, the phone rang. With a deep breath, Terri perched on the edge of the bed before she picked up the receiver and spoke a calm hello into the mouthpiece.

"Hi, darling."

Christopher's voice came over the line, not Jeremy's. Terri experienced a pang of letdown.

"Where were you tonight? I called at seven and at about eleven-fifteen."

His attempts to reach her had obviously been timed so as not to interfere with his own social activities during a Saturday evening, but she didn't voice that insight, surprised that it was objective. ''I kept two children tonight at their home, a five-year-old and an eight-year-old. You probably missed me by a few minutes each time you called.''

''For God's sake, Terri, you're not taking jobs as a sitter?''

''I didn't accept any money. It was a favor, mostly to myself.'' The opening was there to tell him she did have a regular job working as a gas station attendant, but after tonight, she might be unemployed. If Jeremy wanted her to quit, of course she would. The train of thought brought a heavy sigh. ''I was about to go to bed, Christopher. It's late.''

''You seem down in the dumps, darling. I wish I were there to hold you in my arms. Or rather, I wish you were here.'' His voice had lowered and softened. ''Come home, Terri, where you belong. Let me love you and take care of you. I know it's what you really want.''

''No, it isn't. Not anymore.'' The denial held sadness and brought a chill of loneliness.

Something had happened to insulate her from Christopher's caressing tone and persuasive words, which tonight left her unmoved. Terri had told herself repeatedly that her marriage was over. Now she knew that it truly was.

''I won't believe that until you tell me in person. If you won't come to Little Rock, I guess I have no choice but to make a trip to the boonies.''

''It would be a pointless trip.''

''Not if I get to see your beautiful face and spend fifteen minutes in your company. Get some rest, sweetheart. Things will look brighter in the morning. Good night.''

''Good night, Christopher.''

Once again nothing she'd said had shaken his conviction that she would come back to him.

Would he eventually seek her out here in Yellville? The

possibility would have raised panic just a week ago. She would have feared for holding on to her strength of conviction in the face of his urgent pleading in person.

But no longer.

Terri was far more anxious about the status of her job and how things stood between her and Jeremy after tonight than she was concerned about dealing with Christopher.

Without realizing that it was happening, she'd moved on into the next phase of her life. She wasn't hiding out in her hometown at this point and biding time until she'd recovered from her divorce. She was here by choice, focused on the present and the future.

A present she hoped would keep her in close contact with Jeremy. And his children. It was too soon to wish for a future centered around the three of them, mainly because Terri wasn't nearly confident enough at this point that she could measure up as combination wife, homemaker and stepmother. Jeremy and his son and daughter were already too important to her to want anything other than the best for them.

Otherwise she would edge out Jennifer Larkins any way she could.

It wouldn't take any plotting, Terri reflected, still perched on the side of her bed. *I would just follow my natural impulses.* Right this minute she would pick up the phone and call Jeremy and make up with him tonight. She would hang on to her job by whatever means it took and let proximity keep the physical attraction between them alive. She would plan outings with Jerry and Mandy and turn them into her allies while she was enjoying their company.

But Terri wouldn't do any of those things, because landing Jeremy wasn't a competition. The name Mrs. Jeremy Wells wasn't a contest title conferred on a winner.

Sighing, Terri snapped off the lamp and got into bed. It was too late now to call Jeremy anyway. Unlike her, he might be asleep. Even if he wasn't, the ringing of the phone might disturb his children.

Sleep soundly, sweet darlings. Terri smiled in the darkness, maternal affection welling up in her heart as she visualized Jeremy's young son and little daughter deep in peaceful slumber. The photograph of Susan Wells came into focus, and it was oddly comforting. *Watch over them, Susan....*

Terri drifted off to sleep.

Chapter Six

Jeremy slept restlessly, waking every couple of hours. At six he got up and brewed a pot of coffee. Jennifer Larkins had mentioned in the course of conversation last night that she was a habitual early riser, but he waited until seven to call.

Her "Hello" sounded alert. Jeremy came right to the point. "I'd like to cancel out on this afternoon, Jennifer. Please accept my apology for accepting when I should have refused last night."

"Bob pressured you into accepting. I regretted putting you on the spot, but short of withdrawing my invitation, I didn't know what to do."

"Bob means well. My main concern was not offending you, and that's my concern now," he stated earnestly.

"You haven't offended me. To be honest, I'm even a tad relieved. Out in the kitchen last night, I stressed to Shirley that I *hadn't* included you and your children because I was interested in dating you, but interested rather in being friends. But I'm sure my words didn't make a dent. People who are happily married find the idea hard to grasp that some of us career-minded types are quite happy being single." She went on, bringing the conversation to a cheerful close. "No problem about this afternoon, Jeremy. When you called, I was just about to take food out of the freezer, so I'll take out less. Bye, now. I'm sure we'll run into each other around town."

"Without a doubt, we will. Bye, Jennifer. Good luck with the new job."

He hung up, a load lifted from his mind. If only redeeming himself with Terri could be as easy, he thought. It was too early on a Sunday morning to call her. She might still be sleeping. He would have to wait at least an hour, suffering the suspense of whether she would answer the phone. If she didn't, well, Jeremy would cross that bridge when he reached it.

Somehow or other, he *had* to communicate with her today, ask her forgiveness, say or do whatever was necessary to regain her trust and respect. In the event she was so disgusted by his behavior last night that she'd decided to quit her job immediately, then certainly Jeremy would release her of any obligation to continue as his employee.

Her disgust wasn't any greater than his own, he reflected, stirring himself to action. Mandy and Jerry would be expecting a Sunday-morning breakfast rather than a bowl of cereal topped with fruit. Earlier he'd gotten a box of pancake mix from the pantry. Now he assembled other ingredients, including a thawed package of blueberries, and proceeded to mix a batter. By the time he'd finished, his son entered the kitchen, yawning. He was still wearing his cotton pajamas and his blond hair was tousled.

"Good morning, sleepyhead," Jeremy greeted him, paternal love welling up in his heart.

"'Morning, Dad." Jerry climbed up on a stool at the island. "I had a dream about Mom. You weren't in it, but Mandy was. And Ms. Sommers, too. She and Mom knew each other and were friends. They were laughing and talking.'' He sighed. ''I was sorry when I woke up.''

''It was a happy dream, then.''

''Real happy.''

Jeremy was getting juice glasses from an upper cabinet. He thought about his own disjointed dreams the previous night. Both Terri and Jennifer Larkins had been in them, in some instances both in the same crazy segment, but not Susan. Before now, it hadn't even occurred to him that she'd been absent. The realization awoke more sadness than guilt.

It was a healthy sign, he knew, that he hadn't dreamed about his wife or felt disloyal because he hadn't. Finally Jeremy was moving on with his life, after being stalled by the tragedy of losing her.

''Hi, Daddy.''

Mandy entered the kitchen, her usual chipper morning self. Her appearance set off tender paternal love.

''Good morning, angel.'' She came over to him, and he picked her up and hugged her before setting her on her feet again.

''What's for breakfast? I'm hungry,'' she declared.

''Blueberry pancakes.''

''Oh, goody!''

''While I'm cooking them, you two set our places and get out the syrup and the jug of orange juice.''

They complied with some normal bickering about who would do what. By the time Jeremy had lifted the last pancake from the griddle, both children were seated at the island, place mats before them.

''You know, we have a perfectly good table,'' he remarked, taking the stool they'd left for him, between them.

The custom of having meals at the island had begun after Susan's death. It had been too painful for him and for Jerry to cope with the empty place at the table in the breakfast nook.

''I like eating here better,'' Jerry stated firmly, pouring

syrup on his pancakes. "It's closer to the cabinets with the dishes and to the dishwasher, Dad, just like you said." Convenience had been the reason Jeremy had given.

"Now that Mandy's older, she provides an extra pair of hands," he replied.

"Yeah, but she drops things and breaks them."

"I do not! At least I don't very often, do I, Daddy?"

"Not often at all, angel."

"Are Mandy and I going to Sunday school?" Jerry asked.

"I'm planning to take you. Why?"

"I just wondered. I need to read my Sunday-school lesson. The pancakes are good, Dad."

"Thanks, son. I'm glad you're enjoying them." Jeremy wasn't fooled into thinking his son's thoughts had drifted. Jerry had deliberately changed the subject. His very resistance to the idea of eating at the table was indication that it was time to bring about gentle change to the routine that had been established for healing.

"Did you have fun last night, Daddy?"

Mandy's inquiry broke into Jeremy's reflections. "I had a pleasant evening," he said, wanting to be truthful and yet positive. He hadn't had fun.

"Do you intend to take that schoolteacher out on dates?" Jerry's question was tense.

"No. Actually, I don't have any such intention."

Relief flooded his son's expression and relaxed his posture. "That's good."

"Why not, Daddy?" protested Mandy. "You can get Ms. Sommers to be our sitter."

Jerry glared at her. "Ms. Sommers can stay with us when Dad has meetings."

"But he doesn't have meetings all that often." The little girl brightened. "Maybe you could join more clubs, Daddy."

"Yeah, Dad."

"Thanks a lot," Jeremy said dryly. "You want me to make myself scarce. Is that the message?"

"No, we just like Ms. Sommers," Mandy hastened to explain. "She can't come and be our sitter if you're here. Because then we don't need a sitter."

"Ms. Sommers has a life of her own. She was kind enough to volunteer to look after you kids last night, but I wouldn't impose on her on a regular basis." Jeremy finished silently, *even if last night had ended differently, with Ms. Sommers and your dad on friendly terms.*

"Why couldn't we just invite her over to visit when you're home?" Jerry eagerly expanded on his idea. "We could ask her to come to supper one night. You and I could grill hamburgers, Dad, like the time Miss Tyler had supper with us. We could eat out on the patio."

Mandy put down her fork to clap her hands excitedly. "Let's do it tonight! Please, Daddy!"

"Tonight is short notice," Jeremy said, hearing his own regretful note. Even if Terri was receptive to such an invitation, and she probably wouldn't be—not after last night—he'd need more time for preparation. "Remember, Mrs. Grambly made potato salad and brownies when Miss Tyler was our supper guest. You two haven't forgotten my attempt to make potato salad, have you?" The question brought responses of disgust from both his children.

"You do want to invite Ms. Sommers to supper, don't you, Dad?" persisted Jerry.

"Yes, I want to."

The answer apparently sufficed as a statement of intention, since Jerry didn't press for a definite commitment. A more truthful reply would have been, *Yes, but not nearly as much as I would like to have supper alone with Ms. Sommers.*

That hadn't been the case with Pat Tyler. It wouldn't have been the case with Jennifer Larkins if she'd been under consideration as a supper guest. Why? Because the element of physical attraction was missing? Because he hadn't been hot to take Pat to bed and the same held true with Jennifer?

That was the only explanation Jeremy had. And it didn't make him at all proud of himself. However, shame didn't lessen any of the male anticipation that quickened his pulse as he headed to his bedroom fifteen minutes later to use the telephone. Even if Terri didn't pick up, he would hear her voice on tape.

She didn't pick up. Jeremy left a message, wondering if she was standing by and listening. "Terri, it's Jeremy calling on Sunday morning. I wanted to apologize for last night. I'll try again later after the kids and I get back from church services. If you're home by then, I hope you'll talk to me."

He waited a few seconds before he hung up.

Terri had gone out to buy a Sunday newspaper. On her return she saw the blinking light on her answering machine and went quickly to play back the message. Since Jeremy hadn't asked her to call him back, she didn't.

Probably he had his hands full getting himself dressed and supervising two children as they got ready for church, Terri reflected. Five-year-old Mandy would require some help with fastening her clothes and combing her hair. Jerry might need assistance with knotting his tie and buttoning his cuffs. It was such an appealing picture to imagine Jeremy doing those things as he would do them, with patience and humor.

He was a good father. A fine man, though human.

Without doubt, Jennifer Larkins would recognize his admirable qualities, as Terri had. More than likely, the new schoolteacher in town had already set her cap for Jeremy.

Terri poured herself a cup of coffee and carried it out to her small front porch, where she'd left the Sunday edition of a Little Rock newspaper. But she barely scanned the pages she usually read with interest and gave scant attention to the ads. What was happening today, in Yellville, seemed of much greater importance.

Would Jeremy also see Jennifer at church, in addition to spending part of the rest of the day with her? Terri wondered. Would the schoolteacher sit with him and Mandy and Jerry, while members of the congregation looked on approvingly?

The jealous speculation made Terri's coffee taste as bitter as gall. *I could attend the service at Jeremy's church instead of my grandmother's church.* "You could, but you won't," she said aloud to herself, tossing aside a section of newspaper.

She *wouldn't* compete for Jeremy, not by resorting to falling back on her looks. In the end, she wouldn't win anyway, because this wasn't a contest based on looks. Jeremy had already been dazzled by Terri's beauty when he'd agreed to the blind date with Jennifer. When he'd made plans to be with her today, not with Terri.

The worst part of it was the possibility that he might have acted wisely, choosing to date Jennifer. If dating led to marriage, she might, just might, make him a better wife than Terri ever could. She might make Mandy and Jerry a better stepmother.

Terri was certain about one thing. If Jennifer became the second Mrs. Jeremy Wells, Terri would envy her a lot more than she'd envied her competitor in the Miss America Pageant who'd walked off with the crown.

"Dad, Archie needs a ride home. I told him we'd drop him off."

"Sure thing." Jeremy smiled at the youngster who'd dashed up to him alongside his son. "I see Mandy headed this way." From her expression she had something on her mind.

"She was over talking to Mr. and Mrs. Peterson."

Jeremy mentally groaned. He hadn't chatted with the Petersons either before or after church service. If Jennifer Larkins hadn't told them differently, they were ignorant of the fact he'd canceled on the cookout.

"Daddy, did you forget to tell us we're going to Miss Larkins's house for hamburgers and hot dogs this afternoon?"

Mandy had called out her puzzled question when she was yards away. Jeremy waited until she'd reached him to answer.

"No, I didn't forget. We were invited, but we're not going."

"Mrs. Peterson said we are. She said she'd see us there."

"She's mistaken."

"But I want to go!"

Jerry spoke up with grim emphasis. "I *don't* want to. Come on, Dad. Archie needs to get home." He led the way toward the van.

"*Please,* Daddy," Mandy pleaded as she and Jeremy followed after the two boys.

"Miss Larkins isn't expecting us, angel. I turned down her invitation."

"Why?"

"Because Dad doesn't want to date her," Jerry said over his shoulder. "Didn't you hear him say that at breakfast?"

"But she invited us, too, not just him."

Jeremy sighed, mindful of the fact that Archie was all ears. "Let's save the discussion for later, since this is a private family matter. Archie, how's your grandfather? I heard he was in the hospital."

"Yes, sir. He had a knee operation."

Jerry joined in the conversation on the drive to their young passenger's neighborhood, but Mandy remained noticeably silent, obviously brooding over missing Jennifer's cookout.

"You okay back there, angel?" Jeremy asked gently after he'd dropped Archie off at his house.

"No, I'm sad," she replied.

"Hey, Ms. Sommers lives just a couple of blocks from

here," Jerry announced. "She drove us by her house last night to show us."

"It's a little blue house, Daddy, with a porch," Mandy piped up, suddenly animated. "You want to see it?"

"Take a right here, Dad."

Jeremy turned the wheel, reluctance overruled by his children's urging. And by his own wish to see where Terri lived.

"Go straight."

"Let me tell him which house," Mandy begged her brother.

"You've already told him what it looks like. And her car will probably be in the driveway if she's home."

"I hope she is home! We could stop and visit her!"

"No, we can't, not without an invitation," Jeremy said in the tone that brooked no arguments.

"Look, her car's just turning in, Dad. She must be coming from church, too. She's getting out. She sees us."

Jeremy didn't need the blow-by-blow. "I have twenty-twenty vision, son." He was using it to note how gorgeous Terri looked in a sleeveless white dress.

"Let's stop and say hi, Daddy! *Please!*"

"Please, Dad. It's only being friendly. I think she wants us to stop. She's smiling and waving."

"Yes, she is, isn't she?" Jeremy said, marveling. "Okay, we'll stop for just a minute and say hello."

His children wasted no time releasing seat belts and scrambling out of the van as soon as he'd braked to a stop behind Terri's white sedan. Jeremy completely empathized with their unrestrained eagerness. He could have bounded out, too, calling out a greeting.

"Hi, Jerry and Mandy! What a delightful surprise!" Terri exclaimed. "You both look so nice, all dressed up."

"Thank you," Mandy said sweetly, accepting the compliment for her and her brother. "We just came from church."

"We dropped off this kid named Archie, who lives just

a few blocks away from you." Jerry took over the explanation. "I gave Dad directions to your house. We were just
going to drive by so he could see where you live."

"Then we saw you and begged Daddy to stop."

Jeremy had walked up by now. "And I didn't need to
have my arm twisted too hard," he said lightly.

Terri shifted her attention to him, the smile still on her
lips. Jeremy's shoulders seemed to grow broader under her
gaze. "Hi, Jeremy. I got your phone message earlier."

"Dad, you called Ms. Sommers after our talk at breakfast?" Jerry sounded not only interested, but pleased.

"It would have been too early to call her before breakfast."

"Did you ask her?" Jerry demanded.

"Ask me what?" Terri inquired.

"Actually, the purpose of my call had nothing to do with
what Jerry has on his mind. He wants you to come to our
house for supper one night."

"I do, too, Ms. Sommers," Mandy put in. "I wanted
Daddy to invite you for this afternoon, but he wouldn't
because Mrs. Grambly hadn't made potato salad. Daddy's
potato salad is awful." She made a face, shuddering.

"I think you have plans for this afternoon anyway."
Terri looked at him questioningly.

"Not anymore," Jeremy told her.

"We're not doing *anything* fun today." Mandy's woeful
expression matched her tone.

"Oh, no, here we go again," Jerry muttered, rolling his
eyes.

Jeremy quickly got in his own explanation before his
children could blurt out their own. "Mandy's upset because
I canceled out on the invitation that I mentioned to you last
night."

"I'm not upset. I'm glad," Jerry said to Terri.

She sighed. "I'll bet you are." Her troubled gaze met
Jeremy's. "I feel responsible."

"You shouldn't. My actions are my responsibility."

"Dad's not interested in dating Miss Larkins. That's why he turned down her invitation for all three of us."

"I'm sure Ms. Sommers has heard enough discussion on the subject. We just stopped to say hi. Now we should say goodbye and not hold her up any longer," Jeremy stated.

"You're not really holding me up. You brightened my day." She smiled at Mandy and Jerry.

"Can *you* make potato salad, Ms. Sommers?" asked Mandy wistfully.

"Yes, actually, I can. I follow my grandmother's recipe."

"Daddy, we have hamburger patties and buns in the freezer, don't we?"

Jerry had followed his sister's train of thought with no difficulty, as had the adults. "Ms. Sommers doesn't want to come to our house and cook."

"Certainly not," Jeremy said.

"Don't I get to speak for myself?" Terri objected.

"Sure." Jerry was quick to give her permission.

"I'm not the best cook in the world, but I'm quite handy in the kitchen. If the three of you decide to invite me over sometime, I would enjoy pitching in and helping with the meal."

"I'd like to invite you over now," Mandy offered without hesitation.

"Me, too," Jerry seconded.

"Then it's unanimous," Jeremy said, casting his vote. "But we'll understand if you already have plans for this afternoon."

"I don't have plans, but—" She broke off, glancing toward the street.

He turned and saw that a delivery van from a florist in Mountain Home had pulled up.

Jerry voiced the obvious. "Hey, Ms. Sommers, somebody has sent you flowers."

"Yes, somebody has." Her voice held a note of resignation. "Excuse me a minute."

While they watched, she walked to meet the driver of the van, a stocky woman bearing a large bouquet of yellow roses.

"Today I caught you home," the woman said cheerfully, obviously recognizing Terri. "He ordered yellow this time. Aren't they beautiful?"

And expensive, Jeremy thought. There were at least two dozen long-stemmed partially opened buds.

"Very beautiful." Instead of taking the bouquet, she lifted out the tiny envelope, but didn't open it. "Could you do me a favor and deliver these to the nursing home? It wouldn't be much out of your way, and you would save me the trouble. I'll tell you the location."

"I know where the nursing home is. No problem."

"Thanks. I really appreciate it."

Jeremy could sense his children's curiosity. He instructed them in a stern undertone, "Mind your manners and don't ask nosy questions."

"Sorry for the interruption," Terri said as she rejoined them.

"Dad sent Mom red roses for their anniversary one year," Jerry said, eyeing her hand holding the envelope. "She was so happy over them she cried."

"I heard some commentary recently that red roses are the unimaginative choice of the majority of men," Jeremy remarked.

"The color doesn't matter. It's the thought behind sending flowers that matters. A little handpicked bouquet can be precious."

"I like picking flowers," said Mandy. "I'll pick you a bouquet sometime, Ms. Sommers."

Terri smiled at her. "What a sweet thought." Her fond glance took in Jerry and finally rested on Jeremy himself. "Back to our conversation, I don't have any plans for this afternoon." But was the invitation extended by his children and him truly unanimous? Or had they put him on the spot? Jeremy read the questions in her eyes.

The answer was yes to both questions. "In that case, we'll wait while you change your clothes," he said.

"Rather than have you wait, I could drive myself."

"Ride with us, Ms. Sommers," Mandy urged.

Jerry offered his persuasion. "We don't mind waiting."

"At least come and sit on the porch," she said, giving in easily. "I won't be more than ten minutes."

The three of them accompanied her to her small front porch, where she paused long enough to pull out the comics section of a Sunday edition of a Little Rock newspaper for Jeremy's children and handed the rest of the newspaper to him.

The top section was the society pages, folded to a column about social events, complete with snapshots. How many of the people were acquaintances or friends? Jeremy wondered, scanning the names in the captions. It wouldn't have surprised him to run across the name Christopher Sommers.

Next on the stack was a section devoted entirely to an advertisement of the latest women's fashions at an upscale department store in Little Rock. The pages were folded in such a way as to tell Jeremy that Terri had looked through this section, too.

Actually, she'd paged through the entire newspaper, but the fact that those two parts of it were on top spoke volumes to him. She missed her life in Little Rock.

Eventually she would go back to that life.

"Dad?" Jerry said in a stage whisper.

"What, son?" Jeremy heard his own disheartened note.

"Who do you suppose sent Ms. Sommers the flowers she didn't want?"

It was Jeremy's policy always to be candid with his children when they were better off hearing the truth or as much of the truth as they were capable of grasping. In this instance that was the case. Jerry and Mandy, like their dad, needed to accept the temporary nature of having Terri in their lives.

"My guess would be Mr. Sommers, her ex-husband."

"Oh. So he still likes her even though they got a divorce? She must not like him, since she's giving his bouquet away," Jerry mused.

"I wouldn't assume she doesn't like him. It might be generosity on Ms. Sommers's part, sharing her bouquet with elderly folks who don't often receive flowers from the florist, the way she does." Terri's motives were undoubtedly more complicated than mere generosity, but it was charitable of her to dispose of her ex-husband's flowers by sending them to the nursing home rather than tossing them into the garbage.

"If they still liked each other, why would they get a divorce?"

"Divorces don't result just from a couple not caring for each other. Sometimes there are serious problems that cause them to split up for a period of time and later they resolve those problems and get back together."

Jerry nodded and provided his own example. "Scott Getty's mom divorced his stepfather and married his real father again."

"Yes, I remember when that happened last year." And need to keep remembering how common the pattern was, Jeremy thought.

"Read me this cartoon, Jerry." Mandy tugged at her brother's arm, and he obligingly turned his attention back to the comics, his curiosity apparently satisfied by his father's replies.

Jeremy felt anything but satisfied himself.

There was little doubt that Terri's husband was the man who'd sent the yellow roses. *He ordered yellow this time,* the delivery woman had said, her words a clue that delivering roses to Terri had become fairly routine.

Christopher Sommers had no intention of giving her up, and Jeremy couldn't blame him.

Mandy slipped her little hand inside Terri's as the four of them walked to the van. "Will you sit next to me, Ms. Sommers?" she asked.

"No, she won't," Jeremy stated in a firm tone before Terri could speak. "Ms. Sommers will sit in the front passenger seat."

"Because she's a grown-up, huh, Dad?" Jerry said. "Grown-ups get to sit in front."

It didn't escape Terri that Jeremy's son preferred to rule out any other reasons, such as the possibility that his father might want her sitting beside him because he found her attractive as a woman.

"Not always," Mandy argued. "Last Sunday I saw Mrs. Peterson getting in the back seat of their car with Heather, and Bobby got in the front seat with Mr. Peterson."

"That's different. Mom used to get in the back seat with you sometimes."

"She did?"

"Don't you remember *anything?*"

"Okay, enough bickering," Jeremy scolded. "Or Ms. Sommers may decide she'd rather not ride with us."

"Not a chance," Terri said with utter sincerity.

She had reservations about the impromptu plans for spending the rest of the day with the Wells family. Primarily she wondered whether Jeremy wasn't acting out of a sense of apology for what had happened last night. Without doubt a guilty conscience had made him cancel out on Jennifer Larkins's invitation. Thanks to his children, he'd ended up here at Terri's cottage after church. She could imagine them urging him, *Please, Dad, let's drive by Ms. Sommers's house!* By sheer luck, she'd seen them and made it almost impossible for him not to stop.

Then his children had railroaded him into including Terri in the family activities for the afternoon. She suspected he was belatedly granting her request of last night that the four of them do something together today that the children would enjoy. It was all too obvious that Jeremy had qualms.

Still, Terri was glad for the unexpected turn of events,

as he escorted her to his van and courteously opened the passenger door. His hand grasping her arm and helping her up into the bucket seat was strong and steady, as he was. Her body had its own memory of a more intimate touch from that same hand, and warm pleasure seeped through her.

"This is a high step from the ground," she said lightly.

"I'll bet you've never ridden in a van before, have you, Ms. Sommers?" Jerry commented, hopping into the back seat with his sister.

"No, I don't believe I ever have. So this is a new experience."

"Mostly mommies and daddies and their children ride in vans," Mandy stated.

Terri looked around and smiled at her. "What a smart little girl you are to have noticed that."

Jeremy hadn't participated in the conversation, she reflected as he came around the front and got in behind the wheel. He had on the same gray slacks and navy blazer he'd worn last Saturday to Pat Tyler's wedding, but with a different tie. In just a week's time, he'd grown even more handsome in Terri's eyes. And more virile. Her feminine response to his clean-cut masculinity had grown stronger. Almost too strong for comfort. She had stroked those broad shoulders. She'd been crushed against his chest, felt his heart thudding in time with her own rapid heartbeat.

"All set?" he asked, starting the engine.

Terri spoke in unison with his young son and daughter. "All set." When Jerry and Mandy both burst out laughing, her laughter joined theirs, and Jeremy grinned in amusement as he backed out of her driveway.

For the first time in months, Terri felt lighthearted.

"That was fun! Let's do it again!" Mandy urged. "You, too, Daddy. I'll count to three. One, two, three—"

"All set," the four of them intoned together.

"One more time!" Mandy begged when her giggles had subsided.

"You hear those words a thousand times when you're a parent," Jeremy said to Terri, but on cue he indulged his little daughter, his glance in the rearview mirror tender and good-naturedly loving.

Observing him with his children at Pat Tyler's wedding reception, Terri had known he was exactly the type of man she wanted for a husband when she married again. The more she was around him, the more she wondered if he wasn't *the* man for her.

Of course, it was too soon to make that judgment. Especially since she was far less certain that she was *the* woman he was looking for to be his wife and Mandy and Jerry's stepmother.

Chapter Seven

"Why are you parking in the driveway, Daddy, instead of the garage?" Mandy asked.

"Because Ms. Sommers is company. We don't want to take her through the laundry room."

"Please don't treat me as company," Terri protested. "Go ahead and pull into the garage."

Jeremy did as she bade, but his reluctance was evident.

"I'll open Ms. Sommers's door for her, Dad," Jerry said. "You don't have to do it."

"Thanks, son." The retort was dry.

"Why don't I open my own door? That's what I'm used to doing most of the time."

"Me, too, now that I'm bigger," Mandy piped up.

Jerry scrambled out anyway, held the van door open wide and slammed it closed for her. "This way, Ms. Sommers." He hurried to the door into the house, opened it and led the way inside.

"What a pleasant, well-designed laundry room," Terri

said, glancing at gleaming white washer and dryer and a table with a bar for hanging clothes. The oak cabinets, the cheery wallpaper and ceramic-tile floor coordinated with the adjoining kitchen. "There's no reason to hesitate about bringing any woman through here, Jeremy."

"Did you hear that, Daddy? Ms. Sommers likes our laundry room."

"Yes, angel, I heard." His exasperation was mixed with humor and his unfailing patience.

"Dad, I'm starving," Jerry announced as he and Terri came to a standstill in the kitchen.

Jeremy and Mandy joined them.

"I'll fix us a snack to stave off our hunger," Jeremy said, slipping off his jacket. "You kids go and change your clothes."

"Ms. Sommers, would you like to come with me to my room?" Mandy asked hopefully.

Terri smiled at her to soften her refusal. "I think I'll stay and give your father a hand."

Jeremy had stripped off his tie. He handed it and his jacket to Jerry, with instructions to put them in his bedroom. Both children hurried off, leaving Terri alone with him.

"You're not angry," he said, without preamble.

"No, I didn't stay angry for long. What happened last night was as much my fault as yours." She hesitated, summoning her courage to be completely honest. "As I admitted, earlier before I dropped off to sleep I'd considered trying to seduce you. Part of me wants to go after you, Jeremy. I like and admire you so much and adore your children."

"Just part of you, though."

"Yes, the selfish part that's looking after my happiness. You and Jerry and Mandy deserve someone like Susan, superwife and supermom and superhomemaker."

Jeremy turned away from her, shaking his head. "I can't listen to this, Terri. It goes against all reason and common sense. You wouldn't be happy married to me, not after the reality set in. If I had only myself to consider, it would be different, but my kids have already lost one mother. When I remarry, the woman has to be someone who will stick with me. Stick with *us*.''

"That really hurts, that you think I might marry you on a whim. I would have stuck with Christopher, Jeremy, if he'd been faithful. The way you would be.''

For a moment she thought he would turn around to face her, but instead he strode over toward the refrigerator. "Mandy and Jerry will be back out here in record time. Let's not have them walk into a tense situation.''

"Shall I make up some excuse and have you take me home?''

"No, they would feel terribly cheated.'' He pulled open the refrigerator door. "And so would I.''

"Include me in that number,'' Terri said, taking what consolation she could in the fact that he wanted her to stay. "Do I still have my job?''

He glanced at her over his shoulder, frowning at her question. "Of course you still have your job. I don't have any legitimate cause for firing you.''

"If you asked me to quit, I would.''

"I would be a poor businessman if I did that. You can quit at any time, though, if the situation makes you uncomfortable. I won't hold you to your unofficial six-month contract.'' He rummaged in the deli drawer of the refrigerator and took out two packages of cheese.

Relieved at the outcome of the discussion about her employment, even if she was deeply dissatisfied with the previous exchange, Terri stood and watched as he brought the cheese over to the center island. Next he got a cutting board and a knife, but paused to unbutton the cuffs of his dress shirt and fold them back over tanned, muscular forearms.

"Why don't you go and change clothes and let me do that?'' she suggested, moving over to the sink to wash her hands.

"You're our guest," he objected. "Just make yourself comfortable."

"I'm not going to wound myself using a knife, if that's what's worrying you. I may look useless, but I'm not." Terri walked over beside him and proceeded to slit the clear plastic packaging on a block of cheese. "Were you planning to serve this with crackers?"

"Yes. I'll get them from the pantry."

"I can locate them myself. Just run along. And take your time."

But he observed her another thirty seconds at least while she sliced cheese, before he finally left the kitchen.

Jerry soon came in with Mandy on his heels, both of them eager to carry out Terri's directions. By the time Jeremy returned, wearing jeans and a cotton knit shirt, she'd finished arranging the ingredients for do-it-yourself canapés on a platter and was placing it in the middle of the table, which was set with place mats, paper napkins and glasses.

"Do you want milk, Dad?" Jerry asked, the gallon jug in his hand.

"Milk's fine." He sounded odd.

"We're sitting at the table, Daddy," Mandy said.

"I see that."

"Is it unusual for you to sit at the table?" Terri asked in surprise.

"We've fallen into the habit of eating our meals perched on stools." He gestured toward the stools placed along the curved outer edge of the island. "But this is much more civilized. The food looks delicious."

"It tastes delicious, too," Mandy assured him. "We sampled it."

"Have a seat, Terri." Jeremy pulled out a chair for her.

"Not there, Dad. That's your place. Ms. Sommers can sit across from you in Mom's place."

For a split second Jeremy seemed frozen, before he quickly recovered. "Let's change things up, just for the sake of variety."

"Yes, I'm for that," Terri said, sinking into the chair in which he'd sat at family meals served to him by his wife. "Habit can make life very dull." Not to mention painful, when habits were tragically altered. Now she understood why the charming dining area had been abandoned in favor of the island.

It was deeply touching and humbling that young Jerry was willing for her to occupy his mother's former place at the table. He was conferring the highest possible honor on Terri. But only because he didn't view her as having any designs on his father.

Jeremy had balked, and Terri was grateful that he had, even while she wondered about his reasons.

Seemingly oblivious to the undercurrents, Mandy climbed up into the chair on Terri's left. "I don't care where I sit as long as it's next to Ms. Sommers."

Jerry scooted into the chair on her right before Jeremy could pull it out. "You're too slow, Dad," he taunted, grinning up at him.

"Looks like I'll have to be happy with sitting across from Ms. Sommers."

"I've never been so popular before in my life, and I'm loving every minute," Terri declared, topping a wheat cracker with cheese and a dill pickle slice.

The last was a true statement, despite misgivings and the underlying awareness that today was probably a very special one-time occurrence.

The others followed her example, helping themselves, and the four of them munched companionably and sipped from their glasses of milk.

"We'll clear the table and clean up, Terri," Jeremy said when the contents of the platter had been demolished. "You can relax in the living room, if you like."

"I don't like," she replied, rising to her feet. "Why don't you relax in the living room, instead? Put up your feet and watch sports on TV?"

"Yeah, Dad. Take it easy."

"Watch a baseball game, Daddy."

"Thanks, but no, thanks. Getting rid of me isn't that easy," he retorted.

They cleaned up together and afterward everyone participated in making potato salad, lengthening the whole process rather than saving time with the assignment of duties. Terri could have operated a lot more efficiently working alone, but not had nearly so much enjoyment.

"You seem quite at home in the kitchen," Jeremy observed, with some surprise.

"Probably the most fun I had as a child was helping my grandmother cook. Some of my happiest memories involve mixing up batches of cookies for her church's bake sales."

"Didn't you have fun playing with other children?" Mandy asked.

"I really didn't play with other children much. My grandmother's nerves were bad, and she couldn't tolerate noise and childish energy. Also, she didn't like for me to get dirty." Terri made a face as she added ruefully, "Plus she bragged on how much prettier I was than the other little girls, and that offended the mothers."

Jerry spoke up, revealing that he'd been following the conversation, "I'll bet you were prettier."

"Sounds like a fairly lonely childhood," Jeremy reflected. "And I imagine your grandmother didn't stop bragging about you when you were a teenager winning teen beauty titles. She must have kept offending the same mothers of your peers."

"I was her pride and joy. It's hard to blame her when she devoted so much time and attention to bringing me up. Looking back, I realize I should have been a stronger individual and rebelled at some point against entering beauty pageants. But I didn't, and I survived."

"You must have had to beat the boys off with a stick."

"With a *stick!*" Mandy repeated, giggling.

"Dad doesn't mean Ms. Sommers really used a stick. He means she had lots of dates."

"I didn't have lots of dates. Not in high school. In fact, I had very few."

"How come?" Jerry asked.

"Because I had the reputation of being stuck up. Underneath I was shy and didn't know how to flirt and be friendly. My social life picked up in college and afterward, though. Are you two finished peeling the hard-boiled eggs?" she asked the children.

The purpose of the inquiry wasn't to change the subject. Talking about her past wasn't distressful, not under the present circumstances.

"We're on the last ones," Mandy said, her chubby fingers busy picking off bits of shell.

"Good. Once they're chopped up, we can mix in the mayonnaise, and we're all finished except for popping the bowl into the refrigerator."

"Then what are we going to do, Ms. Sommers?" the little girl wanted to know.

"I'm not necessarily the one to decide," Terri replied, amused and slightly taken aback.

"You and I could go to my room and play with my dolls and toys."

"No way," objected Jerry. "That's really selfish, isn't it, Dad?"

"Yes," Jeremy answered. "But we all have selfish impulses occasionally."

Terri's heartbeat quickened as she met his candid blue gaze, in which she read the admission that he was totally in sympathy with Mandy's ploy to monopolize her company.

After some discussion of outdoor games the four of them could participate in, they went outside into the shaded backyard, where Jeremy strung a badminton net. After some argument between the children about who would team up with Terri, she and Jerry squared off against Jeremy and Mandy. The competition was more humorous than serious.

Eventually Terri and Mandy retired to the sidelines to sit

in comfortable lawn chairs and sip cold drinks while father and son played each other awhile longer. It was obvious to Terri and endearing that Jerry wanted to show off his athletic prowess for her benefit. Typically, Jeremy let him, and bestowed praise that bolstered his confidence.

The woman in Terri got as much pleasure in being a spectator as did the maternal part of her. She took full advantage of the excuse to gaze at Jeremy and admire his manly physique. Mandy's happy chatter added another level of enjoyment. *This is what I've never had and what I want so much,* she thought. *Family life.*

As a little girl she'd yearned to be a part of a traditional family unit, and the yearning was still strong inside her; only now the role she coveted wasn't daughter and sister, but mother and wife. All the bouquets of roses in the world couldn't make up for the fact that for her, a marriage without children was empty. A life-style devoted to adult entertainment, adult interests, adult society, no matter how luxurious and affluent that life-style was, would never satisfy her deep-seated needs for Sunday afternoons like this one.

"This is so delightful," she declared when Jerry flopped down on the grass at her feet and Jeremy pulled up a chair nearby after they'd both tossed aside their rackets. "I hate to think that I could be spending this afternoon alone instead of with the three of you."

"You should spend every Sunday with us," Mandy said.

"Yeah, Ms. Sommers. Shouldn't she, Dad?"

"Nothing would suit me better, but I don't think Ms. Sommers meant to lock herself into a weekly arrangement. Is anybody else getting hungry?"

His question brought positive responses, including her own, and he got up to go and light the grill.

Terri took heart in his words, which had been the man speaking *Nothing would suit me better.* The father, ever on guard, had evaded the issue of including her in their lives on a regular basis. It was the father she would have to win over once she'd conquered her own self-doubts.

"I wish we didn't have to take you home," Mandy lamented as they loaded up in the van. "It's not my bedtime yet."

"But it is time for you to have your bath and get ready for bed," Terri replied, barely able to hide her own regret. She would have liked to stay and help Mandy with her bath, tell both children good-night and then have a half hour or so alone with Jeremy to finish out the marvelous day.

Next time she would drive her own car so that she could stay later.

There just *had* to be a next time.

"I'm glad Archie happened to live in your neighborhood," Jerry said, not sounding much more cheerful than his sister.

"So am I."

"Hey, let's not end on a down note," Jeremy chided. "You'll make Ms. Sommers feel bad."

"It's easy for you, Dad. You'll get to see her every day at the station. We won't."

"Unless we come to the station to visit her! Please, Daddy, will you take us one day?" Mandy begged.

Terri waited for his answer as hopefully as the children did.

"Sure, I guess that's only fair," he said.

The atmosphere lightened considerably.

When he pulled into her driveway and had switched off the engine, she stopped him as he was about to open his door. "Don't bother to get out. I'll just say my good-nights and steal a few hugs and kisses here in the van."

Mandy didn't require any urging to undo her seat belt and slip forward to hug Terri around the neck. Jerry was shyer, but he brought his face close for her to kiss him on the forehead and give his shoulder an affectionate squeeze. Only Jeremy remained. Terri smiled at him, beckoning with her forefinger, as she leaned toward him. He met her half-way, and when she pressed her lips to his cheek she heard his intake of breath.

Before she could pull back, he circled the back of her neck with his hand, holding her head close to his. During those few seconds, Terri shared his frustration that they had a audience and he couldn't kiss her on the mouth the way he urgently wanted to.

"Good night, Terri," he said, releasing her. His voice was rough.

"Good night, Jeremy. See you tomorrow."

Walking quickly to her cottage in the beam of his head-lights, Terri knew he was experiencing the same dissatisfaction she felt at parting like this.

"I was the only one who gave Ms. Sommers a hug," Mandy stated with a smug satisfaction. "She likes hugs. I can tell."

"Little kids go around hugging everybody," Jerry said with scorn. "You didn't see Dad hugging her, either."

"I would have liked to, though," Jeremy admitted candidly, backing out of Terri's driveway after she'd gone inside. The urge had been strong inside him all day to put his arms around her, to touch her, to kiss her, and had made the pleasure of her company also a torment.

"So why didn't you, Daddy?" Mandy inquired.

"Because adults can't always do what they would like to do."

"And she probably didn't want you to hug her, huh, Dad?" The answer Jerry wanted was clearly *yes*. "Just Mandy. And maybe me."

"Definitely you and Mandy, but I don't think she would have minded a hug from your dad." The intuition made it all the harder to keep his distance.

"I think she would mind, but she might be nice and not tell you. You would probably just embarrass her, Dad."

"I don't think Ms. Sommers would be embarrassed. I

think she likes Daddy a lot.'' Mandy put in her two cents'
worth.

"What do you know about anything?'' the young boy
jeered. "You're just a dumb five-year-old.''

Jeremy called a halt. "That's enough. Let's drop the subject.'' Not that he could drop Terri from his thoughts.

They rode along in silence for several minutes.

"Dad, I remember how you used to hug and kiss Mom,''
Jerry said with a sigh.

"I'm glad you have those memories, son, along with
many other wonderful memories of her. I loved your
mother very much. Nothing can ever change that, including
my marrying again at some future time.''

"Why don't you marry Ms. Sommers, Daddy?'' Mandy
suggested brightly.

"Just *shut up* about Ms. Sommers!'' Jerry spoke vehe-
mently to her. "If you weren't so *stupid,* you'd know that
both people have to want to marry each other. Ms. Sommers isn't interested in marrying Dad.''

"Daddy, did you hear Jerry call me 'stupid'!''

"I'm sorry I called her 'stupid,' Dad,'' Jerry muttered
before he could be reprimanded.

"Apologize to your sister.''

"I'm sorry, Mandy.'' The apology was terse and miserable.

"Jerry, it's highly unlikely that I will marry Ms. Sommers. So cheer up, son.''

Jeremy heard his bleak note and tried to take his own
advice.

The phone started ringing as he herded his children from
the garage into the house. Jerry hurried to answer it.

"For you, Dad. Mrs. Grambly.''

Bad news, Jeremy thought, his gut tightening with dread.
Mrs. Grambly wouldn't call on a Sunday evening to chat.

"Help your sister run water for her bath,'' he requested
of his son, taking the receiver.

"Sure, Dad. Come on, Mandy.''

Mrs. Grambly broke down in tears as she explained that she was packing her things to travel to Texas the next day. Her daughter's husband was on his way to Yellville to get her. "Cindy has a tumor on her right ovary, and her doctor is afraid it's malignant, Jeremy. She's scheduled for surgery on Tuesday. I hate to go off and leave you in a bind like this, but I need to be there to help out."

"Of course you do," he assured her with complete earnestness and heartfelt sympathy. "And Cindy needs you with her for moral support. Don't worry about us. We'll manage. And we'll remember you and your daughter and her family in our prayers."

"You're such a fine man. I knew you'd understand after all you've been through. I wish—" She didn't finish her statement, but said a tearful goodbye and hung up.

I wish you would find yourself another wife had been her partially expressed thought.

"I wish the same thing, Mrs. Grambly," Jeremy said wearily, replacing the receiver.

He didn't have any doubt that he would manage somehow without her capable help, but it wouldn't be easy. Thank heaven he'd hired Terri this past week and wasn't also shorthanded at the station, or he truly would have been in a bind.

His immediate concern was making arrangements for his children for the following day. At ages five and eight, they were too young to be left on their own at home.

Half a dozen phone calls later, Jeremy hadn't had any luck. With a glance at the clock, he abandoned any further efforts until the next morning and phoned Terri, instead, to fill her in on the situation.

"Poor Mrs. Grambly," she said, her compassion coming over the line. "How frightening for her and her daughter. I hope the doctor turns out to be too pessimistic."

"I hope so, too."

"In any event, she'll be gone several weeks, I would think."

"That's what I'm assuming. So far I'm batting zero on getting someone to come and stay with the kids tomorrow."

"What about letting them each visit a friend for the day?"

"No success there, either. I may end up having to bring them to the station with me."

"Why don't you just plan to do that? They wouldn't be a problem. They're such well-behaved children."

"They'll be underfoot. You didn't bargain for running a day care center when you took the job as attendant."

"I'll enjoy having them underfoot. And the experience will be good for them. They'll see their dad in his work environment."

"Okay. I'll bring them and concentrate on other arrangements for Tuesday. Thanks for being so flexible, Terri."

"Don't worry any more about it tonight," she urged. "I'll gladly do everything I can to help out while Mrs. Grambly's away. Plus you have friends and neighbors to rely on. That's a big advantage of living in a small town."

"You're so right. I shouldn't have to be reminded."

"It's all right not to be strong and perfect all the time, Jeremy," she said gently.

"I'm a long way from 'strong and perfect.'"

"I disagree. You're closer than any man I've ever known before. Good night. Give Mandy and Jerry a kiss for me. Here's one for you." She made a kissing sound.

Jeremy closed his eyes and recaptured the touch of her lips against his cheek earlier. "I needed that," he said, his voice soft with gratitude. "Mark it down that I owe you a hug. According to my daughter, you like hugs."

"A hug can do wonders when nothing else helps. Believe me, I'll collect sometime. See you tomorrow."

Hanging up after he'd said good-night, Jeremy felt considerably more prepared to deal with several weeks of Mrs. Grambly's absence.

Ten minutes after Terri had gotten off the phone with Jeremy, Christopher called. "Where the hell have you been?" he asked with barely controlled exasperation. "I've been trying to reach you all afternoon and all evening."

"I listened to your messages when I got home a half hour ago." Terri's tone was none too patient. "This has to stop, Christopher. The phone calls. The flowers. Our marriage is over. You need to accept the fact that we're divorced."

"You were with the gas station owner, weren't you?"

"With him *and* his two children. Not that it matters at this point, but how did you spend your Sunday?"

His brief silence before speaking was an eloquent answer in itself. He'd had a woman for company.

"Let's not trade accusations. Tell me what I'm up against here. Are you having an affair with this guy? How old is he anyway? And what's his name?"

"No, I'm not having an affair with him. He's not the type of man who gets involved in affairs. As for his age, he's in his midthirties. His name is Jeremy Wells. You might be interested to know he's my boss."

"Your *boss?*"

"Last week I began working at his gas station as an attendant. I mainly handle the cash register. It's a self-service station."

His murmured curse fully conveyed his appalled reaction. "My *wife* is employed as a *gas station attendant?*"

"Your ex-wife. Don't worry. No one in Little Rock has to know. When I come to visit my great-aunt or go shopping or whatever, I won't breathe a word to anyone I happen to run into. My purpose isn't to embarrass you."

"Your purpose is twofold. To be around Wells and drive me crazy with jealousy," he accused in a grim tone. "I never expected you to fight this dirty, Terri."

"This isn't a fight, Christopher. My actions no longer have anything to do with you. Please get that through your head."

"Quit the damned job. I'll put a check in the mail to you tomorrow for ten thousand dollars. Or I'll wire the money directly to your account if you'll give me the account number."

"I don't *want* any money from you!"

"Look, I'm about at the end of my rope. I've respected your need for some space. But you're going too far. I can't put up with much more."

"Do us both a favor, then, and get on with your life. I'm not the right woman for you, Christopher. I never was." And he wasn't the right man for her.

"And I suppose you think you *are* the right woman for this Jeremy Wells? Be serious, Terri. The guy's looking for a sweet little homemaker type and nanny. He won't marry you if he has any sense. He just wants to get you into bed."

"If that were the case, he wouldn't have too much trouble! And how would you know what a man like Jeremy wants in a wife? You and he are as unlike as two men could possibly be! Now, I'm hanging up! I've had as much of this conversation as I can stomach. Good night, Christopher."

Terri cut off the connection and hurled the cordless phone on the bed to vent some of her irritation.

"I'll get an unlisted number! And if he keeps harassing me, I'll report him to the police!" she fumed aloud.

Just as in the previous night when she'd flared up at Jeremy, Terri's anger quickly died, leaving her vulnerable to her emotions. Christopher's words mocked her: *And I suppose you think you* are *the right woman for Jeremy Wells?*

She'd wanted so badly to shout yes, and not for the purpose of antagonizing him.

His skepticism had stung all the more because of Terri's own deep-seated lack of confidence that she was well suited to be Jeremy's wife.

Chapter Eight

Jeremy could hear the conversation outside his cubicle of an office, where he sat in front of his computer, entering data from invoices into the spreadsheet program he used instead of an outdated ledger system.

"I finished putting out more candy bars, Ms. Sommers," Jerry reported.

"And I finished handing them to him," Mandy said.

"Great job. Thanks to you two, I'm all caught up with restocking candy and gum." Terri's voice was warm with approval, evoking a clear mental picture of her smiling at his children. Both the vision and the sound of her voice sent a surge of pleasure through him. *Lucky kids to be out there with her.*

"I'll bet you're glad we came to the station with Daddy today," Mandy speculated.

"Very glad. And not just for your help."

Jeremy dropped the invoice in his hand and got up from his desk to go and stand in the doorway. "So how are

things going out here?'' he asked, eyeing Terri inquiringly.
Any excuse to look at her would do. She was so incredibly
lovely. Today she was wearing a slim, white denim skirt,
with the hemline just above the knees, and a pale-yellow
sleeveless blouse. Either she'd forgotten to don a uniform
jacket or decided against it. Try as he might, Jeremy
couldn't keep his gaze from roving admiringly up and
down her slender, but lush, figure.

"Things couldn't be better out here," she replied. "How
are you doing?"

"I'm about caught up."

"Here comes a customer wanting to pay for his gas. Can
I operate the cash register, Ms. Sommers?" Jerry begged.

"Sure you can. He's such a bright boy," she said to
Jeremy. From her note of pride, she might have been prais-
ing her own offspring. "He handles cash and credit card
transactions every bit as well as I do. As soon as he's old
enough, you can hire him as your attendant during the sum-
mers."

With her arm draped around Jerry's shoulders, she accompanied him behind the counter. Watching, Jeremy was
hard put not to envy his son.

The customer was a stranger, a muscle-bound man in his
late twenties wearing a cropped T-shirt and ragged cutoff
jeans that fully exposed his thighs at a level with his crotch.
He swaggered into the station, leather sandals scuffing the
floor.

"Hi, beautiful," he addressed Terri, not so much as
glancing at either child or at Jeremy.

"Hello, how are you today?" she answered him pleasantly. "Your gas was eighteen dollars even. Did you need
anything else?"

He grinned, pulling out his wallet and extracting a
twenty-dollar bill. "Just your name and phone number."

Terri's smile didn't falter. She took the money and
handed it to Jerry, accepted the change back and counted

the two bills into the fellow's palm. "We appreciate your business. Come back again."

He lounged against the counter. "Name's Larry. Larry Seager."

"It's nice to meet you, Larry. This is Jerry. And Mandy. And Jeremy Wells, the owner and my boss." She'd indicated each of them in turn, her eyes widening when she came to Jeremy. He realized he was scowling and both his hands were clenched into fists.

"Anything else we can do for you today?" Jeremy asked, stepping forward. The inquiry was anything but friendly.

Larry straightened. "It's like that, is it?" he drawled, glancing from Jeremy to Terri and back to Jeremy. "You're some lucky son of a gun, man. I'm out of here." Raising a hand in salute, he backed away and swaggered out.

"Dad, I thought you were going to take a swing at that guy!" Jerry exclaimed. "What did he mean, anyway, when he said you were 'some lucky son of a gun'?"

Terri spoke up and made the explanation. "He assumed that I was your dad's girlfriend because your dad stopped him from making a worse nuisance of himself." She turned to Jeremy. "Thanks for coming to my rescue, but you'll lose customers like that."

"You don't have to tolerate that kind of sexist treatment."

"What's 'sexist treatment'?" asked Mandy.

"It has to do with men not showing the proper respect for women," he explained to his daughter.

"And vice versa," Terri put in. "Your dad was offended because Larry wasn't very courteous to me."

"Like calling you 'beautiful' instead of 'miss' or 'ma'am,'" Jerry said.

"Exactly."

Another customer about the same age of the macho Larry entered, halting the conversation. He was a local man. Jeremy responded to his greeting and retreated to the doorway of his office, looking on while the fellow paid with a credit card and carried on lame conversation with Terri, all the while gazing at her like a dog hungrily eyeing a bone.

"Mighty hot weather we've been having."

"Well, it's August, isn't it?" she replied, smiling at him.

"Er, it sure is. Hasn't been a wet summer."

"No, but we haven't had drought conditions, fortunately. I hate it when everything's brown and the plants look thirsty."

"Uh-huh, know what you mean."

"Sign here, please."

He scribbled on the charge slip, took his copy and stuffed it into his pants pocket. Then he stood there, obviously reluctant to leave. "Er, maybe I'll have a soft drink."

Jeremy had to clench his jaws to keep back the words on his lips. *Buy yourself a soft drink somewhere else.*

Terri glanced at him, mild reproof on her face, as she replied pleasantly, "We have a big selection in the coolers along the wall. Help yourself." Coming from behind the counter, she said to Jeremy, "Could I talk to you privately in your office?"

"Sure. Jerry can handle the register while you take a break." A long enough break for the guy to buy his soft drink and be on his way.

She rolled her eyes at Jeremy's grim tone. He got a whiff of her perfume as she sailed past him in the doorway, her arm brushing his chest.

"What *is* the matter with you?" she asked when he'd followed her inside the small room and closed the door. "You're acting like a bouncer in a nightclub. There was nothing out of line in that man's behavior."

"He was salivating looking at you."

"People don't get thrown into jail for what goes on in their minds. Women get used to men 'salivating,' to use your term. We take it in stride and are guilty of it ourselves on occasion."

"I guess you're thinking I'm a prime example of the pot

calling the kettle black,'' Jeremy said with a grimace. "But at least I don't undress you with my eyes.''

"Your eyes pay me nice compliments. The pleasure's mutual because I like your looks just as much.'' A teasing smile signaled a lightening of her mood, and whatever she was about to say seemed to cause some slight embarrassment. "In fact, I can't claim to be as virtuous as you are. Yesterday when you and Jerry were playing badminton, I imagined you without your shirt on. But I didn't strip you below the waist.'' She made a movement to go.

Jeremy stopped her, clasping her shoulders. "You're going to tell me that and leave?''

"We can't stay in here with the door closed and leave your children to run the station.''

He moved his fingers in a massaging motion, battling the powerful longing to take her into his arms and kiss her. "No, you're right. We can't.''

"Forgive me, Jeremy.'' She stroked his cheek.

"Forgive you?''

"I know it's not fair to use physical attraction to rush you into a relationship.''

"You haven't exactly come on to me, Terri.''

"Just now that was my clumsy version of coming on to you,'' she confessed. "Although I honestly didn't ask you in here to get you alone. And tempt you to…'' Her husky voice drifted off.

Jeremy's hands had taken on a will of their own as they slid up to frame her face and tilt it back. "Tempt me to kiss you?'' he murmured, bending his head and bringing his lips to hers.

Just one chaste kiss was the thought in his mind, a thought that was drowned in sweet pleasure as he savored the luscious softness of her mouth. He might have had a chance of sticking to his plan if she hadn't kissed him back, her breath warm on his face. Soon their tongues found each other, rough and wet and intimate. His groan mingled with her soft sound of feminine desire. His arms went around

her and her arms slipped around his neck, holding him
tight. All consciousness of time and place faded as he ravished her lips and she ravished his and mated with his
tongue.

Need exploded inside Jeremy, the way it had on Saturday
night in his living room. He lifted Terri off the floor, holding her tight against him. Her breasts pressed against his
chest, soft mounds of femininity, and her hips were welded
to his groin. Existence centered around the urgency to make
love with her.

From far away a faint knocking penetrated the thick haze
of passion.

"Daddy?" called a childish voice. "Are you and Ms.
Sommers still talking?"

*Mandy was knocking on his office door. Both children
were outside.* The return to reality was abrupt and harsh,
like having a bucket of ice water poured on his head. Equal
amounts of frustration and shame flooded Jeremy as he and
Terri hastily ended the kiss together, pulling apart.

"Just a minute," he called after sucking in a breath. His
voice was rough and strained. "Some father I am," he said
to Terri, releasing her. "When I get you in my arms, I even
forget about my kids."

"It was my fault."

"No, it wasn't your fault. I should have more sense than
to think I can kiss you without getting aroused. Are you
okay?" he asked gently, straightening the collar of her
blouse. She looked as dazed and out of sorts as he felt.

"As okay as you are." She smiled at him, reaching to
wipe his mouth with her thumb. "You probably have more
lipstick on than I do."

"Daddy? Has a minute passed?"

"Yes, you can open the door now and come in."

Jeremy retreated behind his desk, and Terri went out,
rumpling Mandy's curls as she passed her. Mandy promptly
stopped in her tracks and followed after Terri, leaving him
to finish his work after his body calmed down.

A flow of customers came and went and Jeremy could hear snatches of conversation. Jealousy flared up in him, hot and strong, when a male customer lingered longer than necessary—something that happened too often. It was a new emotion for Jeremy. He'd never been a jealous, overly possessive husband. Susan had certainly gotten her share of admiring looks from other men, but always he'd been certain of her love, certain that he was *the* man in her life.

That certainty didn't exist with Terri. And it was never likely to develop. Jeremy accepted that fact. Reason told him he had no grounds whatsoever for jealousy. He was her employer, on a temporary basis. *Temporary.* The key word to keep in mind at all times.

Jeremy's problem was keeping anything in his mind when he was in sight of Terri—or even earshot. And once he took her into his arms, once he started kissing her, he stopped functioning as a rational being. Conscience and morals and duty to his children were swept aside by passion.

He was appalled at his behavior and yet a shameful part of him yearned for more stolen kisses, more opportunities to test his self-control and lose out to the burning desire to make love to her.

Terri had been completely honest. Yesterday she'd admitted outright to having mixed feelings about getting involved with him. *Part of me wants to go after you*, she'd said.

That "part" of her was the same "part" of Jeremy that wanted to throw aside caution and common sense and succumb to sexual attraction. Fortunately she was too conscientious a person not to consider his well-being and that of his children.

The hell of it was that Jeremy didn't feel in the least fortunate for being spared the guilt and loss of self-respect that a fling with Terri would surely cost him.

* * *

"I have some errands to run. Kids, why don't you come along with me?"

"Do I have to, Dad?" Jerry asked. "I'd rather stay here at the station and help Ms. Sommers."

"Me, too, Daddy," Mandy said.

"Let's give Ms. Sommers a breather." Jeremy's tone didn't encourage any argument. "I'll be back in a couple of hours, Terri."

With long faces, his children accompanied him. Terri's expression was none too cheerful, but she didn't intervene on their behalf as he sensed she wanted to do.

Jeremy had figured he was doing her a favor. While she genuinely seemed to enjoy his young son and daughter, she wasn't used to being around children for extended periods of time. He'd assumed she would appreciate a break during the afternoon. However, she gave no indication of being appreciative.

Was it possible that Jeremy had misjudged Terri? That some of his other assumptions regarding her were wrong, too?

She'd stated with conviction that her marriage was over. Maybe she would stick with the divorce and not reconcile with her ex-husband. Maybe she wouldn't return to Little Rock, but decide to stay right here in Yellville, where she seemed to be quite content.

Maybe...

Cautious hope flickered to life inside Jeremy, putting a spring into his step.

"Dad, Mandy's sick to her stomach. She just threw up. I don't think she'll feel like going to stay at Brittany's house today."

"I'll go check on her. Finish fixing yourself a bowl of cereal." Jeremy had set down the cereal box and was already halfway to the door of the kitchen, concerned about his daughter.

She'd made it back to her bed from the bathroom and

lay curled up on top of rumpled sheets. "Daddy, I feel bad," she complained fretfully.

He smoothed her tousled hair back from her pale little face and laid his hand on her brow. To his relief she wasn't hot to the touch. "You don't seem to be running a fever, angel. Just crawl back under the sheet."

With his help, she obeyed his gentle instructions even as she protested, "But I have to get dressed and go to Brittany's."

"Not unless you get to feeling a lot better in the next thirty minutes."

"Who'll stay with me?"

"Let Daddy worry about that." He straightened her sheet, hesitant about leaving her alone and returning to the kitchen. The responsibility of sole parenthood rested heaviest on Jeremy's shoulders when one of his children became ill. "Will you be okay for a few minutes, angel?"

"I don't know, Daddy. I might have to throw up again."

Feeling helpless as well as anxious, he sat down on the edge of her bed and held her little hand in his, pondering whether he should stay home with her himself or try to get someone. His day was fully scheduled, but Mandy came first. The problem was Jeremy's own sense of inadequacy as a nurse. He'd depended upon Susan to gauge the seriousness of the children's ailments. She'd somehow seemed to be able to judge when a trip to the doctor was in order or just a dose of over-the-counter child's medicine.

Jerry appeared in the door. "Dad, aren't you going to eat your breakfast?"

Mandy's hand clutched his. "Not just yet," Jeremy answered.

"You're supposed to drop me off at Mitch's house at eight o'clock," Jerry reminded him. "Is Mandy going to be well enough by then to ride with us?"

"I doubt that she will."

"Remember that Mitch's mom can't pick me up. She doesn't have a car to drive today."

"We may have to call Mrs. Zimmer and tell her you'll be late."

"Dad, I can't be late! Mitch and I are supposed to go hiking with his uncle Brad, who's coming from Jasper."

Jeremy sighed. "We'll figure out some transportation for you somehow. Bring me the cordless phone and the phone book."

Jerry returned after a couple of minutes without either item. "I took care of it myself, Dad. I called Ms. Sommers. She said she'd be happy to pick me up and drop me off at Mitch's house."

"You shouldn't have done that without my permission, son." The reprimand lacked sternness because Jeremy acknowledged to himself that he would have gone along with appealing to Terri for a favor. Oddly, she seemed the logical person.

Mandy had stirred and rolled over on her back. "Ask Ms. Sommers to come in and see me, Jerry," she requested, not opening her eyes.

"Ms. Sommers probably won't want to risk catching a stomach virus, angel."

"No, Dad, she's not worried about catching anything. She was just real upset that Mandy was sick, and plans on coming in and seeing her. She'll be right over."

Relief swept through Jeremy at the news that Terri would soon be there, looking in on Mandy. He welcomed Terri's diagnosis and advice. Her moral support.

Mixed in with the paternal reaction was a purely male gladness that Jeremy couldn't squelch during the short wait before her car pulled up outside.

Jerry let her into the house. Soon she appeared in the doorway of Mandy's room, all concern. Jeremy vacated his spot and she immediately took it, crooning, "Poor darling." He stood by while she touched her hand to his little daughter's face, obviously testing for fever, and asked questions he hadn't had the presence of mind to ask.

"Are you having pains in your tummy?"

"No. I just feel sick."

"Did you have a chill during the night?"

"No, I don't think so." Mandy opened her eyes and rolled her head to locate him. "Daddy, you can go eat your breakfast now that Ms. Sommers's here."

"Okay," Jeremy agreed, glancing at his watch to calculate the time factor. "Then Ms. Sommers will have to leave, angel, and drop Jerry off."

"Why don't you take him, instead?"

"I was going to suggest that myself," Terri said. "Who's going to stay with Mandy today? She's obviously not feeling up to spending the day with her little friend."

"I haven't had a chance yet to make any arrangements. Do you think she's sick enough to go to the doctor?"

"We should be able to tell better by the time office hours open. We might just need to get some medical advice over the phone and let her rest comfortably." She caressed Mandy's cheek. "Children get upset tummies."

Her matter-of-factness was enormously reassuring for him, even if it was meant to reassure his daughter. Would it be taking unfair advantage to ask Terri to act as nurse today while he ran the station? he was wondering.

Just then Mandy requested wistfully, "Would you stay with me today, Ms. Sommers?"

"Your father has to make that decision, darling."

"Can she, Daddy?"

Would you mind? Jeremy asked Terri silently.

She telegraphed her answer without hesitation. *Of course, I wouldn't mind. I want to.*

"Yes, angel. For the first half of the day anyway, Ms. Sommers can stay with you." A full morning of tending a sick child might be all Terri could handle. He wanted to give her an out for the afternoon.

Business was brisk at the station. Jeremy had his hands full the first hour and a half. Finally there was a brief lull and he had a chance to call his house to get an update on Mandy. Terri filled him in, seeming very calm and in control of the situation. His daughter had had one more bout of throwing up, but was feeling slightly better.

"She's a dear little patient," Terri declared with affection after explaining that she'd spoken on the phone with Dr. Gloria Hollis, the children's pediatrician, and was following her instructions, which included administering doses of a children's over-the-counter medicine for upset stomach. "We've moved into the living room and she's lying on the sofa and watching a kiddie program."

"If you decide you want to swap places, just let me know. I can get one of my mechanics to cover for me for fifteen or twenty minutes."

"I'm happy where I am."

Jeremy was struck by her word choice. It occurred to him that he could so easily be happy to have her where she was, in his home, and not just when she was needed as a nurse for one of his children.

Maybe he'd been too negative in his outlook about a future that might possibly include Terri. Maybe Jeremy should date her and gamble on a relationship with her. After all, life held no guarantees, no promises of permanency. Losing Susan was tragic proof of that.

Jeremy's reflections made the flicker of hopefulness that had been ignited the previous day burn brighter.

At noon he checked in with Terri again, and learned that Mandy had eaten soup and kept it down and was napping. "She seems to be over the nausea. It won't surprise me if she's feeling well enough to play quietly this afternoon. Before you ask, I'm not ready to be relieved of my nursing duties," Terri added firmly.

"In that case, I won't offer to relieve you."

"What arrangements have you made for the children tomorrow?"

"None so far. I'm batting zero with hiring someone to replace Mrs. Grambly until school starts."

"Would it be an easier matter to get someone to fill in for me at the station? A high-school student, perhaps?"

"Why, yes, but—"

"Go ahead and do that," she suggested. "Let me fill in for Mrs. Grambly. I know I'm not as capable, but I'll do my best."

"Terri, I wouldn't ever expect you to do what Mrs. Grambly does. She cleans house and cooks and keeps up with the laundry in addition to looking after Jerry and Mandy." Jeremy's voice expressed his shock at the idea of her as housekeeper.

"It may surprise you to learn that I can run a vacuum cleaner and operate a washer and dryer. And my potato salad was edible, wasn't it?"

"Your potato salad was tasty," he assured her with sincerity. "I'm not questioning your ability in any of those areas, but you wouldn't need to do housework. I can get help with that and manage meals myself. My problem is a mature daytime sitter for the kids. I'm tempted to snap up your offer," he admitted.

"We'll consider the matter settled, then."

She sounded glad, and Jeremy knew his children would both be delighted.

Certainly a load was lifted from his mind. By the time school started, hopefully Mrs. Grambly would have returned. Jeremy would still need the good-hearted woman on a modified schedule, even though Mandy would be in kindergarten.

Mrs. Grambly's sudden departure had caused him some headaches, but the way things had turned out, it had a fortunate side. A few weeks as daytime sitter should give Terri a good idea of what being a stepmother to his children on a day-to-day basis would be like. No child was lovable all the time, and his two were no exception.

After only a couple of days, Terri might well realize that she wasn't cut out for the role of stepmother to an eight-year-old and a five-year-old. If so, her interest in Jeremy would die a natural death, since he and his kids were a package deal. Better to find out as soon as possible, he thought, before he'd built up his hopes any higher.

As it was, he'd already built them up higher than he should have.

Mitch's uncle had brought Jerry home, so Jeremy drove directly to his house when he left the station at six o'clock. He was surprised to see his son outside, playing tag football in a neighbor's yard instead of being indoors with Terri. Had he misbehaved and gone outdoors to sulk after being scolded? Jeremy wondered with a pang of parental anxiety.

Jerry spotted him and dashed over, wildly waving his arms. Somewhat reassured by the boyish exuberance, Jeremy put on the brakes.

"Dad, isn't it *great* that Ms. Sommers is going to take Mrs. Grambly's place while she's gone?" the young boy exclaimed as he skidded to a stop.

"She's doing us a big favor. I expect you and Mandy both to be very cooperative and mind her just as you do Mrs. Grambly."

"Sure, Dad." Jerry brushed aside the fatherly lecture with a hint of impatience. "Ms. Sommers will probably tell you what a big help I was to her when I got here. I folded part of the laundry and showed her where to put it away. She was going to leave your clothes on your bed, but I told her Mrs. Grambly always opens your dresser drawers."

"Ms. Sommers did the laundry?"

It was a dumb question, since obviously she had, but some response was expected of him and Jeremy could hardly speak his thoughts. He was imagining Terri in his bedroom, putting away his clothing, including his underwear. Having Mrs. Grambly perform the same service had never seemed intimate.

"Uh-huh." Jerry was bobbing his head. "She changed Mandy's sheets, and since she was washing them, she did the rest, too. I wanted to help her make supper, but when

Jamie rang the doorbell and asked if I could come out and play, she wouldn't let me say no.''

"Ms. Sommers is cooking supper?"

"Mashed potatoes and meat loaf and green salad. Mandy wanted mashed potatoes. I hope you can talk Ms. Sommers into eating with us. She's not planning to."

"I'll certainly try to persuade her. Come on in now and wash your face and hands."

"Why do you think I came running over, Dad? I was waiting for you to get home."

"Sorry to insult your intelligence." Jeremy reached through the open window and ruffled his son's hair, empathizing with his eagerness to go inside and enjoy Terri's company.

Mouthwatering aromas hit him when he entered the kitchen behind Jerry, who bounded out of the room. A glance over at the table revealed it was set for three. A timer went off, and soon Terri came hurrying in.

"Hi," she greeted him with a welcoming smile, heading directly to the gas range.

"Hi. Supper smells terrific. I got a preview of the menu outside."

"I hope it tastes good."

"I bet it'll taste delicious. But you really didn't have to go to the trouble of cooking." He went over to stand near her under the pretense of inspecting the meat loaf she was taking out of the oven.

"Throwing a meal like this together isn't much trouble. The mashed potatoes are in a Pyrex dish in the microwave. Just heat them up when you're ready to eat." She removed her oven mitts and laid them down. "Let me say goodbye to Mandy and Jerry, and I'll be going."

"Won't you join us for supper?" Jeremy asked quickly, lightly clasping her arm to stop her. "All three of us would like you to."

She faced him, looking uncertain. "As long as you don't

feel obligated to include me as a regular habit. I'm sure
Mrs. Grambly doesn't have supper with you every night.''

Jeremy still held her arm, since he couldn't quite bring
himself to drop his hand. What he wanted to do very badly
was draw her a half step closer, close enough to bend his
head and kiss her on the lips. The urge softened his voice
as he said, ''I promise not to include you out of obligation.
Okay?''

Terri nodded, drawing in a deep breath that lifted her
breasts. Jeremy had glanced down before he could stop
himself. When he raised his gaze and looked into her eyes,
he knew her pulse had quickened, too.

''Boy, I'm hungry. Aren't you, Dad?'' Jerry had returned.

''Starving,'' Jeremy said, his fingers caressing Terri's
warm, soft skin before he reluctantly released her.

''Hi, Daddy. I'm feeling better.'' Mandy entered.

''Hi, angel. That's really good news.'' He paused to pick
her up and give her a hug and kiss before he washed his
hands at the sink and helped with serving the appetizing
meal Terri had prepared. In the process he bumped into
Terri once or twice and the contact heightened his contentment, even while it intensified the hunger in him that
couldn't be satisfied by food.

I'm happy where I am, she'd said earlier today. Certainly
she looked happy and content supervising in the kitchen
and then sitting down to supper with them. Jeremy put aside
thoughts of the future and immersed himself in the pleas-
ures of eating and enjoyment of the companionable family
atmosphere.

Jerry related the high points of his hike with Mitch and
his uncle, suffering Mandy's interruptions with unusual
brotherly patience. Jeremy shared a couple of amusing incidents that had occurred at the station, telling them primarily for Terri's benefit. Ordinarily supper conversation
consisted of his listening to his children, he realized. For

all his interest in them, it was limiting to be the sole adult, the sole parent on a regular basis.

"This is awfully nice, evening up the odds," he said to Terri. "Two adults instead of one."

She smiled and nodded. "I can imagine."

Jeremy sensed that she *could* imagine and understood his meaning without any more explanation. The moment of rapport warmed him and yet sharpened the awareness of how much he missed being married and carrying on unspoken communication with a wife who was in tune with him and he in tune with her.

Could Terri be happy over the long term being his wife? Jeremy's serious doubts were eroding, eroding far too rapidly.

Deliberately he conjured up a vision of the expensive bouquet of yellow roses and replayed the telling comment of the delivery woman from the florist, then his son's voice and then Terri's own voice revealing her ambivalence.

He ordered yellow this time.

Scott Getty's mom divorced his stepfather and married his real father again.

Part of me wants to go after you, Jeremy.

He needed to make a mental tape and keep playing it over and over for at least another month.

Chapter Nine

"*Jeremy, your hands feel so wonderful on my body. Make love to me...*"

"*Someone's at the front door.*"

"*They'll go away.*"

But the persistent knocking continued.

"Please don't bother us now!" Terri murmured, and awakened herself with the words spoken aloud in her sleep. She'd been dreaming, such a wonderful, arousing dream in which Jeremy was on the verge of making love to her in his bedroom after the children had gone to bed and were asleep. "Why did I have to wake up?" she muttered in dismay, curling up on her side and hugging herself.

Her breasts felt heavy, the hardened nipples thrusting again the silk of her nightgown. Between her thighs she was wet and ready for Jeremy's lovemaking. If she'd kept on dreaming, he would have filled the aching emptiness and satisfied the need that was more than sexual. Lovemaking had never been purely sexual with Terri. It was bound up with closeness and emotional intimacy.

Knock. Knock. Knock.

There *had* been someone knocking on *her* front door, she realized, raising her head from the pillow. With a sigh, she tossed aside the sheet and got up and slipped on the silk robe that matched her nightgown.

Who could be visiting her at eight o'clock on Saturday morning? she wondered, having verified the time with a glance at her digital alarm clock. Jeremy and the children weren't supposed to pick her up until ten. Surely they weren't this early. Were they?

The slight possibility brought a flush of anticipation as she hurried to open the door. On her porch stood two young boys about Jerry's age, who both looked familiar.

"Hi, Ms. Sommers," said a youth with carrot-red hair and a liberal sprinkling of freckles on his face. "Remember us? We saw you at the ballpark. I'm Archie and he's Pete."

The mention of the ballpark helped Terri to place them and served as a pleasant reminder that she'd become a regular fan at Jerry's softball games the past couple of weeks. "Hi, boys. What can I do for you, Archie and Pete?" she inquired, smiling at them.

Archie, obviously the spokesman for the two, jabbed a thumb at his shyer pal as he explained, "Pete here's selling Christmas candles to raise money for his Sunday-school class to take a trip. You order 'em now and pay him the money when he brings 'em to you in time for Christmas."

Pete drew a colored brochure from behind his back and proffered it to Terri with a mute hopefulness that sold her on purchasing a candle more than a sales pitch could ever have done. "These would make lovely small Christmas gifts," she commented, and selected several candles.

The money would go to a good cause, and it was worth the cost to see the grins spread across both boys' faces. As she watched them lope across her small yard on the way over to the Williamses' house, the thought occurred to Terri that she hadn't hesitated to order items that would be delivered in December. Just three weeks ago when she'd attended Pat Tyler's wedding, she couldn't have said definitely that she would still be living in Yellville in December.

The uncertainty had completely vanished. She'd committed herself to staying for at least six months when she'd taken the job as Jeremy's station attendant. Her verbal contract wouldn't be up until January, and she couldn't foresee wanting to leave then. There was nothing drawing her away from her hometown and a great deal to keep her right here, namely Jeremy and his two children.

Life had suddenly become so rich with promise, when it had been so empty on that Saturday Jeremy had sat down beside her in the church on Pat's wedding day. Miraculously, what Terri most prized and wanted—a decent, faithful husband, a real home, a family—seemed to be within her reach. It was almost too good to be true.

Christmas, Terri thought, still standing in her open doorway and gazing out at the quiet street. What fun it would be decorating Jeremy's house and shopping for presents and planning a special meal, in general making the special holiday a happy, festive occasion for him and Jerry and Mandy, as it surely had been when Susan was alive and probably hadn't been since.

But she was thinking too far ahead. Thanksgiving came before Christmas. Terri could visualize the four of them sitting down to a feast. A traditional meal with a golden brown roasted turkey and dressing and all the trimmings. They would eat in the dining room.

"November," she said, her vision making her wistful and also bringing to life impatience and anxiousness.

By Thanksgiving, surely she and Jeremy would have gone through a period of dating each other and she would have conquered his reservations about her as a wife and stepmother. Perhaps he would have proposed by then, and maybe they would even have gotten married. Terri was ready to say yes if he asked her today.

Jeremy needed her. Mandy and Jerry needed her. And she loved ministering to their needs. Never before had she felt as productive and rewarded for her efforts and her labor. And with every day that passed, she grew more deeply attached to father and children.

Terri still couldn't say to herself with utter confidence that she could make Jeremy as good a wife as he deserved or make his son and daughter as good a stepmother as they deserved, but she knew she would put her heart and soul into doing her best, given the chance.

Her phone was ringing. "Probably Christopher," she said, sighing and closing the door. After a two-week silence, which she'd welcomed, he'd phoned last night and left a message, ending it with the promise, *I'll call you in the morning, darling.* His use of his favorite endearment, which fell off his tongue so easily, had set Terri's thoughts down a path that wouldn't have pleased him at all. She'd imagined Jeremy calling her "darling" and had gotten goose bumps.

Sincerity made such a difference in a man's voice, she reflected now as she picked up the phone in her living room. Sure enough, her caller was Christopher.

"How are you?" he asked.

"I'm well. And happy."

"Come on, darling," he chided. "You can't be 'happy' working at a gas station, no matter how dull and upright the owner is."

"Jeremy *isn't* dull. He's personable and intelligent. For that matter, I haven't been working at his station. I've been taking the place of the woman who's his combination sitter and housekeeper and cook."

A brief silence conveyed his stunned, appalled reaction before he said with disbelief in his voice, "The guy has put you to work cleaning his house and cooking his meals? And you went along? My God, Terri, you need to see a therapist. Please, darling, come back to Little Rock before you screw up your life."

"He didn't 'put me to work.' I volunteered to fill in when Mrs. Grambly, the woman I referred to, was called out of town on a family emergency." Terri's explanation was patient. She couldn't help feeling a little sorry for Christopher, who was genuinely bewildered and concerned. In his own way, he did care for her, although he didn't understand her needs and never had. In some part of her heart, she would always care for him and be concerned about his welfare.

"I definitely won't be moving back to Little Rock, Christopher," she stated. "I'm hoping to marry Jeremy, and if I do, I'll live right here in Yellville."

"You're 'hoping' to marry him? He hasn't proposed to you?"

"No, not yet. We haven't actually dated up to this point." Or slept together, but Terri didn't doubt that love-making with Jeremy would be satisfying and wonderful.

"You don't love this guy. You still love me. As angry and hurt as you were when you left me, you didn't really want a divorce or you would have gone out and hired yourself a big-gun divorce lawyer. Instead you agreed to let my attorney handle the legal procedure for both of us, knowing I would drag things out as long as possible. Now, isn't that true?" Christopher demanded.

"A big-gun divorce lawyer wouldn't have taken me on as a client, because there wouldn't have been any profit motive. I wasn't contesting our prenuptial agreement and was walking away with nothing. Since I wasn't involved with anyone or even interested in dating, it hardly mattered whether you delayed the proceedings. I knew eventually the divorce would be final."

"You wanted to give me the chance to move heaven and earth to get you back. Can you honestly deny that?"

Terri couldn't. "Fortunately for both of us, I was strong enough to hold out for what I knew was best."

"Holding out wasn't best for you or for me. Terri, don't throw our marriage away on some crazy fantasy about being Susie Homemaker. I'm on my knees, begging you to come back to me on your terms. We'll do away with the prenuptial agreement. You can have a baby, if that'll make you happy. I'll hire a live-in nanny to free you up. I'll do *anything* you say, for God's sake."

She bit her lip. It would be too cruel to speak the truth: *I don't want your baby anymore.*

"Let's make a fresh start," he implored. "I need you."

"No, you don't need *me*. You need the woman I tried to be to please you. Wife of prominent attorney, former beauty queen and former model, gracious hostess, fundraiser for charity and the arts. I want a whole different identity."

"Wife of gas station owner in Yellville, Arkansas? That's the other end of the spectrum, all right. When the novelty wears off, you won't be happy with shopping at the supermarket and attending PTA meetings. If this Jeremy Wells is intelligent, as you say he is, he has to realize that, too."

"You can be sure he won't marry me until he has overcome any qualms."

"He's in love with you, of course."

"No." The admission was surprisingly painful. "Not in the sense of romantic love. He's a very caring person, and I think he cares about me." *I'm certain he desires me,* she could have added.

"And you care about him?"

"A great deal. And I adore his children, Jerry and Mandy."

"So you envision the four of you becoming one big happy family, like some heartwarming TV drama, which is the sole basis of your ideas about family. Reality is a lot different. Whether I can ever win you back or not, I can't stand by and let you make this mistake. Goodbye, darling. I have to get to the club for a nine o'clock tee-off time."

He hung up, giving her no opportunity to answer and combat his corrosive skepticism.

What if he was right and Terri *was* indulging in fantasy, building up unrealistic expectations? Not just her own, but Jeremy's, too. What if she was deluding herself into believing she could be a good wife to him, a good stepmother to his children? Failure was unthinkable in view of the damage she could do to the three of them, especially when they'd already survived tragedy.

Did Christopher know her better than she knew herself?

Troubled, Terri made coffee and got dressed. Her soul-searching spoiled much of her anticipation for the excursion to Mountain Home.

Jeremy obviously sensed that something was wrong, even though she made an effort to behave normally. Terri caught his questioning glances at her.

"What's the matter?" he asked when they'd arrived at a mall and the children had run ahead in the parking lot, giving him and Terri their first opportunity for private conversation. He caught her hand and linked her fingers with his. "You seem to have something on your mind."

Terri sighed, glad to drop the pretense of being cheerful. "Christopher phoned this morning. He'd left me alone for a couple of weeks."

"He's still trying to get you back?"

She nodded. "It's no wonder he's a successful litigator. He just keeps battering away at my will, and when I don't cave he takes another tactic and tries to undermine my confidence in my own judgment about the kind of future I want."

"Does he know about me?"

"Yes. Much of our conversation this morning was about you." Terri took her courage in hand, continuing, "He ridicules the very notion that I would make you a suitable wife and be happy living in Yellville. He's convinced I would eventually grow bored and dissatisfied."

Jeremy's hold on her hand tightened, almost painfully,

before it eased and he finally said, "I wish I were convinced he's wrong."

"Don't you be negative, too!" Terri cried in dismay. "I could use a vote of confidence."

"So you aren't sure yourself?"

"I was starting to be sure, but it's difficult with you and Christopher both believing I'm incapable of determining what will make me happy." Terri pulled her hand free.

"God knows I don't *want* to side with him on anything, least of all on the subject of you and me. I'd like to put a stop to his phoning you and sending you roses and having any contact with you whatsoever."

She glanced over, taken aback by the vehemence that combined with the frustration in his voice. But it was his disheartened expression that flooded Terri's heart with emotion, that dissipated her sense of hurt. She slipped her arm in his. "Let's don't allow Christopher to ruin our whole day. That's not fair to the children."

As though in response to her calling attention to them, his son and daughter skidded to a halt some twenty-five yards ahead and waited for their father and Terri to catch up.

"Why're you walking so slow?" Jerry asked, frowning as he eyed their linked arms.

"We were walking at a normal pace for adults," Jeremy replied.

"And we were walking at a normal pace for children, huh, Daddy?" Mandy fell into step so that the three of them walked abreast, while Jerry dropped to the rear.

"Did you run out of energy all of a sudden?" Terri inquired, smiling at him over her shoulder. He didn't smile back.

"Shopping for school clothes is boring."

"Not for me," Mandy said. "I think it's fun."

"What do you know about anything? You're only a little kid starting kindergarten."

"I bet I know more things than you knew when you were five years old!"

"That's enough squabbling," Jeremy stated, intervening.

Terri eased out a sigh, comprehending all too well the sudden change in Jerry's mood from high-spirited and carefree to glum and surly. Despite his liking and affection for her, he strongly rejected the notion of her and Jeremy forming a couple.

As though she didn't face a large enough hurdle in conquering her self-doubts and winning Jeremy's trust, his son wasn't any more ready to accept her as a stepmother than he'd been ready to accept Pat Tyler or Jennifer Larkins.

Inside the mall the four of them entered a department store together, but after brief consultation Jeremy headed to the boys' clothing department with Jerry, while Terri and Mandy went in another direction in search of little girls' clothing. Terri's low state of morale was soon boosted by the pleasure of outfitting her charge, who preened and admired herself in the mirror of the dressing room.

"I look cute, don't I?" Mandy inquired with innocent vanity, fluffing her black curls as she modeled pink corduroy pants and matching pink pullover blouse.

"You look precious." Terri couldn't resist hugging her tight, affection welling up.

As arranged, they met Jeremy and Jerry in the shoe department, where the latter was trying on high-top athletic shoes.

"Did you leave any clothes for other little girls?" Jeremy asked his daughter teasingly, raising his eyebrows at two oversized shopping bags Terri carried. "Looks like you and Ms. Sommers bought out the department."

"We got carried away," Terri admitted. "But you and Jerry must have done all right, too, if those bags in the chair there are yours."

"Dad got me this real neat sweatshirt, Ms. Sommers," Jerry volunteered eagerly. "I'll be glad when the weather gets cold and I can wear it to school."

"You'll have to show it to me. Along with everything else."

The earlier strain was gone. Jerry had returned to his normal lovable self. Setting down her bags to inspect the shoes for small girls, Terri felt the swell of happiness. *This is what I want,* she thought as she had numerous times since she'd met Jeremy and his children and become a part of their lives.

Christopher was wrong. She hadn't idealized the special joys of having a family. Along with those joys came worry and irritation and stress. Not every day was a good day for a parent. If Terri needed proof of the flip side of the coin, all she had to do was listen to the harried mother scolding a fretful little girl about Mandy's age who was being uncooperative about trying on a pair of shoes.

Finally the woman gave up. As she hustled the child away in defeat, threatening a spanking when they reached their car, Mandy let out a loud giggle.

Jeremy frowned at her. "That's not polite to laugh at people, angel."

"I wasn't laughing at them, Daddy. I was remembering something funny that happened. A lady who works in the store thought Ms. Sommers was my mommy. And we didn't tell her she was wrong."

"That's not funny," Jerry said, scowling at her. "You should have told her that our mom died. That's like lying."

"Was it like lying, Daddy?" She poked out her bottom lip.

"More like a harmless fib. Let's not make a big deal out of nothing, son. Which pair of shoes do you want to buy? The black high-tops?"

"I don't *care* which pair! I'm going out to wait for you in the mall." He got up and stormed out.

"You should punish him, Daddy, and not let him go to the movies with Jamie and sleep over at his house tonight. He's a bad boy, isn't he, Ms. Sommers?"

"No, he isn't a bad boy," Terri answered, her heart aching for Jerry. "He's just loyal to the memory of his mother. Now, sit down in the chair, sweetie, and let's see which of the shoes we picked out for you fit best."

"I'll pay for these black high-tops and then go out and wait with him, if that's okay," Jeremy said, his voice somber.

"Of course it's okay," she assured him.

It wasn't necessary to add, *Don't be too harsh with him.* She had utter confidence in Jeremy's ability to deal wisely with any situation that came up with his children. What she admired most about him was his being such a wonderful father, the kind of father she would have foolishly hoped Christopher would become if she'd borne his child.

Thank heaven he hadn't given in to her wish to be a mother.

For all Terri knew, she might not have been able to conceive. Not every woman was lucky enough to be fertile. She might marry Jeremy and a few years down the line discover that nature had never intended her to experience pregnancy and childbirth. Being a stepmother to Mandy and Jerry would allow her to take such a disappointment in stride.

But if she was fertile and became pregnant with Jeremy's baby and gave birth to a little brother or sister for them...

"These shoes pinch my toes, Ms. Sommers."

"Do you have those in the next larger size?" Terri asked the male salesclerk.

She gave her full attention to Mandy and the here and now, pushing aside thoughts of an imagined future so beautiful it might be a mirage.

Jeremy located his son sitting on a bench in the mall, shoulders slumped and eyes downcast. "How about giving me a hand with these bags?" he asked. "We'll take them out to the van. Then we won't have to lug them around the mall while we finish our shopping."

Jerry promptly got up, responding to his father's matter-of-fact request. He didn't speak until they were striding along side by side in the parking lot. "I guess you're mad about the way I acted in the store."

"I'm not proud."

"It's not right that we should forget Mom."

"I'll never stop treasuring my memories of your mother. But as life goes on, I'm hoping that you and Mandy and I will collect other happy memories, too."

There was no reply until they'd almost reached the van. "You said you weren't going to date Ms. Sommers."

"So far I haven't."

"It'll spoil everything if you do, Dad!"

"Why should it spoil everything for Ms. Sommers and me to become closer friends? You and Mandy would certainly be included most of the time. Occasionally I might hire a sitter and take Ms. Sommers out for an evening, but not frequently."

They stowed the bags and headed back the way they had come, with Jerry sunk in stubborn silence. Jeremy considered and rejected different new approaches to the discussion, hampered by his inner conflict about dating Terri. How could he sell his son on the theory that Terri's presence in their lives could be the greatest possible blessing, when Jeremy wasn't one hundred percent sure it wasn't a temporary blessing?

Less than two hours ago she'd admitted to him right here in this same parking lot that she suffered doubts about whether she could be content making her home in Yellville.

"I expect you to be polite," he said. "Ms. Sommers is being kind enough to spend her Saturday with us. The least we can do is act appreciative."

"It's not that I don't like Ms. Sommers. I like her a whole lot." Jerry sighed. After a moment, he asked, "Can we go back in the store and buy those black high-tops, Dad?"

"I already bought them. I could tell they were your first choice."

Jeremy squeezed his shoulder, and the gesture of fatherly affection and forgiveness seemed to do wonders for his son's posture.

Minutes after they'd reentered the mall, Terri and Mandy emerged from the store and came over to join them. Jeremy was aware of the admiring glances Terri attracted from females and males alike. Two boys in their late teens did double takes and looked her up and down. One middle-aged man passing by was so intent on staring at her that he bumped into the plump woman with him, who snapped, "Will you watch where you're walking, Roger!"

It would take some getting used to, if he was married to Terri, to having men of all ages openly lusting after his wife. Without any grounds for being annoyed, he found himself glaring at the teenage boys and the middle-aged man.

"Is Jerry being punished?" Mandy demanded.

The sight of her brother apparently reminded her of the incident in the shoe department. Or maybe it was the sight of his own expression, Jeremy realized, smoothing out the frown on his brow.

He tugged a curly black lock of her hair. "How about letting me take care of being the father? You have your hands full being Mandy."

She smiled up at him. "Your precious little girl, huh?"

"And sometime busybody."

"Am I punished, Dad?" Jerry asked worriedly.

"Do you think you should be?"

"Probably, unless I behave myself the rest of the day."

"I'll go along with that. Now, where to next?"

Jeremy heard the answers, even as he directed an unfriendly look at a man about his own age who, headed for the exit carrying a fancy-wrapped package, no doubt for his wife, cast an appreciative glance at Terri.

"Stop it," she scolded in an undertone as Jeremy fell into step with her, the two children walking ahead. "Just don't pay attention."

"Didn't your husband mind?"

"Mind? He loved every minute out in public places."

"I'm afraid I wouldn't."

"No, you're different." She slipped her arm in his, but then almost immediately drew away, her gaze falling on Jerry.

Jeremy restrained himself from reaching for her hand, mindful, too, of not wanting to upset his son. "Jerry's spending the evening with his friend Jamie. Would you keep Mandy and me company tonight?" he asked. "Before you answer, I should warn you I promised to rent a video to watch with her."

"She told me, and I was hoping to be included."

"Consider yourself automatically included in whatever goes on at the Wells house."

"Until further notice, I will." She looked and sounded quietly thrilled by his offhanded, but earnest, words.

"Can we go into this store, Dad?" Jerry turned around at that moment to ask. They'd come abreast of an electronics store that sold intriguing gadgets.

Jeremy gave his permission and steered Terri toward the entrance, touching his hand to her back and satisfying the aching need to connect with her physically. After that he took every opportunity to play the male escort, brief touches being better than nothing.

Inadvertently he heeded her advice about ignoring the attention she attracted, because it was so easy to restrict his attention to her and to his children, enclosing them in a small, charmed group.

"Don't stop the movie," Jeremy said, getting up from the sofa. "I'll answer the phone out in the kitchen." He was already halfway to the door.

"You'll miss the ending, Daddy," Mandy protested.

"We'll wait for him anyway," Terri consoled the little girl, picking up the remote control and pressing the pause button.

He returned in about five minutes.

"Bad news?" Terri asked with concern, reacting to his somber expression.

"Not good news. I'll tell you later."

"Start the movie up again," Mandy urged, oblivious to the undercurrents.

Jeremy took his place again on the sofa, with Mandy occupying the spot between him and Terri. Up until the interruption, the three of them had been absorbed in the well-acted drama involving children and a dog, but Terri could sense that Jeremy was only gazing at the TV screen and thinking his own thoughts now, while she puzzled over who had called and the nature of the "not good" news. Common sense ruled out an emergency involving Jerry or a catastrophe like a fire at the gas station, because Jeremy wouldn't be calmly sitting there.

"That was a real good movie!" Mandy exclaimed as the credits began to scroll following the finale. She slid off the sofa and stretched, yawning, before she held out a hand to each of them and said sweetly, "You can both tuck me in. Then Ms. Sommers can read to me tonight, since you read me a story last night, Daddy. And you can listen, too, if you want."

He rose and accompanied them to his daughter's bedroom, but after kissing her good-night, he left.

Mandy barely stayed awake until the last page of the book she selected had been read. "Good night, Ms. Sommers," she said sleepily, hugging Terri around the neck.

"Good night, precious."

"I love you."

The words spoken with childish simplicity took Terri completely unawares. Tears stung her eyes and clogged her throat as she answered, her voice coming out in a whisper, "I love you, too." *And your brother. And your father.*

What she felt for the three of them went much deeper than fondness.

Jeremy wasn't in the living room. Terri looked for him

in the kitchen and finally found him out on the patio. He stood with his hands in his pockets, gazing up at the sky, which was wreathed by clouds. "Here you are," she said, joining him. "Mandy's asleep."

"Out like a light?"

"Yes." Her tone was tender. She was still under the spell of the good-night scene with his small daughter. "What was the phone call about? I could tell it disturbed you."

"Mrs. Grambly has decided to live permanently in Texas to be near her daughter and grandchildren. She phoned to let me know she would be returning for only a few days, long enough to put her house up for sale and take care of the details of moving."

"Her daughter is doing okay? The diagnosis that her tumor was benign hasn't changed, has it?"

"No, and she's apparently doing fine, recovering from the surgery. Reading between the lines, I think the fear of cancer changed her outlook and Mrs. Grambly's about being separated by hundreds of miles, when there's actually nothing preventing Mrs. Grambly from relocating. They've found a small house for her, and she sounded excited. I'm glad for her, but replacing her is going to be well-nigh impossible." He drew his hands out of his pockets. "Shall we go back inside?"

"I'm enjoying the fresh air." Terri was adjusting to the development that troubled him but didn't trouble her at all, and she welcomed the screen of darkness. "You can rely on me to continue in Mrs. Grambly's job."

"No, I can't. I haven't liked taking advantage of you on a short-term basis." He went on, thinking aloud, "Now that I'm offering permanent employment, I'll stand a better chance of getting household help. But I was counting on Mrs. Grambly being here in the afternoons when the kids came home from school."

Terri took in a deep breath, summoning her courage. "I'm sure Mrs. Grambly's a wonderful person, Jeremy, but Jerry and Mandy would be better off coming home to a stepmother, not a housekeeper.'' Bravely she met his gaze in the darkness, hoping that he couldn't hear her heart thumping in her chest.

"I agree completely."

"Hiring one or more people to replace Mrs. Grambly isn't a real solution."

"No, of course it isn't. Not for my children or for me. I need a wife as much as they need a stepmother, and not for housework." He'd thrust his hands back into his pockets.

Terri plowed on. "Don't you think it's time you started considering whether I might not make a satisfactory wife and stepmother? You seemed to rule me out right from the start. By now haven't I shown you that there's more to me than a face and figure? The way I see it, we have a lot going for us. You and I get along well. We're attracted to each other. You're my ideal of the perfect husband and I would do my best to try to be your ideal of a perfect wife. Last but not least, I love your children—"

"Terri, we've known each other only a few weeks," he said.

He'd interrupted her before she could add, *And you, too.*

"Yet I feel like I know you very well," she said simply.

"Marriage is a permanent commitment."

"A commitment I'm ready to make."

He turned toward her, bringing his hands to her shoulders. Terri had been willing him to touch her, but his firm clasp seemed designed to hold her stationary where she couldn't retreat or edge closer. "Just today in Mountain Home you told me you weren't sure you could be happy living in Yellville," he reminded her. "What if you aren't happy? I can't see myself wanting to uproot my children and raise them in an urban environment like Little Rock."

"Jeremy, I truly believe I would be happy making a life with you and Jerry and Mandy anywhere."

His hands gradually ceased holding her and were caressing her, instead. Terri tilted back her head, absorbing the pleasure of his touch.

"You haven't even been to bed with me," he said.

"No, but I'm dying to. This morning I was dreaming about making love with you, when I was awakened by those two boys knocking on my door. I wanted so badly to go back to sleep." She moved closer, and he let her. Curbing the urge to move closer still and slip her arms up around his neck, she placed her hands on his chest. His heart was beating as fast as hers was. "I'm not pressuring you to propose to me tonight, Jeremy. Or take me to bed tonight. Although I'm ashamed to admit the thought occurred that the coast would be clear with Jerry at his friend's house and Mandy fast asleep."

"You think the same thought didn't occur to me? I want you so much, Terri." The words conveyed his intense yearning. "It's impossible to keep a clear head when I think about a future with you. Right now I shouldn't kiss you, because that will be the end of this discussion. I know from experience that my judgment flies out the window."

But he was going to kiss her.

There was time enough before his mouth found hers for anticipation to grow like a flower unfurling its petals in seconds. When his arms gathered her close, a whole joyful bouquet exploded into bloom.

Anything that feels this right has to be right, Terri thought before the thinking part of her brain shut down and made way for passion and joy.

Chapter Ten

"Make love to me, Jeremy." Terri uttered the same plea she'd spoken to him in her dream. Her body was in the same aroused state it had been upon waking that morning, the peaks of her breasts protruding against the lace of her bra as they had against her silk nightgown. Hot desire kindled by his passionate kisses had pooled between her thighs. She couldn't press close enough to him to soothe the aching emptiness that he could fill.

"It's been a long time for me, Terri. You can feel how I'm shaking." He hugged her tighter against him, quivers running through his strong muscles.

The reluctance in his voice stemmed from a lover's fear of not satisfying his partner. Jeremy had put aside his other reservations and in his mind had already become her lover. The intuition thrilled Terri and added an almost unbearable sweetness to her physical urgency.

"That's not all I can feel." Her intimate tone pinpointed the contact of his tumescent manhood pressing against her lower body. "Don't worry. You'll satisfy me. Please, let's go inside."

They sought the privacy of his bedroom, taking a route familiar to her now as well as to him, but one they'd never taken together before. Her hand tightly clasping his, Terry rejoiced in the inner certainty that Jeremy, like her, was also taking a step into the future she'd outlined for him on the patio. Eventually—hopefully soon—she would become his wife when he'd grown to trust her.

"I've fantasized about this when I was vacuuming your carpet and dusting your furniture," she confessed when they'd reached his spacious bedroom and the door had been closed behind them.

"In your fantasy, do I take your clothes off?" he asked, stopping with her beside his bed, which had been made up each morning on Terri's arrival.

"We start taking yours off first." She unbuttoned his short-sleeved striped cotton shirt, letting him pull it free of his waistband. While he was stripping it off broad shoulders, Terri explored his bared upper torso, tanned a golden brown. "Your heart is beating fast again," she observed, resting her palms against his chest.

"It hasn't stopped beating fast since you stepped out on the patio earlier." He bent his head and kissed her neck, his breath warm on her skin. Terri tilted her head sideways to give him total access, hot shivers of delight rendering her momentarily passive. Then his hands found her breasts, fondling them with exquisite gentleness and cupping and squeezing.

She whispered his name, expressing her intense pleasure. It was the desire for the even greater pleasure of feeling his hands on her naked flesh that stirred her to urgent action again. She grasped her knit blouse at the waist, and Jeremy paused to help her peel the snug-fitting garment up and over her head. The intention to remove her bra foundered when he gazed at her, saying with reverence as well as passion, "You're so lush and beautiful."

Once again she surrendered to helpless delight while he caressed her cleavage with fingertips that were unsteady and located her nipples and rubbed them with his thumbs. The ecstatic sensations wrung a soft moan from her throat, restoring momentum to the whole procedure of undressing, but it was Jeremy, not Terri, who unfastened her bra and freed her breasts from their silk-and-lace prison. After feasting his eyes briefly, he gathered her into his arms and hugged her tightly, a great shudder rippling through his body.

Terri hugged him back, reveling in the intimacy of bare flesh pressed against bare flesh, her woman's softness yielding to his muscular hardness. "At this point in my fantasy, we rip off the rest of our clothes and dispense with foreplay," she said when his embrace loosened.

"I'll be lucky to last thirty seconds, sweetheart. I'm sorry—"

She cut the premature apology off with a tender kiss and gazed into his face, knowing that her face must be aglow with the thrill of his calling her "sweetheart." "Thirty seconds will probably be fifteen seconds too long."

They moved far enough apart to undress themselves, Terri's full attention on him and his on her. "Wait," he said, stopping her when she was down to her bikini panties. She obediently waited while he shed his briefs and sat, fully aroused, on the edge of the bed. He reached for her and drew her by her waist to stand between his knees.

"Isn't this foreplay?" she questioned, and sucked in her breath as he leaned forward and kissed her on her abdomen, his hands shaping the curve of her hips.

"I don't know what the definition is," he answered, fondling her buttocks. "But I think we've switched to my fantasy."

He stroked her mound with his palm and Terri's legs relaxed apart in invitation, which he took, sliding his hand between her thighs and staking possession of what was already surrendered to him. "I like your fantasy, too," she breathed, caressing his shoulders.

"Your gorgeous hair color *is* natural." He'd eased down her panties and was combing his fingers through red-gold curls.

"Yes..." Terri murmured, not so much in answer but in rapturous response to his fingertips stroking between her legs. Then he delved one finger into her molten heat, and she had to cling to him for support, gasping out a plea for him to cease the stimulation that had her on the verge of climaxing.

He rose and Terri reached and stroked his jutting manhood. *"Sweetheart,"* he whispered, grasping her shoulders.

His expression reflected the same mixture of pain and bliss that was in his voice. Gazing into his eyes, she read another emotion that filled her with tender elation. Jeremy cared for her in addition to wanting her.

"Take me to bed," she said, the desire to satisfy him adding to her own urgency to couple her body with his.

While he was attending to sheathing himself, his movements hurried, Terri turned down the covers and lay on her back in his bed. The sheets were cool against her heated skin. She held her arms out to him, and he positioned himself over her, but paused to kiss her breasts. Terri arched her back with the onslaught of pleasure as he delayed longer to suck her nipples and taste her sensitized flesh with his warm, rough tongue. He wasn't stimulating her unnecessarily with additional foreplay, she knew, but rather succumbing to his own male pleasure in acquainting himself intimately with her body.

"You're so sexy as well as beautiful," he said, raising his head and gazing down at her. His voice resonated with the stark need in his face. "It's been sheer torture wanting you and knowing I couldn't have you."

"I'm yours, Jeremy." She embraced his shoulders, drawing him down on top of her.

He looked into her eyes as he entered her, pushing deep

in a strong, but gentle, thrust. The incredible sensations brought Terri perilously close to the peak of ecstasy. "Hurry! I'm almost there!" she cried out in joy, writhing her hips to take him even deeper still. Her abandoned response seemed to snap his restraint. Suddenly he was devouring her mouth, mating his tongue with hers. Terri kissed him back and gloried in the driving power of his lovemaking all too briefly before she climaxed just seconds ahead of him.

Afterward she lay nestled in his arms, happy and utterly content. "Now I have been to bed with you," she said, remembering their conversation on the patio. "Just as I expected, you're a wonderful lover."

He kissed her forehead. "Normally, you should be able to count on more staying power."

"Any more staying power this first time would have been too much." She planted a kiss on his shoulder and then nuzzled the spot with her lips, luxuriating in her freedom to kiss him, to touch him at will.

Jeremy's hand began to caress her back and soon Terri's complacency turned into languorous anticipation. They made love again at a much more leisurely pace, but with no less intense pleasure. If anything, her satisfaction was all the sweeter because of the conversation that had been sandwiched in with its indirect references to a lifetime of intimacy.

"I wish I could sleep with you tonight," she said, cuddling against him a second time in a state of total satisfaction. "I hate sleeping alone."

"I do, too."

He was quiet, and some somber quality in his silence awoke a faint anxiousness in her that she wanted to dispel. "What are you thinking about?" she asked.

"About us. And about you and Sommers. There are some things that bother me about your relationship with him now. I certainly understand why he wants to win you back, but he's being awfully persistent."

"You're wondering if I'm not giving him some subtle encouragement, keeping his hopes alive."

"Yes," he conceded quietly. "Perhaps without even realizing it."

Terri sighed. The last subject she wanted to discuss right now was her ex-husband, but it was important to deal with Jeremy's lingering reservations. "I never consciously held out any hope of salvaging our marriage, but Christopher made some remarks in our phone conversation this morning that indicated he has construed my actions all along as signs that I wasn't really serious about divorcing him. Even after the divorce he continued to believe I was bent on negotiating a different marriage arrangement on my own terms. It's not true. I wasn't driving a 'hard bargain,' to use his terminology."

"What particular 'actions' on your part?"

"I didn't hire an attorney, mainly to avoid the expense, but instead let Christopher's attorney act for both of us. I had willingly signed our prenuptial agreement and felt bound by it, so the only service a divorce attorney could have performed was to get an earlier court date. Time really wasn't of the essence then, whereas if my divorce weren't final now, I would be in a great hurry."

Her explanation wasn't putting his mind at ease, Terri could tell. She went on, "Christopher figured I was giving him ample opportunity to persuade me to reconcile with him. In weak moments I did actually consider a reconciliation, but I knew I would be fooling myself if I expected him to change. I would have to turn a blind eye to his involvements with other women, as so many wives of unfaithful husbands do to keep their marriages afloat." Terri kissed his chest. "Thank heaven I found the strength to hold out. I wouldn't have been happy."

Jeremy turned over on his back. "How long has it been since you've seen Sommers?"

"Over two months. I moved here in June."

"For the sole purpose of getting away from him."

"And to avoid running into mutual friends and acquaintances and avoid being pestered by men who wanted to date me. I wanted to escape the limelight and shore up my courage for moving on with my life."

"Have you been back to Little Rock since you left in June?"

"No, and I feel no great desire to go. Any more questions?" Terri asked lightly.

"How often has he been sending you bouquets of roses and phoning you?"

"The roses arrive every week or two. He was phoning more often until recently, when he tapered off."

"Do you phone him?"

"Mainly just to ask him not to keep sending flowers and to stop calling and leaving messages. You're probably thinking that I could have gotten an unlisted number, but, knowing Christopher, he would have learned the number somehow. And I found that dealing with him on the phone was a kind of curative therapy, helping me get over him. I am over Christopher now," Terri added.

Jeremy sat up and swung his legs to the floor, his back to her. "Won't you have to see him before you can be positive?"

"No, but I will see him, if you want me to."

"I don't *want* you to go anywhere near Sommers, but I can't marry you with the fear that you'll wake up and discover you're not over him. In the meanwhile, I would rather keep Jerry and Mandy in the dark about us."

"In other words, pretend nothing's changed after tonight? Jeremy, you *do* want to marry me?"

"More than anything."

His earnest words salved some of her hurt and disappointment that he still had no confidence in their chances for happiness as a married couple. "Of course I'll go along with whatever you judge to be best for Jerry and Mandy," she said.

While they were both getting dressed, she broached the

subject of the following day. "Are the children going to Sunday school in the morning?"

"I plan to take them. Then the three of us will attend the eleven o'clock church service. What about you?"

"Instead of attending church at my grandmother's, I would like to attend your church and sit with you and Jerry and Mandy, if that's okay."

"Of course it's okay. Why don't I come and get you shortly before eleven? The kids can save room for us on a pew."

She agreed without hesitation, and they went on to discuss their options for doing something fun with the children in the afternoon. Terri jumped at Jeremy's suggestion that they change into casual clothing following church and drive up to Bull Shoals for lunch in a family restaurant, then rent a boat to take a boat ride. "I'll bring along sunscreen," she promised.

"I'll get some fishing gear together in the morning," he said. "We might even hook an unsuspecting fish."

Formulating plans with him did wonders for curing Terri's sense of dejection. He accompanied her out to her car, which she'd driven to his house after their return from the shopping excursion in Mountain Home. His good-night hug and kiss restored most of her previous optimism about the future.

For the time being, Terri's optimism had to suffice for both her and Jeremy. He obviously had qualms about whether her divorce marked a final breakup with Christopher. Like Christopher, he also questioned whether she was suited to a small-town life-style, whether she would be happy and contented as his wife and his children's stepmother.

Ironically, the two men were unlikely allies, eroding her confidence.

They were both wrong. They *had* to be wrong, because so much was hanging in the balance. Terri would simply be forced to hold out against them alone, clinging to faith in herself, until Jeremy crossed over and joined her.

The vision of what could be was wonderful enough to sustain her. Marrying Jeremy and being his wife, being a stepmother to his children, the four of them forming a close family unit that might eventually expand to include a tiny fifth member.

It was a vision that Jeremy needed to embrace, too, in order for it to become true. Surely he would.

Terri had decided on a dark-green sheath to wear to church, but she'd removed it from the hanger and draped it across her bed to slip on at the last minute. She'd just finished applying her makeup and was attired in black bra and panties and sheer black panty hose, when she heard an automobile pull into her driveway.

Jeremy must have come a few minutes early to pick me up, she thought, glancing at the clock. Her heartbeat quickened with her surge of gladness that he'd arrived and she would be seeing him. Should she hurriedly put on her dress or just throw on a robe and go and let him in?

Terri decided on the latter, remembering that the children weren't supposed to be with him. She couldn't resist reaching for a black silk and lace negligee.

So certain was she of opening the front door to Jeremy that Terri didn't even peek out the window. After dealing with the lock, she pulled the door wide. Her smile of welcome froze on her face and she blurted stupidly, "Christopher! It's *you!*"

"Hello, darling. I decided to deliver these personally." He held a huge bouquet of red roses.

"You drove from Little Rock?" She glanced beyond him at his sleek, expensive car.

"I was up at the crack of dawn. Can I come in? I hope you have coffee made." He stepped up close and bent to kiss her on the mouth. Terri was still too stupefied to turn her head aside.

"I'm getting ready to go to church," she objected, but he brushed past her anyway and entered her living room.

"I'll go with you. My suit jacket is in the car, and I brought along a tie." He wore charcoal gray slacks with a faint-red pinstripe and a white dress shirt unbuttoned at the neck. Once Terri's heart would have glowed with wifely pride at his dark, suave handsomeness.

"After church, I'll take you to lunch," he went on before she could get a word in. "I have reservations at Gaston's resort in Bull Shoals. I'm told it's one of the few decent restaurants in a fifty-mile radius of your hometown."

"You can't go to church with me! I'm going with Jeremy Wells. And I've already made plans for the rest of the day."

"Have a heart, darling. I've come all this way to see you." He set down the bouquet on her coffee table.

"You shouldn't have come without any warning."

Terri still stood with the door open. She closed it, some of her initial surprise fading. In view of last night's conversation with Jeremy, Christopher's unexpected arrival, however unwelcome, was convenient in a way. *Won't you have to see him before you can be positive?* Jeremy had asked when she'd stated that she was over Christopher.

As much as she'd looked forward to today's excursion to Bull Shoals, here was the opportunity to set Jeremy's mind at ease.

And maybe get the point across to her ex-husband once and for all that their divorce had marked an end to their marriage.

"I'll just skip church," she said. "There's coffee in the kitchen. You can pour yourself a cup while I finish getting dressed. Jeremy will be here soon."

"That's probably him if he drives a minivan." Christopher was looking with narrowed eyes through the window overlooking the street.

"He does." Terri's nerves tightened as she listened to the sounds of an automobile pulling into her driveway. She wished she'd had a chance to put on her dress and shoes before Jeremy arrived and found her dressed in a black negligee with Christopher ensconced in her living room.

"His transportation fits the image of a family man." The remark was cutting.

"It fits his image perfectly. Jeremy's a family man through and through." Her words were spoken in proud defense, even as she noted that the van engine continued to run after the tires had crunched to a halt. Terri could visualize Jeremy gazing with surprise at the unfamiliar car parked outside her cottage. He would naturally be puzzling over the identity of her Sunday-morning visitor.

He finally killed the engine. The slam of his automobile door brought Terri out of her immobile state. "I expect you to be civil, unless you want your trip from Little Rock to be a wasted trip," she said over her shoulder as she reached to open her front door for the second time in the past five minutes.

Despite the awkwardness of the situation, the sight of Jeremy approaching her porch warmed Terri's heart and quickened her pulse. He wore gray slacks, too, and a white shirt, with a red tie knotted at his throat. His sandy hair, streaked with blond highlights, was neatly combed, and he was clean-shaven and wholesome and manly. The only change in his appearance that would have made him more attractive in her eyes was a happier expression on his face and a possessive glint in his blue eyes.

He wasn't smiling, and instead of looking puzzled, he looked grim. When he spotted her in the doorway, he stopped in his tracks, his gaze going over her and his frown deepening.

"Hi," Terri greeted him. "The car belongs to Christopher. He took it upon himself to pay me a visit and showed up a few minutes ago."

The mention of Christopher hadn't come as any surprise to him. While she waited for him to reach the porch and climb the steps, Terri remembered that she'd told Jeremy the make of Christopher's automobile several weeks ago, the same day she had taken the job as attendant. Obviously he'd remembered, and had concluded for himself who was inside her cottage.

From immediately behind her, Christopher spoke. "Invite your gas station owner inside, darling, so he and I can square off and try to outglare each other."

"We can square off out here on the porch, Sommers, while Terri puts on some clothes." Jeremy's voice was dangerously quiet, and his hands had clenched into fists.

"Nobody's going to 'square off,'" Terri declared. She addressed Christopher indignantly, "You don't tell me what to do and stop calling me 'darling.'" When he shrugged and turned away, she looked back at Jeremy. "Would you please come in?" *And control your hostility, for my sake?* she added in silent pleading.

He nodded and stepped over the threshold, passing close to her. Terri noticed that his gaze went immediately to the large bouquet of red roses that Christopher had set in the center of her square mahogany coffee table, which, like the sofa and two chairs, had belonged to her great-aunt.

"Christopher Sommers. Jeremy Wells." She performed the briefest of introductions, and they responded in kind with no handshake.

"Sommers."

"Wells."

The mutual animosity between the two men, so strong it seemed a tangible force in her small living room, heightened Terri's awareness of the contrast between them, a contrast that went much deeper than one man being dark haired, dark eyed and urbane and the other fair haired, blue eyed and straightforward. Also gentle. Also loving. Also trustworthy. The list of Jeremy's attributes went on and on, Christopher's presence making Terri appreciate those qualities all the more.

"I need to talk to Jeremy privately," she said to her ex-husband.

"Of course, darling. I'll take you up on that offer of coffee and make myself scarce in the kitchen." He made a show of consulting his gold Rolex. "Our reservations at Gaston's are for one o'clock, so we're not pressed for time." Pointedly ignoring Jeremy, he left the room, but not without making a further statement by giving her arm a proprietorial squeeze when he walked by her.

Terri held her tongue, not wanting to delay his departure a second longer than necessary. "Don't let Christopher get under your skin," she urged when she and Jeremy were alone. His hands had balled up into fists again.

"What's going on here, Terri?"

"Nothing's 'going on.' He drove up barely five minutes before you did." She went on quickly, explaining, "I heard his car and thought you'd arrived early. I rushed to open the door and there he stood. I was flabbergasted and not at all happy to see him."

"But you invited him in, dressed like that?"

"He invited himself in. And it's not as though he hasn't seen me in less. We were married six years."

He gestured toward the bouquet of roses. "When were those delivered?"

And not sent along to the nursing home.

"They weren't delivered by a florist. Christopher brought them."

"Did you offer him coffee? Are you having lunch with him at Gaston's?"

"He asked for coffee. When you drove up, I told him to go to the kitchen and pour himself a cup, just to get rid of him so that you and I could have a few minutes together. And, yes, I did agree to have lunch with him after I remembered our conversation last night and your insistence that I should see Christopher in person as a test. Plus I'm hoping he'll finally get the message that I'm not coming back to him."

Jeremy shook his head. "Sommers breezes in here with his hundred-dollar bouquet of roses. You cancel out on your day with me just like that." He snapped his fingers. "And he's supposed to get the message that you're over him."

"I *am* over him! I didn't want to cancel out on the day we'd planned! I would much rather go to Bull Shoals with you and Jerry and Mandy!"

But he didn't believe her.

"I have to go," he said, glancing at his watch. "The kids will be out of their Sunday-school classes by now and sitting in church."

Waiting for him and Terri to come and sit beside them on the pew. She could visualize them, dressed up in their Sunday best, and was struck by deep regret for what she was missing out on today. It wasn't too late to do an about-face, but Jeremy's jealous reaction only emphasized the necessity for proving that Christopher wasn't a threat to him.

"Be sure and tell them I'll definitely be attending church with you next Sunday," she said.

"No, I won't tell them that," he replied.

Because he wasn't certain she would be attending church with him. It was another case where words weren't good enough. Only actions. She had to spend the day in Christopher's company and return to Jeremy, as eager as before to marry him.

"Remember, you owe me a hug." Her reminder was wistful. "I would collect right now if I wasn't afraid of soiling your white shirt with my makeup—" She broke off in surprise, as the sounds of a choir singing a hymn could suddenly be heard, coming from the kitchen. Automatically Terri turned her head in that direction and so did Jeremy. "Christopher must have tuned in a church service on my boom box," she commented with annoyance, using the slang name for the portable radio with CD player and tape player that she'd bought to serve as a stereo.

"Where is he playing it?"

Jeremy's harsh question with emphasis on *where* reminded her that he'd never been inside the cottage before and wasn't familiar with the layout of rooms. "In the kitchen. Not my bedroom. He doesn't have quite that much nerve." She stepped forward, took one of his clenched hands in hers and raised it to her lips, kissing his knuckles. "I'll miss you today. And Jerry and Mandy, too. Will you still take them to Bull Shoals?"

He nodded. "They have their hearts set on a boat ride. On the way to Sunday school it was all they could talk about. Next time I won't—"

He broke off, but Terri could finish his thought for herself. Next time he wouldn't mention to his children ahead of time plans that he'd made with her for their entertainment.

"This won't *ever* happen again, Jeremy. I promise you."

"I have to run." He kissed her on the cheek and squeezed her shoulder with his free hand.

"I hope you guys catch a big fish." Her woebegone words were spoken to his back as he walked hurriedly to the door.

The church service had already begun. Jeremy located Jerry's blond head next to Mandy's black curls. Beside her was a space large enough for him and Terri. Taking the most direct route to join them, Jeremy moved quietly up an outside aisle, trying not to look as sick at heart as he felt.

Both children eyed him in bewilderment when he appeared alone. Jeremy touched his forefinger to his lips, cautioning them not to blurt out questions. Mandy waited until he'd sat down beside her before she asked in a stage whisper loud enough to be heard several pews away, "Where's Ms. Sommers? Is she driving herself?"

Jeremy shook his head. "She couldn't come," he whispered back.

"But she said she was coming," Mandy persisted, dismay written on her face.

Jerry had leaned around his sister and followed the communication. He mouthed his most pressing worry. "Dad, are we still going to Bull Shoals, without Ms. Sommers?"

"Yes," Jeremy mouthed back with an affirmative nod.

Mandy didn't seem consoled by the news that the day's outing hadn't been postponed. Jeremy mustered a smile and winked at her, giving her chubby clasped hands a comforting squeeze. "We'll have fun, angel," he whispered in her ear.

Terri's words played in his mind: *Be sure and tell them I'll definitely be attending church with you next Sunday.* Jeremy wouldn't make any such promise to his children, even though he didn't doubt her sincerity at the moment she'd voiced her intention. He didn't doubt she'd been sincere last night when she'd made plans with him for today, plans she'd canceled when Sommers had shown up.

Now, instead of accompanying Jeremy and his kids to a family restaurant that served a buffet, she would be accompanying Sommers to Gaston's first-class resort on the White River. She would ride in his luxury automobile and on arrival be seated at a table overlooking the unspoiled natural scenery. Instead of iced tea, she would sip a glass of fine wine with her meal, ordered from a menu featuring tempting soups and appetizers and salads as well as a variety of entrées to please the most sophisticated palate. The service would be excellent and the ambience relaxed and enjoyable.

Jeremy could easily visualize the setting, since he was familiar with the restaurant, having patronized it on special occasions himself. He would have liked to be the one to take Terri there, but before he got the chance, Sommers had beaten him to it, cleverly zeroing in on the perfect dining experience in the general vicinity of Yellville that would whet her appetite for the amenities of city life.

I'll miss you today, she'd said to Jeremy, meaning the words. But thoughts of him would fade as Sommers filled her in on everything going on in the lives of people back in Little Rock who were her friends and acquaintances. He would do everything in his power to charm her, amuse her, make her fall for him all over again.

Would he succeed? By the end of the day would Terri be willing to talk reconciliation?

A terrible fear inside Jeremy told him she would. It told him that the reasons she'd given him and herself for spending today with Sommers were honest rationalization. Deep down, Terri wanted to be with Sommers, despite the fact that she'd pledged herself to Jeremy last night.

There Jeremy sat in church, unable to pray because his prayers would be bitter and reproachful. *I need her more than he does. He doesn't deserve her as his wife. He cheated on her. Why would You let her choose him over me?*

The prayer Jeremy did utter silently was one that had been granted countless times since Susan's death: *Help me get through this day and be a good father.*

"You can change the radio station now," Terri said from the doorway of the kitchen. "Jeremy's gone."

Christopher's smile was sheepish. "You wouldn't want Mr. Goody Two-shoes to be late for church, now, would you, darling?"

"He's not Mr. Goody Two-shoes."

"Evidently not, or he wouldn't be trying to steal my wife."

It was on the tip of Terri's tongue to reply, *The wife you ran around on,* but she would only be beginning a conversation they'd had too many times already. "Your ex-wife, Christopher. We're divorced. Now, if you'll excuse me, I'll finish getting dressed."

"There's no hurry." He snapped off the radio, which sat on top of the refrigerator. "Let me pour you a cup of coffee, and we'll go into your living room and talk. I have a lot to tell you."

"It won't take me long to put on a dress and pair of

shoes. I'll join you in the living room." She turned to go to her bedroom.

He caught up with her, clasping her waist and halting her. "I've missed you so much," he said softly. "And you've missed me, haven't you?"

"Not lately," she replied, resisting the instinct to pull away from him. This was a part of the test, to let him touch her and try to seduce her. "I've been too busy and happy."

"Happy being Wells's housemaid and riding herd on a couple of kids?" he scoffed. "What a waste."

"I don't think it's a waste."

"I know someone else who would agree with me. Angela Partridge. I ran into her the other day, and she asked me for your phone number and address. She'll be contacting you."

Angela Partridge was the driving force behind the Partridge Agency, which contracted with models and actresses to do TV commercials and print ads for clients. Terri had done many modeling assignments for the Partridge Agency during the couple of years between leaving college and marrying Christopher. He hadn't wanted her to have a career, so she'd stopped accepting jobs, willing to put all her energies into what she considered a more rewarding career—that of wife and, eventually, mother.

"If you run into her again before she does contact me, you can tell her I'm not available."

"You're looking so beautiful. So sexy in black silk and lace." He slipped his arms around her waist and drew her back against him.

"Christopher, don't."

"I can't help myself. I want you too much." He kissed her neck and nuzzled her skin beneath her ear. "It's been an eternity for me since we made love. Tell me the truth. Hasn't it been an eternity for you, too?"

She sighed. "It was a whole lifetime ago. Please, don't subject us both to a wrestling match."

His arms dropped away. "You've slept with Wells," he accused.

"Yes. And I'm going to marry him as soon as he proposes to me." She went on, with no vindictive motive, "I would rather be with Jeremy today, Christopher, and with his children, not with you. What we had together is dead. Let's part friends and wish each other well."

Without answering, he stalked away into the living room.

Chapter Eleven

Terri stood motionless, waiting for the sound of the door slamming behind Christopher. Instead she heard him pacing back and forth. He hadn't left in a huff and headed back to Little Rock. She could almost sense him regrouping, much as he would if he'd been handed an unfavorable ruling by a judge.

Whether or not she'd gotten through to him, Terri had learned what she needed to know in order to reassure Jeremy: she *was* over Christopher. His touch hadn't affected her. When he'd spoken to her in a tone of voice like a warm caress, she hadn't melted. Without a reason to stay in Yellville, she could move back to Little Rock tomorrow, confident that she was immune to her ex-husband's charm and magnetic personality.

So why deprive herself of going along on the excursion to Bull Shoals with Jeremy and his children? She could get rid of Christopher and be waiting at Jeremy's house when he and Jerry and Mandy arrived home from church.

Her thoughts making her eager, Terri walked to the doorway of the living room. "Christopher, I've changed my mind about lunch."

He'd halted in his tracks and pivoted to face her, every inch the trial attorney thinking on his feet. Terri was reminded of times she'd sat in the courtroom and observed him in action with wifely pride.

"It would mean a great deal to me if you didn't change your mind," he said. "You said you wanted to be friends. Today's a chance to establish some basis for friendship."

"You don't want to be friends with me," Terri objected.

"Maybe I could be a better friend than I was a husband. Although I wasn't a totally rotten husband, was I?"

"No, you weren't," Terri readily admitted, her hopes of salvaging the day slipping away. "But nothing's going to change the fact that you're my ex-husband now."

"Our marriage won't even be a topic of conversation," he promised. "Please."

Terri thought longingly of slipping on casual clothes and going over to Jeremy's house. But she had already agreed to go to lunch with Christopher, and it was difficult to refuse his request—put to her in a humble, beseeching manner—that she stick to her agreement. He'd come over a hundred miles. Today was just one day out of her entire future. Couldn't she afford to be kind to him and help him adjust to the reality that he could never win her back?

Spending hours in his company instead of minutes, she could be that much more convincing when she stated to Jeremy, *I want you as my husband, not Christopher.*

"Okay," she said, resigned to donning the dress laid out on her bed. "I'll be ready in a few minutes."

"I'm sure you've kept in contact with your great-aunt," Christopher commented when they'd left Yellville behind and began the picturesque drive to Bull Shoals on two-lane highways that climbed rugged foothills and dipped into valleys.

"I talk with her on the phone at least once a week."

"How is she getting along?"

"She seems to have adjusted well to living at Magnolia House, which is a very nice nursing home, not at all depressing. She has her own private room and even a little kitchenette. She's taking a crafts class and has made friends with a couple of other elderly women."

"Why the worried note in your voice?"

"Aunt Evelyn has fallen a couple of times lately," Terri explained. "Her doctor has instructed her to use a walker, but she insists on using her cane, instead."

"A cane is more dignified."

"Exactly. I really must make a trip to Little Rock soon and visit her. And do some shopping while I'm there." She would buy Mandy a cute outfit and Jerry a present at a sporting-goods store. And she would buy a gift for Jeremy. Or two gifts, one to give him when they were alone, just the two of them, celebrating a future together.

"You're smiling," Christopher observed. "Does the prospect of returning to civilization put you in a happy frame of mind?"

"Mainly because there's also the prospect of coming home to Yellville."

He looked skeptical. "Realistically, how long would you be content to live in your hometown if your romance with Wells went sour?"

"It isn't going to go sour." *Ever.* Not after years of being married.

"You didn't answer my question. Isn't Wells the big attraction in Yellville? You haven't suddenly become fascinated with small-town life."

"Before I got to know Jeremy, I couldn't quite imagine living permanently in Yellville," Terri admitted. "Now I can easily imagine it."

"But not without Wells."

"No." She refused to imagine life without Jeremy, period.

Apparently satisfied with the responses he'd pulled from her, he switched the conversation back to her projected trip to Little Rock, asking, "Will you plan to stay a couple of days when you come to visit your aunt?"

"Probably so."

"There's no need for you to put out money for a hotel room. You're welcome to make use of the guest house. You could come and go as you please, and you would have my word that I wouldn't intrude on your privacy."

"That's nice of you to offer, but—"

He cut in before she could refuse. "You don't have to decide now. The offer's open, and if you do take me up on it, I would feel a little less guilty about the raw financial deal you got when you divorced me. I didn't pay you a penny of spousal support."

Terri visualized the lovely interior of the separate guest quarters. She could bring her great-aunt there for a visit and have her stay overnight, if Aunt Evelyn was so inclined. There wouldn't be the same option with a typical hotel room, and Terri certainly wouldn't feel indebted to Christopher, since, as he'd pointed out, she hadn't exactly taken him to the cleaners financially. "I'll consider it an option," she said.

"In any event, I'll leave you a key."

She didn't argue, figuring she could decline to accept the key when the time came, depending on how things went today. They talked of other subjects, including Bull Shoals, their destination, a fishing mecca and popular retirement locale. Not surprisingly, Christopher proved to be well-informed, imparting interesting facts and figures such as the enormous size of Bull Shoals Lake, which had been created by damming the White River. The many fingers of the lake extended a hundred miles along the Arkansas and Missouri borders and constituted some forty-five thousand acres of water teeming with bass and trout.

Terri had never been bored with Christopher's company, and she wasn't bored today. He was a skilled conversationalist, just as he was a skilled driver, a skilled host, a skilled attorney, a skilled lover. The list went on and on, but it didn't include faithful husband, devoted father, family man.

She could still admire Christopher as much as ever for his brilliant mind and his other good traits, of which he had many. She could still appreciate his charisma, but she was no longer susceptible to it. Marrying him had been a mistake. He never had been the right man for her.

And Jeremy was.

Terri's insight allowed her to relax and adopt a patient attitude during the remainder of the ride and the long, leisurely lunch at Gaston's resort. Afterward she didn't balk when Christopher proposed taking a different and roundabout route back to Yellville.

"Just so long as I'm home by four or four-thirty," she stipulated, calculating that Jeremy and the kids should be returned by then.

They drove through spectacular mountain scenery, passing few habitations. Fortunately, the winding two-lane highway had brought them near the town of Mountain View, when they rounded a sharp curve and Christopher suddenly gripped the wheel, cursing and putting on the brakes.

"Damn! I've got a flat tire!" he exclaimed as the car rolled to a bumpy stop.

Terri worriedly pointed out the obvious. "It's too dangerous to stop here and change a tire. There's no shoulder to speak of."

"I doubt I could loosen the lug nuts by hand anyway. They put them on with impact wrenches. I'll just have to drive slowly on the tire until we get to a safer spot."

"You'll ruin it, won't you?"

"Cut it to ribbons. Here's hoping we can locate a replacement, because there's no way I'm driving to Yellville on the spare."

"It's Sunday. If Mountain View has a tire store, it'll be closed."

"I'm hoping there's a gas station open with a mechanic on duty."

"I wonder if Mr. Sommers has gone yet. Could we drive by Ms. Sommers's house and find out, Daddy?" Mandy asked.

Jeremy had explained to his children, doing his best to be matter-of-fact, that Terri's former husband had come from Little Rock today to see her.

"No, I'll phone her when we get home," he replied to his small daughter. He didn't think he could bear discovering that Sommers's sleek status symbol of an automobile was parked in her driveway.

It was five-thirty, and Jeremy and his kids had just reached the Yellville town limits, returning from Bull Shoals.

"Be sure and tell her I caught a big fish, Dad," Jerry said with a self-satisfied air.

"It wasn't a big fish," Mandy objected. "It was just a bigger little fish."

"You didn't catch any size fish," Jerry taunted her. "And you got your line all tangled up, like a dumb girl."

"I'm not dumb! And I'd rather be a girl than a boy. Boys are stupid and mean."

"Are you calling Dad 'stupid'?"

"He's not a boy. He's a man, and men are smart."

"Not all men are smart. Are they, Dad?"

"No, son, and very few men are smart all the time."

Your dad's a prime example, Jeremy added silently, anger at himself burning like a steady, destructive fire, as it had throughout the day. He deserved to be miserable and frustrated and eaten up with jealousy. Right from the beginning he'd sized up the situation with Terri and known to stay clear of her. Common sense had told him that since she'd married her high-powered lawyer husband in the first place, she must have been attracted to the kind of man he was and the kind of life-style he offered. An entirely different life-style from the one she would have with Jeremy, who was an entirely different type of man.

Not for a moment had he ever truly believed she would be content for any length of time away from the social whirl and fine restaurants and exclusive shops a city like Little Rock offered. And yet he'd harbored foolish hopes, like a grown man spinning a fairy tale. The small-town gas station owner marries the beautiful divorcée and lives happily ever after.

Sure. Right.

Sommers had shown up today and she'd opted for lunching with him in style, just as eventually she would succumb to the lure of returning to Little Rock, where she belonged. Maybe she was packing her things right this minute, thinking of a kind way to break the news to Jeremy that she'd decided she couldn't marry him after all.

It would be devastating news even without the element of surprise, but not nearly so devastating as marrying her and having her leave him in a year or two because she was unhappy. To submit his children to the rejection they would experience from his failed marriage would be criminal on his part as a father.

Jeremy needed to start heeding his judgment and be a smart dad, if not a smart man.

"I want to call Jeremy." It was five-thirty. Terri and Christopher were in downtown Mountain View, waiting for the new tire to arrive and be mounted on his car. They'd walked to the courthouse square, where an audience was enjoying a free bluegrass concert.

"There must be a pay phone close by. Let's walk around the courthouse square," he suggested.

He spotted a phone and accompanied her to it, standing ten or twelve yards away while she placed the call to Jeremy's house. No answer. Terri sighed in disappointment as she hung up.

"I'll just stand here and try again in five minutes," she said.

He shrugged and paced up and down.

When five minutes had dragged past, Terri went through the whole process again and got a busy signal. "Jeremy's phone is busy," she reported to Christopher, hanging up again. "He may be calling me."

Her nerves stretched thin while she forced herself to wait another five minutes. To her relief the phone rang.

"Hello." Jerry's boyish voice came over the line.

"Hi, it's Ms. Sommers. Is your father there?"

"Dad's out in the garage, putting away the fishing stuff. We just got back from Bull Shoals. He called your house, and you weren't home yet."

"I'm still not at my house."

"Where are you? I hear music."

"I'm in a town called Mountain View. There's a bluegrass band playing here. But could you please get your father?"

"Sure. Are you there with Mr. Sommers? Dad told us he came to visit you."

"Yes, we've had car trouble."

"Before I get Dad, I'll just tell you real quick I caught five fish today. One of them was a big trout. We didn't keep any of them. We threw them back in the water. Mandy didn't catch a single one, and neither did Dad, but he didn't really try. He mostly helped her and untangled her line."

Terri's mental picture of Jeremy and the two children out on the water in a boat roused wistfulness and strong regret. "Tomorrow you'll have to tell me all about your fishing adventures."

"You aren't coming over tonight?"

"It'll probably be too late for me to come over."

"That's too bad. Hold on."

Terri could hear him shouting, his voice fading in volume as he raced out to the garage, probably having answered the phone in the kitchen, "Dad! Telephone! It's Ms. Sommers. She's not coming over!"

After what seemed like an hour, Jeremy spoke a tense "Hello" into the phone.

"Hi," Terri said. "I guess Jerry filled you in briefly. Christopher's car had a flat tire this afternoon in the vicinity of Mountain View. We were taking a longer, scenic route back to Yellville. He had to keep driving slowly until we could pull over in a safe place, and ruined the tire. It took forever for someone to come along and give us a ride into town, where we had to search out a wrecker to pull the car to a gas station. On a Sunday afternoon, rousing a mechanic wasn't easy. Then came the long drawn-out process of locating a new tire and paying someone to go pick it up in Batesville. I'm hoping we'll be on our way by seven-thirty or eight, at the latest. I didn't want you to be worried when you didn't find me home."

"Thanks for calling." The words were terse.

"How was your day? I could tell Jerry had fun."

"Both kids seemed to enjoy themselves. Look, I won't keep you. I gather you're at a pay phone and Sommers is probably nearby."

"He is and champing at the bit. This has been a frustrating ordeal for him. I'll talk to you later tonight whenever I get back to Yellville. Providing it isn't too late," she added.

He didn't take her cue and encourage her to call however late the hour.

"Let's stop at that pizza place we passed coming into town and pick up a pizza for supper," Christopher suggested as they were leaving Mountain View.

"I'm not hungry," Terri replied, glancing at her watch. It was a quarter to eight. She wanted to get to Yellville, send him on his way and phone Jeremy.

"It'll take us at least an hour to get to your house. By

then I'll want to eat something before I make the drive back to Little Rock. I'll just stick around long enough to heat the pizza up in the oven and eat a couple of slices,'' he assured her in a weary tone.

''Okay.'' Terri gave in, since refusing seemed ungracious.

During the thirty-minute wait in the car while Christopher went inside the pizza restaurant, the regret she'd experienced throughout the long day welled up strong. It welled up even stronger on the seemingly endless drive along dark, steep mountain highways with hairpin curves and long, isolated stretches with forests crowding in on both sides.

I could be with Jeremy at his house right now, she thought longingly.

A dozen times she'd consoled herself with the thought that this was just one day in her life, but giving up today with Jeremy and his son and little daughter seemed a huge sacrifice in retrospect.

At nine-fifteen Christopher pulled into the driveway of her cottage. Terri's primary goal as she located her keys in her purse was going inside and heading directly for the phone. She wanted to hear Jeremy's voice. The sound of it would sustain her for another thirty minutes until she could call him and have a longer conversation.

Inside, she gave Christopher hurried instructions for heating the pizza and left him on his own while she made a beeline for her bedroom, where she hurriedly punched out the familiar digits of the number she hoped would be *her* number soon.

Jeremy answered on the second ring.

''Hi, it's me,'' she said. ''I've made it home. I was never so glad to reach the town limits of Yellville.''

Before he could answer, a click sounded on the line, followed by a series of beeping sounds. After a puzzled moment, comprehension dawned. ''Christopher must be trying to use the phone in the kitchen,'' Terri explained.

"Sorry, I didn't realize you were on the phone, darling," Christopher apologized. "I'll hang up." A *click* indicated he'd been as good as his word.

"Sommers is still there?" Jeremy demanded, his tone both incredulous and outraged. "Is he spending the night with you?"

"No, he isn't spending the night! We picked up a pizza in Mountain View and he's heating it up in the kitchen. I just wanted to make a quick call to say I would phone you after he had left."

"The kids are in bed, and I'm beat. It's been a stressful day and a stressful evening."

In other words, don't call, he was telling her indirectly. "I won't keep you."

He hung up.

The dial tone buzzing in her ear increased Terri's deep dismay. "Don't be like this, Jeremy!" she pleaded.

"Was that Wells on the phone with you?" Christopher asked when she joined him in the kitchen.

Terri nodded.

"I'm sorry," he apologized again. "I picked up, assuming the line was free, and didn't check. Judging from your expression, he wasn't too happy about my interrupting your conversation."

"No, he wasn't happy at all that you were still here." She got a plate for him from a cabinet and placed it on the table, along with a fork and knife and paper napkin.

"Am I eating alone?"

"I'm still not hungry." Any appetite she might have had was gone.

"In that case, I think I'll skip the pizza. I'm not that hungry, either."

"Pizza always gave you heartburn anyway," she reminded him. Out of consideration for his feelings, she tried not to appear as relieved as she was that he was leaving immediately.

"Thank you for taking pity on me and favoring me with your company today," he said at the door. "And for being such a trooper. Most women would have whined and complained."

"It wasn't your fault that your tire picked up a nail. I'm sure you could have done without the expense." All told, the new tire had cost him several hundred dollars.

He shrugged. "I owe you a dinner when you come to Little Rock. There's a new restaurant called the Poseidon that opened recently. The food's marvelous. Also, there's an excellent watercolor exhibit at your favorite art gallery. It got rave reviews. I would also enjoy taking you to see it, if you have time."

"Christopher, I'm hoping to be engaged to marry Jeremy very soon. I don't think he will want me going to dinner with you."

"Let's wait and see whether you are engaged. Wells struck me as a pretty levelheaded guy. Oh, before I forget, I left the key to the guest house on your kitchen table."

"Don't leave it with me," she objected. "I'll go and get it."

"Keep it. You don't have to use it. Good night, dearest. I've got to run." He kissed her on the cheek and departed.

As soon as she'd bade him an answering good-night, Terri closed the door, not overly concerned about having the key in her possession. She could return it by mail or drop it off at his house when she went to Little Rock.

What was of major concern was talking to Jeremy tonight and making things right between them. She also wanted to *see* him. She wanted to be with him at least an hour or two and hear about his day.

It wasn't late, just nine-thirty. He'd said both children had gone to bed. *I'll go over to his house,* Terri decided, and went quickly to change clothes.

During the short drive, she vacillated between feeling eager and feeling apprehensive, between being relatively certain he would be glad to see her and being not so certain.

The emotional tug of war heightened when she pulled into his driveway and noted that lights were still on in the main part of the house and in the master suite. It seemed likely that he was in the living room and would hear her car engine and notice her headlights.

As she got out of her car and walked to the front entrance, Terri was expecting him to open the door any second, saving her from having to knock quietly in lieu of ringing the doorbell, which might awaken Jerry and Mandy. Disappointingly, the door didn't swing open. Nor did she glimpse any movement within through the windows. Had Jeremy dropped off to sleep on the sofa? she wondered, peering into the foyer through the glass panels on either side of the door.

She knocked and waited. No response. She knocked again, harder, and rubbed her bruised knuckles while she waited, straining to hear footsteps.

No response.

Wherever he was and whatever he was doing, he obviously couldn't hear her. How should she alert him to her presence? A neighbor might spot her walking around the house and peering in windows, trying to locate him. *I have a key*, Terri thought. *I could just unlock the door and let myself in, the way I'm used to doing.*

Before she took out her keys, she knocked once more, with the same results.

Inside the foyer she said as loud as she dared, "Jeremy?" Walking from room to room, she repeatedly spoke his name. He wasn't in the living room, the kitchen, the laundry room or garage. Nor was he out on the patio. By process of elimination, Terri concluded that he must be in his bedroom.

Surely he wouldn't have gone to bed and left all the lights on, she reflected, heading down the hallway. The doors to the children's bedrooms were closed and no light showed under each one. Reaching the door to the master suite, she found it standing wide open.

"Jeremy?" she said, entering.

The door to his bathroom was also open, and she was able to solve the puzzle of his whereabouts. He was in the shower.

Terri's heart was already beating faster than normal. Its rhythm quickened with a different kind of anticipation as she visualized Jeremy standing naked and male, water coursing down his body. The temptation was strong to venture boldly into the bathroom and have a towel ready.

Instead she closed his bedroom door and went over to sit on the edge of his bed, which he'd made up, but not as neatly as usual. Soon the sound of water stopped. Her throat muscles had tightened with nervousness. She swallowed to relax them before she spoke.

"Jeremy, I'm in here. I came over, and when I couldn't rouse you I used my key to get in."

There was no answer for what seemed an eternity. Then she couldn't gauge his reaction when he said, "Just a minute."

It was fully three minutes before he appeared in the doorway with a towel wrapped around his waist. Terri's heart sank at his grim expression.

"You must have eaten pretty fast," he remarked.

"I didn't eat. Neither did Christopher. He's on his way back to Little Rock," she added, noting that he'd combed his hair. Even wet, it had blond streaks. His tanned upper torso and legs were a deeper shade of golden brown from being outdoors in the sun today. He looked healthy and virile. Gazing at him awoke a possessive pleasure and urgency to get the conversation over with.

"Do you want to wait for me in the living room while I put on some clothes?" he asked, striding to his dresser, where he pulled open the drawer that held his underwear.

"No, not really," Terri replied truthfully. "What I want is to kiss and make up." She rose and walked over to him.

Abruptly he turned his back to her, a pair of briefs in his hands. "Terri, don't use sex to cloud the issue."

"What issue? There isn't any, in my mind." She slipped her arms around his waist and hugged him. "I missed you today and wished I were with you and Jerry and Mandy."

"You could have been with us, but you chose to be with Sommers."

"I didn't *choose* to be with him. I agreed partly to prove to you that I'm over him and partly because he appealed to my kind streak. If I'd had any inkling you would get this upset, I wouldn't have agreed." She kissed his back, inhaling his clean male scent. "Will you forgive me?"

"It's not a matter of forgiving you. It's a matter of my heeding common sense and good judgment rather than giving in to wishful thinking. You wouldn't be happy for long as my wife."

"I think I would happy for a whole lifetime."

"Eventually you would get bored with living in Yellville year in and year out."

"I'm hoping we'll squeeze in a trip somewhere with the kids at least once a year, and Little Rock isn't that far away that I can't go there if I get the urge. Yellville's not the North Pole." Terri sighed. "Did you miss me today?" she asked wistfully.

"You know I did. I thought about you all day, with Sommers."

"There's no reason for you to be jealous of Christopher. Seeing you two in the same room worked to your advantage in every respect, not his."

"It sure didn't feel that way. He was the one who stayed behind at your cottage while I left with a picture in my mind of you in that sexy black robe."

"I slipped it on, thinking that you'd arrived early. When I opened the door and saw Christopher, I was disappointed. And tonight I'm here, aching for you to kiss me and hold me. And make love to me," she said softly, concluding her case.

"Making love won't solve anything."

But he was turning around as he spoke. Terri's arms went

up around his neck and her lips met his, while his arms gathered her to him in a crushing embrace.

There was no punishment in his kisses, no vestige of anger and resentment in his caresses as they made love. But when he coupled their bodies, he was claiming her and cherishing her as his own with a possessiveness that thrilled Terri. She let her passionate and tender response convey her apologies for the lost day and soothe his needless insecurities.

Afterward, lying in his arms, she used words to bolster her reassurances. "Don't ever be jealous of Christopher again. He's not nearly the man you are."

"He's the epitome of the successful, high-powered professional, with his gold Rolex and custom-tailored clothes and high-priced automobile. And he has no intention of giving you up. That was obvious to me."

"I think he saw the handwriting on the wall today and realized our marriage was really over," Terri stated.

"Did he say as much?" His tone was doubtful.

"No, but the ground rules for the day were that we wouldn't discuss our marriage, and he stuck to them. When he left tonight, he kissed me on the cheek."

"He called you 'darling' when he made that phony apology for picking up the phone and ensuring that I knew he was there."

"That really was a mistake, and the 'darling' slipped out. He'd been careful not to call me 'darling' all day. But let's not talk anymore about Christopher other than noting the fact that I have seen him in person now and wasn't affected. I still want to be Mrs. Jeremy Wells as badly as before. Haven't your qualms been eased enough for us to become engaged to be married?" she inquired, sounding as hopeful as she felt.

Disappointingly, an answer wasn't immediately forthcoming, even though his arms tightened around her.

"My qualms don't just involve Sommers. Remember last Sunday when the kids and I waited for you on your porch?

You'd gone out earlier and bought the Little Rock newspaper. I couldn't help noticing that you'd read the society section and looked at the ads for women's fashions.''

"I looked through the whole newspaper, but not with any particular interest. Do you want me to go to Little Rock, Jeremy? Is that another test I have to pass?" she demanded.

"I wish with all my heart I could say, 'Let's get married immediately,' but I have to think about how harmful divorce could be for Jerry and Mandy."

Terri sighed. The earnestness in his words helped to alleviate some of her hurt. "I need to make a trip to Little Rock and visit my great-aunt anyway. Actually, I was tentatively planning to go soon. I'll go next weekend."

"You haven't mentioned any tentative plans," he said.

"Today Christopher inquired about Aunt Evelyn and I began to feel guilty when I was explaining that she'd fallen a couple of times lately. She's my only living family and has always been so good to me. I'm looking forward to taking you and Jerry and Mandy to meet her after we're married. There're some fun things to do with the kids in Little Rock."

"Have you told your great-aunt about me? About us?"

"No, not in any great detail," Terri admitted. "Nor have I broken the news that I might be living permanently in Yellville. She was against my moving here even temporarily. Like you and Christopher, she sees me as a city person."

"What was her reaction to your divorcing Sommers?"

"She's old-fashioned and against divorce, in principle. Her advice was to turn a blind eye to Christopher's dalliances with other women. Apparently she weathered a stormy phase of her marriage to my uncle Randolph when he had an affair."

"So she's not likely to encourage you to marry me."

"No, but showing her pictures of Jerry and Mandy will weaken her opposition. She adores children, particularly little girls. I can win over Aunt Evelyn," Terri said with certainty. "Winning you over is my big challenge. I'm starting to wonder—" She broke off.

"Wonder what?" he pressed.

"Whether there's not some deeper reason you're so cautious about remarrying. Maybe a deep-seated loyalty to Susan. Or fear about being vulnerable to tragedy again."

"There's no guilt about loving you, and as a parent, I'm vulnerable to tragedy every minute of every day."

Terri was recovering from the thrill of his first statement, spoken soberly. "You've never actually told me you love me," she said.

"I do love you."

"And I love you."

At her words, he hugged her so tight she could hardly breathe. Terri broke the emotion-charged moment, her voice happy. "Would it be overly optimistic of me to shop for a new dress when I'm in Little Rock next week, a dress I could have handy to get married in?"

"If you come back from Little Rock with a dress to get married in, we'll set a wedding date."

Terri decided to ignore his use of *if* instead of *when*. "A proposal of sorts, at last!" She raised up and kissed him on the lips before she snuggled in his arms again. "What color do you like best on me?"

"Any color you've worn around me. You'd look beautiful in a dress made of brown butcher paper."

"Sounds horribly unbecoming." She breathed a sigh of contentment. "I'll buy a dress for Mandy to wear at our wedding, too. Should I get a new tie and shirt for Jerry? I don't want him to feel left out."

"He'll probably have to be coerced into being present. He isn't going to be a happy camper. You are prepared for that?"

"Yes, but hopefully he'll come around fairly quickly.

Everything's going to work out well for us in time, Jeremy. I'm confident of it.'' *Confident enough for both of us,* she added silently when he didn't make any reply.

Chapter Twelve

Terri hummed along with a song on the radio as she drove to Jeremy's house the next morning. There was a touch of autumn in the crisp air. She glanced at familiar landmarks along the way and waved back to people who waved to her, none of whom she knew personally: an old man sitting in a rocking chair on his porch with a dog at his feet, a woman with her hair in pink plastic curlers who was raising the red flag on her mailbox, a pudgy teenaged boy wheeling his bicycle out to the street.

Jeremy probably knew them by name, she reflected. He seemed to know everybody who lived in Yellville and the surrounding vicinity. In time she probably would, too. She would meet other mothers at school functions. Other mothers. The phrase had such a wonderful ring to it! She would enlarge her group of acquaintances by attending church with Jeremy and participating in church and town social events. She would become friends with other wives of local businessmen and with local businesswomen, as well.

Terri didn't intend to be shy or retreat behind a poised facade when she encountered female distrust or unfriendliness. She was determined to be liked for herself or at least accepted for herself, for the person she was. It would become obvious to everyone in Yellville, man and woman, that she wasn't interested in any other man except Jeremy.

Her husband.

She and Jeremy would be friendly with other couples, like the Petersons. They would occasionally have people over to their house, sometimes with their children and sometimes with just the adults. They would occasionally be invited to other homes and accept. *Occasionally* was the key word, because family activities would claim the lion's share of their evenings and weekends, with enough social interaction mixed in to keep a good balance. Admittedly, Terri looked forward to hiring a sitter every now and then and having a night out with Jeremy for dinner and maybe a movie.

Life seemed so rich when she looked into the future. Today she had no doubt about the answer to the question she'd asked herself less than a month ago: *Could I live permanently in my hometown?*

The answer was *Yes, with Jeremy.*

Turning onto his street, she noted the houses of his neighbors, who would be her neighbors soon. Parking in the driveway of Jeremy's handsome brick home, she felt both eager and impatient for the time when she could pull in and know she was returning to her own home.

Their home, hers and Jeremy's and his children's. *Their children.*

Yes, the future was wonderful, almost too wonderful to believe. Finally, life wouldn't be about appearance and surface values and superficial glamour.

At the front door, Terri singled out the key, noticing absently that one of the keys flanking it was the key Christopher had left with her. She'd slipped it on her key ring for safekeeping, figuring that she would drop it by his house and leave it with the maid next weekend when she was in Little Rock.

"Good morning," she called in the foyer to announce her presence.

"Here in the kitchen, Terri," Jeremy answered.

The sound of his voice made joy swell inside her. As she headed for the kitchen, she thought there was danger of her smile splitting her face.

Father and son and daughter had eaten breakfast and were loading the dishwasher. Terri dropped her purse and keys on the built-in desk beneath the wall telephone and went over to join them.

"Hi, Ms. Sommers," Mandy greeted her with a welcoming smile.

"Hi, sweetie." Terri bent to give her a hug, and the little girl hugged her around the neck. Straightening only partially, Terri smiled at Jerry and tapped her cheek with a forefinger. "How about a kiss from the fisherman in the family?"

He blushed and gave her a peck. She pressed her luck and stole a quick hug, which he permitted.

Jeremy had closed the door of the dishwasher by this time and was standing by, watching. Terri stepped up close to him. "Hi," she said.

"Hi."

She could tell he wanted to give her a good-morning hug and kiss as much she wanted to do the same. When he didn't make the first move, she impulsively raised up on her toes and kissed him on the mouth. His arms came around her then, enclosing her in a strong, warm embrace.

Mandy giggled in the background and exclaimed, "Daddy, Ms. Sommers kissed you and you're hugging her! That's *funny!*"

"It's *not* funny," Jerry denied in a fierce, strangled voice.

Terri could feel Jeremy's muscles go lax in a reflexive response and was prepared for him to release her immediately, but instead he kept one arm around her waist as she turned.

"You and Mom used to hug and kiss like that, Dad!" Jerry burst out, fighting tears. His words were part accusation and part protest. "You said even if you got married again, Mom would always be the love of your life! Remember?"

"Yes, I remember, son."

"Are you and Ms. Sommers going to get married, Daddy?" Mandy's inquiry conveyed her delight over the idea.

"We haven't set a wedding date, but we've discussed getting married. It's not definite yet," he added.

She hopped up and down in childish excitement, clapping her hands. "Please, *please* get married! Then Ms. Sommers could live with us all the time!" Her shining brown eyes widened and a bigger smile broke out. "When you marry Daddy, can I call you 'Mommy,' Ms. Sommers?"

"*No*, you can't call her 'Mommy'!" Jerry shouted. "She *isn't* your mother! Mom was your mother!"

"That's enough," Jeremy said sternly.

But his son was too upset to heed parental authority. "I *hate* Mandy!" he shouted. "I hate *you*, Dad! I hate *everybody*—" He ran from the room, sobbing.

"Poor little boy," Terri murmured, her heart heavy with her empathy.

Jeremy sighed. "I'll go and talk to him." He left the room.

The scene had had a subduing effect even on Mandy. "Let's you and I go and make up your bed, dear," Terri suggested, trying to convey with her tone and manner that everything would be all right.

The earlier happiness had been effectively doused.

Jerry lay across his bed, Susan's photograph clutched to his chest, sobs racking his slim body. "I don't care if you punish me, Dad,'' he cried when Jeremy had closed the door quietly and gone over to sit beside him.

"Your mother wouldn't want you to be unhappy like this.'' He stroked his son's back.

"Nobody remembers her but me. I look at her picture and think about her every day, and you don't. Not anymore, since you met Ms. Sommers.''

The accusation, punctuated by sobs, was true.

"During the period of time I did think about your mother every day and grieved for her, I was just as unhappy on the inside as you are right now. The only bright spots in my life were you and Mandy. It was an effort for me to smile then. You wouldn't wish for me to remain in a state of grief, would you?''

There was no answer, but the sobbing gradually abated.

"I'm not going to the wedding if you marry Ms. Sommers. You can't make me.''

"As I said out in the kitchen just now, Ms. Sommers and I haven't set a wedding date. But I hope we do soon, and, of course, I would want you and your sister to be present at an event that important to me. And important to both of you as well, since you would be gaining a stepmother.''

"I won't ever call her 'Mom.'''

"If you don't want to call her 'Mom,' I'm sure she wouldn't expect you to.''

"Are you going to let Mandy call her 'Mommy'?''

"That would be for Mandy and Ms. Sommers to decide. If and when Ms. Sommers and I are married,'' Jeremy added, reemphasizing the element of uncertainty, which still remained. He gave his son's back a loving pat before asking quietly, "Can I rely on you to be cooperative with Ms. Sommers today while I'm at work? And polite to her and your sister?''

Jerry sat up and nodded. At the sight of his tearstained face and woebegone expression, Jeremy enveloped him in his arms and hugged his slim body tightly, paternal love a painful emotion in his chest.

"I don't really hate you, Dad. Or Mandy." The confession was mumbled against Jeremy's shirt.

"I know you don't, son."

"Or Ms. Sommers."

"I'm sure she realizes that. Ms. Sommers is a very understanding person."

Jerry heaved a sigh. "If only you didn't want to marry her...." He pushed out of Jeremy's embrace and reached behind him for his mother's picture. "Can I just stay in my room today?"

"Until you're feeling more cheerful." Jeremy gave Jerry's small shoulder a squeeze before rising.

At Jerry's request, he closed the bedroom door behind him.

Terri and Mandy were across the hall in his daughter's room, one on either side of her neatly made bed. They both looked up from plumping throw pillows when he appeared in the doorway.

"Is he okay?" Terri asked anxiously.

"He has calmed down and will spend some time in his room thinking things over. I don't expect you'll have any problems with misbehavior, but if you do, don't hesitate to call me at the station."

"I'm not worried about his misbehaving." *I'm worried about him.*

Jeremy read the silent communication and offered what silent reassurance he could muster. *It'll work out. I'll deal with this.*

As he left his house and drove to his place of business, he thought about how much better he could deal with his son's rebelliousness if he himself wasn't still plagued with doubts about the wisdom of marrying Terri. It had been on the tip of his tongue to say to Jerry, *Just think how happy we'll be as a family, you and Mandy and me and Ms. Sommers, eating meals together every day, going places and*

*doing things. Think about how much fun holidays like
Thanksgiving and Christmas and Easter can be again.*

Jeremy had to buy into that future unequivocally before
he could sell it to his son as a real possibility. First he had
to let Terri make her trip to Little Rock next weekend, a
trip that had suddenly materialized the very day Sommers
had shown up. She'd been quick to schedule it immediately, labeling it as a "test," which Jeremy supposed it was
in his mind.

If she came back with a dress to wear to their wedding
and still in the same positive frame of mind that she could
imagine herself living contentedly in Yellville, then Jeremy
would be all for getting married right away. That *if* loomed
too great, though, for him to dare to fantasize about sharing
the rest of his life with her.

Something continued to tell him, even when he held
Terri in his arms after making glorious love to her, *Stay
alert. Stay cautious or you'll be sorry.*

After Terri had left last night, he'd had trouble falling
asleep, mulling over her suggestion that losing Susan might
have made him afraid of being happily married again and
laying himself open to tragedy. It was true there was fear
at the heart of his doubts, fear of trusting blindly in the
future and harming his children.

His cautiousness stemmed from parental responsibility.
The fear would disappear when the doubts proved to be
unfounded, as Jeremy hoped with all his heart they would
prove to be.

"Mr. Wells, telephone."

Jeremy was in the garage, standing with his chief mechanic and a customer beside the latter's pickup truck, with
the hood propped open to reveal the engine. He looked
around at Kevin Planter, the high-school boy he'd hired to
fill in for Terri. "Who's calling?" he asked.

He'd spoken to Terri about thirty minutes earlier. If
someone other than her or one of his children was on the

phone, he would return the call later, since he was in the middle of a consultation about repairs on the pickup.

"It's long distance. Some man in Little Rock."

"Little Rock?" Jeremy repeated.

"Sounded real educated and important, like a doctor or lawyer. He said it was 'imperative' that he speak to you."

"Probably somebody selling something," offered Mike, the mechanic, wiping his greasy hands on a rag. "Salesmen call from Timbuktu these days on them eight hundred numbers."

"Hope it ain't no family emergency," put in Red Sanderson, the customer.

"I don't have any family in Little Rock." But Terri did. The call might concern her great-aunt. Perhaps her aunt Evelyn's physician or attorney was trying to track Terri down. "Excuse me," Jeremy said to Red and Mike, and went hurriedly inside the station to pick up the phone in his office.

"Jeremy Wells speaking."

"Wells, Christopher Sommers here."

Sommers. Jeremy's hand tightened on the phone, a picture of Terri's ex-husband appearing clearly in his mind. Darkly handsome, arrogant, exuding assurance and success.

"What can I do for you, Sommers?" he asked tersely.

"The real question is 'What can I do for you?'"

"I can't imagine that you could do anything for me. Nor am I naive enough to think you would want to."

"I can give you the benefit of my observations of Terri yesterday, pass on conversation that she and I had, in the interest of helping you clarify your relationship with her and form realistic expectations. For example, I questioned her about settling down in her hometown, to which she hadn't returned once during our six-year marriage. Would you care to hear her answers?"

No, I wouldn't. Jeremy couldn't get the words out. His jaw was clenched too tight, making his teeth grind against each other. He could visualize Sommers seated at a power desk in a power office in a high-rise building that was a power address in downtown Little Rock.

"I'll take your silence as *yes,*" Sommers said, and went on, "Terri indicated that she'd had no firm intention of living permanently in Yellville, before she met you. Now she's sold on marrying you, it seems, even though small-town life has no greater appeal in itself. I asked her point-blank, 'Can you picture yourself living in your hometown without Wells?' and she said, 'No.' It goes without saying that my view isn't an unbiased one, but I can't picture her being happy for any length of time and I frankly doubt you can, either. You didn't strike me as a man lacking in perception."

"I'm perceptive enough to realize you would like nothing better than for me to break off with Terri and send her back to Little Rock to you."

"If you broke off with her, she wouldn't waste much time before she moved back here. I wish you had seen her face light up when we discussed her making a trip soon and she mentioned wanting to go shopping."

"You've made your point, Sommers." Jeremy couldn't bear to hear any more details, all of which rang true. "I have a customer waiting."

"One other thing I wanted to make sure you were aware of. If Terri marries you and buries herself in Yellville for a year or two, she'll be sacrificing an opportunity to resume a lucrative career doing commercials and modeling for print advertisements. A top agency in Little Rock is clamoring to get her under contract again. She quit her career when she became my wife, and didn't miss the glamour and excitement because our life-style kept her in the limelight. Her wardrobe filled a walk-in closet the size of an average room."

"As my wife Terri wouldn't have any need of a wardrobe that big and our life-style wouldn't provide much glamour, but she would have a husband who's faithful.

From what she has led me to believe, that's very important to her."

There was silence from the other end of the line. Whatever satisfaction Jeremy might have gotten from delivering his own verbal punch to the gut was negated by his verb tense. *Wouldn't,* not *won't.*

Sommers wouldn't have missed his conditional wording.

After he'd hung up, Jeremy took a minute or two to get a grip on his emotions, then returned to the garage, where Mike and Red were waiting. Following some further brief discussion, Red accompanied Jeremy inside his office to get a detailed breakdown on the cost of parts and labor. When he left, the computer printout folded up and stuck in his shirt pocket, it was close to noon.

Mike stuck his head in the office door to ask, "Jeremy, you want a hamburger or something from the Front Porch? Kevin's callin' in an order." The Front Porch was a restaurant on the edge of town that served a large buffet for lunch, but also had a menu with burgers and sandwiches.

"No, thanks, Mike. I think I'll go home and grab some lunch."

He wanted to see for himself how Terri was coping with the situation with Jerry and check in on his son, who at last report was confining himself to his room.

And despite everything, including the phone call from Sommers, he simply wanted to see Terri, period.

At his house he entered through the laundry room and found her in the kitchen, making sandwiches. "Hi," he said, pausing in the doorway and watching her spread mustard on a slice of bread with a small wooden spatula.

"Hi." She smiled at him. "Shall I make one of these for you, too?"

"Please." Her movements were competent and she seemed intent on her domestic task, yet it was all too easy to imagine that his kitchen was the set for a commercial and large cameras were aimed at her. She was so beautiful, so desirable. "Is Jerry still in his room?" he asked.

"Yes, but he has the door open now. When I asked him if he was hungry and wanted lunch, he answered yes. So that's a good sign. Mandy's down at Tommy's house, playing his new video game with him." Tommy was a five-year-old who lived several houses away. "I was just about to phone and tell his mother to send her home. You can do it for me, if you don't mind. The number's written there on a notepad."

"I'll call in a minute." Jeremy was torn between seizing the moment of privacy as an opportunity to bring up Sommers's phone call or taking advantage of it in a different way that quickened his pulse. The latter won out. "First I want to say hi again," he stated as he walked over to her.

Terri stuck the spatula in the mustard jar and turned toward him. "Hmm. I'm all for that," she said, tilting her head back for his kiss. When Jeremy put his arms around her, she slipped her arms up around his neck.

Aware of how quickly and easily things could get out of hand, he didn't deepen the kiss, but instead prolonged it with a tender, seeking pressure, thrilling in the responsive softness of her lips as she kissed him back with a matching tenderness. A sweet sense of leisure relaxed some inner tension inside him.

They ended the kiss, and Jeremy drew her close. She hugged him back, whispering in a happy voice, "I love the feel of your arms around me like this."

"I love holding you tight."

"Just think. Jerry and Mandy will be having their lunch in the school cafeteria during the weekdays. You and I can steal some time together like this at noon. Won't that be nice?" She rubbed her cheek against his jaw.

"*Nice* isn't quite the word."

"We haven't really discussed whether you'll want me to return to work at the station next week. Of course it would be part-time. I'll still have the housework and laundry to keep up with, and I'll need to be here when the children get home."

"Whether you work part-time at the station or not, I'm going to hire some household help."

"Don't you dare. I won't have some other woman invading my territory." She drew back and kissed him on the mouth. "Now, I'd better finish making these sandwiches before the bread goes stale. You can phone Tommy's house and then maybe have a word with Jerry and tell him lunch is ready."

Jeremy dropped a kiss on her nose before he released her. "My, you're bossy," he teased. "You're starting to sound like a wife."

She smiled sheepishly. "Would you please phone Tommy's house and then tell Jerry lunch is ready? Is that better?"

"Much better."

Jeremy's level of optimism about a future with Terri had never been higher as he walked over to the wall phone to summon his daughter to lunch. The few minutes of warm intimacy followed by the lighthearted exchange had done wonders for his morale. Maybe he'd been far too negative up to now. Maybe Terri knew her own heart and mind better than he did. Maybe—just *maybe*—she might be happy as his wife.

Her purse and key ring lay on the desk beneath the phone, where she'd set them that morning. Next to the key ring was the pad with the telephone number. A glance at the number refreshed his memory. While he waited for someone to pick up at Tommy's house, he absently gazed at Terri's key ring, recognizing the key to the station and the key to his house.

He'd given them to her with the knowledge that she would be returning them when she left Yellville and moved back to Little Rock. What a wonderful thought it was that both keys might have a permanent spot on her key ring.

Tommy finally answered the phone and explained that his mother was outside, taking sheets off the clothesline, and he hadn't wanted to put down the control to his video game because he was just about to be the victor over Mandy. He promised to relay Jeremy's instructions for Mandy to come home promptly.

"One assignment accomplished," Jeremy said, hanging up.

Terri was taking small plates down from a cabinet. "I'm amazed that you're in this good a mood," she remarked. "When you came in just now, you looked so sober I figured you'd had a trying morning at the station on top of that bad scene with Jerry."

"The only trying thing that happened at the station was a long-distance phone call from your ex-husband, of all people."

She set down the plates with a little *clunk*, her surprise evident. "Christopher called you? What on earth for?"

"In general, to advise me how unwise I would be to marry you. I'll tell you about the conversation in more detail later when we have time to talk."

"You don't need to. I can guess what he said. 'Terri won't be happy living in Yellville.' Well, he's mistaken."

"According to him, you've been contacted by some agency in Little Rock to do modeling and commercials."

"The Partridge Agency. They haven't contacted me yet, but supposedly are going to. The first I'd heard of it was yesterday." She was placing a sandwich on each plate. "The nerve of Christopher, calling you. I'll make sure it won't happen again."

"If it does, I can handle it." The idea of more phone calls from Sommers was a lot more tolerable than the idea of her in communication with her ex-husband. "I'll go and get Jerry."

"I'm here, Dad." Jerry announced his presence in a glum tone as he entered the kitchen.

Jeremy registered the fact that his son must have heard the last part of the conversation between the adults about Sommers's phone call. Or all of it if he'd paused outside and eavesdropped, which Jeremy suspected might be the case from the way Jerry avoided meeting his eyes.

In the interest of harmony, Jeremy decided to pretend he didn't notice anything amiss. On the positive side, his son had at least emerged voluntarily from his room.

Mandy burst in and greeted him excitedly, "Hi, Daddy!" She chattered nonstop about her video game session at Tommy's during the last-minute preparations of getting lunch on the table. Jerry helped, but he didn't utter a word. Jeremy caught Terri's glances at his son, full of maternal empathy and concern. She caught his own eye several times and smiled reassuringly.

They had just sat down, when the telephone pealed to life.

"I'll get it! I'm tall enough to reach the phone!" Mandy was already scrambling down from her chair. Normally her brother would have moved faster than her, but he didn't stir from his seat.

"Take it easy," Jeremy cautioned, reaching over to stabilize her glass of milk. "Whoever is calling, get their name and tell them we'll call back." He and Terri both waited patiently while his little daughter dashed over to the wall phone and stood on tiptoes. Jerry had picked up a sandwich half from his plate and begun to eat it with all the enjoyment he might shown if it were compressed sawdust.

Having successfully grasped the phone and dislodged it, Mandy seemed to lose her grip and the receiver crashed to the desk, making Jeremy cringe. In her hurry to scoop it up, she managed to knock Terri's keys to the floor. Finally she spoke an eager "Hello" into the receiver. "They hung up," she reported, her expression comically disappointed.

"Probably to make an appointment with a doctor for a burst eardrum," Jeremy remarked to Terri, and was rewarded with her amused smile.

"I *am* tall enough," Mandy insisted. "Look." She replaced the phone without mishap and then bent to scoop up the keys. Instead of dropping them on the desk, she singled out a key and held it up, asking curiously, "What's this new key for, Ms. Sommers?"

"Don't be so nosy," Jeremy chided, although Terri's reaction made him curious, too. She seemed not only embarrassed, but chagrined. Why?

"I might have known she would notice a new key," she said to him. "She has a fascination with keys."

"I know what every single one of my daddy's keys is for, too," Mandy said proudly. "Don't I, Daddy?"

Jerry spoke up suddenly, breaking his morose silence and asking one of the questions on Jeremy's mind.

"When did you get a new key, Ms. Sommers? Yesterday?"

When she'd seen Sommers for the first time in a couple of months. Had he delivered the key?

Terri's discomfiture had obviously grown. Jeremy came to her rescue, instructing, "Mandy, come and sit down. Let's eat our lunch and not put Ms. Sommers through the third degree."

"It's no big mystery," Terri declared. "The key is to a very nice guest house in Little Rock. My former husband, who is the owner of the guest house, left the key with me yesterday in case I wanted to stay there whenever I go to Little Rock."

"Are you going to Little Rock soon?" Jerry inquired.

"This coming weekend," she confirmed, her anxious gaze on Jeremy, who couldn't hide his stunned, betrayed reaction. *I'll explain later. Don't be upset,* she pleaded silently.

"I'll miss you, Ms. Sommers," Mandy said pensively.

"I'll miss you, sweetie. But I'll be back Sunday night. I definitely want to be here on Monday when you start kindergarten." She smiled a forced smile at Jerry. "And Jerry starts third grade."

"My mom took me to school the first day when I started kindergarten," he said, addressing his gloomy statement to the world at large, not to Terri. He bit into his sandwich, and the rest of them followed suit.

It was an effort for Jeremy to chew and swallow. Bile rose in his throat as he recalled with bitter irony phoning his neighbor's house just fifteen minutes earlier, glancing down at Terri's key ring on the desk, spotting the keys to his place of business and his house and being filled with rosy optimism about the future. Unbeknownst to him, she'd had Sommers's key on her key ring, too.

"Can I be excused?" Jerry asked after draining his glass of milk.

"No, you can sit there a couple of minutes until we're finished eating and help clear the table," Jeremy replied.

"I can't eat the rest of mine, Daddy, or I'll get sick," Mandy said, putting down the uneaten portion of a sandwich half and clasping her abdomen.

Terri laid her uneaten portion of sandwich down, too, and Jeremy did the same. He'd been forcing himself to eat, she knew, just as she had. "I'll clear the table later," she said. "Mandy and Jerry, would you please go outside and play? I would like to talk privately with your father a few minutes before he goes back to the station."

"I don't want to go outside. I want to go back to my room," Jerry said sullenly. "Can I, Dad?"

"No, go outside, as Ms. Sommers asked you to, and get some fresh air and exercise."

Jerry didn't argue with the authoritative reply. "Come on, Mandy. They want to talk about the key."

"Okay." From the little girl's subdued manner, the strained atmosphere had had its effect on her, too. She accompanied her brother.

Terri waited until the door to the garage had closed. "The key isn't important, Jeremy. Christopher left it on my kitchen table yesterday. I slipped it on my key ring so it wouldn't get misplaced. I have every intention of returning it this weekend. I'll stay in a hotel."

"You should have seen your face, Terri, when Mandy asked you about the key."

"I'd forgotten about the darned thing! And I could predict how you were going to react!"

He set aside his plate none too gently. "So you weren't going to mention anything about this guest house to me."

"I didn't have any occasion to mention it to you."

"Last night we discussed your going to Little Rock this weekend, which you sprang on me suddenly after spending the whole day and half the night with Sommers. I find it interesting that when he was giving me a blow-by-blow of your conversations with him, he didn't breathe a word, either, about offering you the use of his guest house."

Terri set aside her plate with a thud. "You're not actually implying that he and I cooked up this trip to Little Rock so that I could play around on you with him?" she demanded.

He pushed back his chair abruptly and got up. "People who're planning to get married don't have secrets." With movements that conveyed the anger in his voice, he reached for his two children's plates and stacked them with his.

"No, they can usually rely on each other's trust and understanding!" she retorted, pushing her chair back and grabbing up her lone plate. "How can you expect me to confide something that's going to make you more jealous than you already are? Jealous for no good reason. There wouldn't be anything wrong with my staying in Christopher's guest house."

He stared at her, and she could sense him recoiling from his own thoughts.

"He left the key because you didn't turn down his offer, did you?"

"I did turn it down, but mainly because of you. I would be much more comfortable there than in a hotel, and—" Before she could explain that she'd been attracted by the idea of a place to entertain her great-aunt, Jeremy cut her off.

"Sommers wouldn't have a key to your hotel room. That's a major factor, in my book. Speaking of things you haven't brought up, did he make a pass at you yesterday morning after I left the two of there at your cottage, with you wearing that see-through robe?"

"Of course he made a pass at me! And got nowhere!"

With the stack of plates in one hand, he gathered up his glass, Jerry's and Mandy's with his free hand, clinking them together.

"This is such a tempest in a teapot!" Terri exclaimed in frustration, following him over to the dishwasher. "You're blowing things out of all proportion!"

"I only wish I were blowing things out of proportion," he said grimly.

"Just leave the dishes and go back to the station! Maybe by tonight we can have a sane discussion!"

He set down the dishes he carried and headed for the door to the laundry room. Terri bit her lip, trying to keep back his name, but it came out anyway.

"Jeremy!"

Immediately he stopped, turned around and came back to her. She met him and went into his arms. He gathered her close, his embrace fierce and possessive. Terri hugged him back, her eyes tightly closed, as she fought with him his battle against his anger, hurt and jealousy.

"I love you," she whispered.

"I love you."

The words, sadly, weren't any magic cure for his suspicion and doubts or her sense of being constantly on trial. Love wasn't enough in the absence of mutual trust and mutual confidence in a workable relationship.

"You have to believe in *us,* Jeremy," she said.

"I want to, Terri, more than anything in the world."

But he didn't have that essential belief.

Could her belief hold out?

Chapter Thirteen

"What's wrong, angel?" Jeremy crossed the lawn to his little daughter, who sat under a tree in the front yard, weeping with quiet despair. He squatted beside her and gently wiped her wet cheeks with his thumbs. "Why are you crying?"

"I don't want Ms. Sommers to go away."

Bands tightened around Jeremy's heart. "Are you talking about her trip to Little Rock? She's going to visit her great-aunt, who is very old and lives in a nursing home. You heard her say she'll be coming back Sunday night."

"Jerry said she might decide to stay and marry Mr. Sommers again. Will she, Daddy?"

"I certainly hope not. She hasn't indicated any such plans to me. But whatever happens, angel, you and Jerry and I will manage."

Her big brown eyes filled with fresh tears that spilled over, and he wiped them away. She gulped out, "I want

Ms. Sommers to marry you, but I don't want Jerry to run away from home. He's my only brother.''

"He told you he would run away from home if Ms. Sommers and I got married?"

She nodded. "He said I'd never see him again until maybe when we were grown-up."

Jeremy sat on the grass, lifted her onto his lap and cradled her in his arms. "I wouldn't put too much stock in Jerry's running away from home. Usually boys don't tell their little sisters when they're plotting something that drastic.''

She sniffled, seeming to mull over his words. "Because little sisters tell their daddies, huh? And the daddies would stop the boys from running away?"

"Something like that."

"Jerry was probably just being mean and trying to make me sad.''

"No, I think your brother's genuinely upset himself. But don't let him make you sad. Okay?"

"Okay, Daddy."

Jeremy set her on her feet and stood up.

"I'm going inside to get a drink of water and see what Ms. Sommers is doing. Bye." She trotted off, black curls bouncing.

He walked to his car, wishing he were as resilient.

Driving away, he caught a glimpse of his son in the backyard, tossing a softball high into the air and catching it. His body language wasn't that of the normal, happy Jerry, but it wasn't despondent.

To some extent Jerry was probably cheered by his speculation that Terri's visit to Little Rock might result in her getting back together with her ex-husband, Jeremy reflected, sighing. Such an event would remove the immediate threat of Jeremy's remarrying. To an equal extent, though, Jerry would be dismayed by the prospect of Terri's going away, because he was as fond of her as Mandy was. Jerry's ideal solution, of course, was to go back to the status quo that had existed only in his mind, with Terri functioning as a stand-in for safe Mrs. Grambly.

It didn't surprise Jeremy that his bright, perceptive son had put together clues and arrived at the conclusion that a reconciliation between Sommers and Terri was a viable possibility. Jerry had been present at Terri's cottage when the florist had delivered her former husband's roses. Then Sommers had visited her yesterday, and she'd canceled her plans with the three of them to spend the entire day with him. Then today the business with the key, which had quite possibly followed Jerry's eavesdropping upon the conversation in which Jeremy had related receiving the phone call from Sommers.

Terri had steadfastly denied that she was open to a reconciliation. Jeremy didn't think for a minute that she was being consciously deceitful, but her actions belied that denial and sent messages not just to him but to Sommers, keeping Sommers's hopes alive and Jeremy's fears and doubts alive, too.

Why couldn't she see that?

Would she really have returned the key, or would she have ended up using it? At this point, Jeremy didn't know what she would have done without all the hoopla. He did know that he *should* have had more confidence in the woman he hoped to marry.

Terri had loaded the few dishes into the dishwasher and was wiping the island countertop, when Mandy came into the kitchen. "Have you been crying, sweetie?" she asked the little girl, noticing her tearstained cheeks.

Mandy nodded. "But I'm not sad anymore."

"What were you sad about?"

"I didn't want you to go away and marry Mr. Sommers again."

Terri's jaw dropped. "'Marry Mr. Sommers again'? Whatever put that idea into your head?"

"Jerry said you might."

"Jerry said that?"

"Uh-huh. I started crying and told him I wanted you to marry Daddy, and he said he would run away from home if you did. Then I cried harder. Can I have a glass for some water?" she asked cheerfully.

Terri got a plastic novelty glass down from a cabinet and handed it to her. "You must have talked to your father just now when he was leaving." Obviously she had, and Jeremy had dried her tears. How had he consoled her? Terri simply had to know. "What did your father tell you, Mandy, to stop you from being sad?"

"That you were going to Little Rock to visit your great-aunt, who's an old lady. And you're supposed to come back Sunday night."

"Anything else?"

"He doesn't think Jerry will run away, because boys who run away don't tell little sisters who might tell their daddies." *What a wise father Jeremy was,* Terri thought. *If only his instincts about her weren't so off base.* She waged a war with herself while Mandy filled her glass with water from the dispenser in the refrigerator door and drank half of it thirstily. *I have to ask,* Terri decided.

"Mandy, didn't your father say something like, 'Don't worry, Ms. Sommers isn't going to marry her former husband again'?"

The little girl screwed up her face, as though searching her memory, and shook her head. "He didn't say anything like that. He said he hoped you wouldn't. You're not going to, are you?" The question was beseeching.

"No, I definitely won't ever remarry Mr. Sommers, sweetie."

"You'll marry my daddy?"

"I can't promise you that."

The way Terri felt at the moment, the overwhelming odds seemed stacked against her marrying Jeremy. It was his pessimism creating the odds.

* * *

"I'll answer it!" both children said in unison, but Jerry raced ahead of Mandy into the kitchen, holding a plastic grocery bag in one hand. All three of them were carrying bags, having just arrived home from a trip to the supermarket.

"He's faster than me!" Mandy complained. "I wish he'd stayed mad!"

"You can help me put away the groceries," Terri soothed.

It was an encouraging sign for her that Jerry had reacted normally to the ringing of the telephone. While he hadn't been sulky or belligerent this afternoon, he also hadn't been himself.

"Just a minute. She's right here. For you, Ms. Sommers," he said, holding the phone out toward her as she entered. "It's some man calling."

"Let me put these groceries down."

Terri made a mental note to work on both children's telephone technique and teach them to inquire politely about the identity of a stranger.

"Would you please put the ice cream in the freezer?" she requested of Jerry as she set her bags on the island, one of them containing a half gallon of ice cream.

He nodded agreeably. "I'll put the milk in the refrigerator, too."

"I'm helping Ms. Sommers put away the groceries, not you," Mandy spoke up assertively.

"Silly, the ice cream will melt. You can carry it and I'll open the freezer door for you."

Terri smiled her thank-you as she took the phone from him.

"Hello." Her tone was impersonal.

"Sounds delightful, refereeing a couple of kids." Christopher's voice came over the line, heavily ironic.

"I happen to enjoy it," she answered after a moment's surprise.

"Wait until the novelty wears off." He went on, becoming seriously matter-of-fact, "I'm calling with some rather bad news about your aunt Evelyn. She fell and broke her hip and has been hospitalized."

"Oh, no! When?"

"Today about noon. The administrator at the retirement home called and left messages on your answering machine. Not knowing how else to reach you, she contacted me, and I assured her I would relay the news."

"Poor Aunt Evelyn! What hospital?"

He named one of Little Rock's hospitals. Terri knew the director personally, since she'd served on the committee of an annual fund-raising event benefiting the hospital.

"You'll be coming to Little Rock to see her, I presume."

"Of course I will. I'll come either tonight or tomorrow. I'm her only family, and most of her friends have died or aren't able to sit with her in her hospital room."

"At her age, this won't be a quick convalescence, and there's danger of complications. It'll be a long haul."

"I realize the gravity of the situation." Terri sighed, turning and watching as Jerry patiently accompanied Mandy to the refrigerator, the two of them transporting a gallon jug of milk. Her trip to Little Rock would surely extend through the weekend and probably beyond that, which would mean missing the rest of this last week before they started school. She wouldn't be here for Mandy's first day at kindergarten and Jerry's first day in the third grade. Plus she would be leaving Jeremy in a bind.

But it couldn't be helped. In this instance, at least, she could rely on his understanding, since he placed so much value on family.

"I have to hang up now, Christopher, and make some phone calls. I appreciate your tracking me down."

"That wasn't too difficult. I suggest you make use of the guest house. It's an easy drive to the hospital."

It was an easy drive, but making use of the guest house was out of the question. Jeremy's supportiveness wouldn't extend that far. "I'll try to get a room in a hotel that's conveniently located," she stated.

"Very well. Why don't I have my secretary find out which hotels are closest and reserve you a room in one of them? It'll save you the trouble."

"I would appreciate that very much. Thank you, Christopher. Do you have the phone number of the hospital handy?"

He gave it to her and got off the line. She immediately placed a call to the hospital and talked to a nurse, who told her that her great-aunt was sedated and resting. The nurse promised to convey to Evelyn Peters when she roused that Terri had been contacted and was making immediate plans to come to Little Rock.

By the time she'd concluded the long-distance conversation, Jerry and Mandy were standing off to one side, looking anxious. They'd overheard enough to piece the story together.

"Your aunt Evelyn's had an accident?" Jerry asked.

"You're going to see her in the hospital?" Mandy followed up with her question.

Terri paused to calmly summarize the situation for them and then gave them permission to watch TV. They headed for the living room, and she made her next call, to Jeremy. From her first sentence, it got off on the wrong foot.

"Hi, Christopher just phoned with some bad news."

"Sommers phoned you—at my house?" he demanded, his tone incredulous and outraged. "What colossal nerve!"

Terri sucked in a sharp breath. "Did you hear the part about the bad news?" she asked, her voice edgy. Right now she needed sympathy and support from him, not anger and suspicion. "My aunt Evelyn fell and broke her hip today. She's in the hospital."

"I'm sorry to hear that," he said, sounding genuinely sorry. "How is she?"

Terri related as much information as she'd gleaned from the nurse.

"Why was Sommers contacted and not you?"

"Apparently attempts were made to reach me at my home number. I wasn't there to answer. The administrator of the nursing home got in touch with Christopher."

"Who seized on the excuse to be the bearer of tidings himself."

"Who took the time out of his busy schedule to track me down," she said, restating his biased version of her ex-husband's motives. "Jeremy, what does it matter *how* I got the news about Aunt Evelyn's accident? I'm more concerned about her health and about having to be away for a week or two. Who's going to look after Mandy and Jerry while I'm gone? How are you going to manage? Those are the things worrying me."

"We'll get along. Don't worry about us at a time like this," he said. "When are you going?"

"Tonight, I think. I'll have supper cooked when you get home, but I won't stay and eat. I'll say goodbye and go and pack my things and leave." Terri was formulating her plans as she voiced them.

"Don't bother with supper. I'll fix it myself. You can bring the kids here to the station now, and they can stay with me the rest of the afternoon. That way you'll be on your way to Little Rock several hours sooner and not have to drive at night."

Also not have much of an opportunity for a private farewell. Didn't that matter to him?

In the background Terri heard Kevin's voice.

"Hey, Jeremy, that schoolteacher you talked to a while ago just brought her car in."

"I'll be with her in a minute," Jeremy answered.

"'Schoolteacher'?" she inquired. "I couldn't help overhearing."

"Jennifer Larkins. You probably don't remember her name. She's new in town—"

"I remember her name quite well," Terri broke in to correct him. "What's wrong with her car?"

"Sounded like the starter needs to be replaced. Back to more important matters, bring the kids here to the station now. I insist."

"In that case I will, of course. You're their father."

"Why that tone of voice?" he asked.

"I rather resent being ordered around as though I were Mrs. Grambly. I was under the impression that my position was a little different from hers."

His sigh came over the line. "I certainly wasn't intending to order you around. If anything, I was trying to make up for not reacting as sensitively as I might have to your family emergency. Forgive me for my jealous remarks about Sommers. They were out of line."

"Your jealousy is so groundless." She hesitated. "Just as the jealousy I'm feeling right now is probably groundless."

"The jealousy you're feeling?"

"Of Jennifer Larkins."

"Good heavens, Terri, it's preposterous that *you* would be jealous of Jennifer. You'll get to meet her when you drop off the kids. I'm giving her a ride back to her house."

Great. She would get to tell him goodbye with Jennifer Larkins as part of the audience. And leave the station with the schoolteacher knowing the coast was clear for the next week or two.

"Couldn't somebody else give her a ride? Let Kevin take your van."

"You have more important things to think about than who gives Jennifer a ride," he chided. "I'll see you in about five or ten minutes."

Terri had little choice other than to summon the children and load them up in her car. Jeremy wasn't simply in a hurry to get her out of town. She knew that. The haste was well-intentioned, and the arrangements the best he could come up with on the spur of the moment. But she really would have preferred her plan.

The station was busy, with several customers pumping

gas. In the garage, one car was suspended in the air and another was being worked on at ground level, its hood open. A jaunty red Jeep was parked in front of the open doors. Surely not the vehicle of a schoolteacher, Terri thought. One of the two, more staid automobiles in the garage must belong to Jennifer Larkins.

"Jeremy's in his office, Ms. Sommers," Kevin announced helpfully when she and the children entered the building. He was handling a transaction at the cash register.

"Thanks, Kevin."

Through the open doorway of Jeremy's office floated the infectious laughter of a woman. Obviously Jennifer was keeping Jeremy entertained while she waited for her ride home. The thought made hot jealousy and resentment flare up inside Terri. Both emotions flamed hotter when she reached the doorway and could see Jeremy, seated behind his desk, smiling ruefully and shaking his head as he said, "That's a hilarious story."

Terri was going off to deal with the suffering of her only close relative, dreading being separated from him and his children, and he was enjoying a visit with another woman.

"If I had time, I would sure like to hear a hilarious story," she said in an icy tone, stepping inside the small room behind Mandy and Jerry.

He stood up quickly, his smile gone, and came from behind his desk toward her. "Good, you're here. Jennifer, I'd like you to meet Terri Sommers."

Not *Terri Sommers, my fiancée,* or any identifying tag to suggest she was anyone special in his life. Just Terri Sommers.

"Hi, Terri." The schoolteacher had risen to her feet, too, from a molded plastic chair. Several inches shorter than Terri's five foot seven, she was a sturdily built brunette with a friendly, outgoing manner. She wore khaki hiking shorts, a T-shirt and leather moccasins. "It's great to meet you," she said with seeming sincerity, stepping forward to shake hands. Her gaze went immediately to the two children, her expression lighting up with interest. "And this must be Jerry and Mandy. Hi, Jerry. I'm Ms. Larkins. I'll probably be teaching you next year in fourth grade." She shook hands with him and then bent to shake Mandy's little hand. "Hi, Mandy. Aren't you a cutie-pie!"

"That's not your red Jeep outside, is it, Ms. Larkins?" Jerry asked.

"It sure is. You like it?"

He nodded. "It's neat."

"I'll take you and Mandy for a ride in it sometime."

"Ms. Sommers is leaving us here this afternoon and going away," Mandy offered.

"That's what your dad was telling me." Jennifer gave Terri her attention again. "Sorry about your great-aunt. If she's in good health otherwise, they'll more than likely do surgery and put in a new hip. After a period of rehabilitation, she'll probably be fine."

"Jennifer's grandmother broke her hip," Jeremy explained to Terri.

"I wondered whether she had also been a nurse."

Jennifer grinned. "When you're from a big family, the way I am, and have a dozen aunts and uncles and forty or fifty cousins, you get familiar with every ailment known to man."

"You definitely have the advantage on me there," Terri said. "I grew up with a shortage of relatives."

"Are you staying with family in Little Rock?"

"No, I have no family there besides my great-aunt. I'll be staying in a hotel," Terri replied.

"Which hotel?" Jeremy asked.

"I don't know yet, hopefully one close to the hospital." He frowned. "Shouldn't you make a reservation?"

"Christopher's secretary is taking care of it for me."

"Why didn't I guess?" he said flatly.

Mandy took advantage of the brief awkward silence. "Ms. Larkins, would you give us a ride in your Jeep this afternoon?" The request was forlorn.

"Ms. Larkins is here because she brought her car to have it repaired," Jeremy explained to his daughter. "In a little while, you and Jerry can ride with me when I take her home."

Jennifer cupped her hands around her mouth and confided to Mandy in a loud whisper, "I have a new puppy at my house."

"A puppy? Can I come in and pet him?"

"Sure you can." She hesitated, looking questioningly at Jeremy. "If Jerry and Mandy would like to, they could come to my house and play with my puppy and watch TV until you get off work. I have a big collection of children's movies."

"I'd like to," Mandy volunteered.

"So would I, Dad," Jerry spoke up. "What kind of puppy, Ms. Larkins?"

"If I could interrupt for just a few seconds, I'd like to say goodbye," Terri said. She knelt and gave Mandy a hug. Emotion clogged Terri's throat when the little girl hugged her back tightly.

"Bye, Ms. Sommers. I'll miss you."

"I'll miss you, precious."

Terri half rose and gave Jerry a hug, which he didn't return, but he also didn't shrug her off. Nor did he turn his face aside when she kissed him on the cheek.

"Bye, Ms. Sommers," he said. "I hope your aunt Evelyn gets all right."

"I'll pass along those words to her when I show her your picture and tell her all about you."

When she straightened, Terri saw that Jennifer Larkins had backed away and Jeremy had stepped up closer. He took her arm.

"I'll walk out to your car with you."

"Okay. Goodbye, Jennifer."

"Have a safe trip, Terri."

As she passed through the doorway, behind her she could hear the schoolteacher's voice.

"Jerry, you asked what kind of puppy I have. He's a black Lab and his name is Elvis."

"Elvis?" Mandy repeated.

"That's a weird name for a dog," Jerry commented.

"You can tell she's used to dealing with children," Jeremy remarked as they walked through the outer room.

"Schoolteachers in the elementary grades usually are." Terri waved to Kevin, and responded to his words of farewell. Outside, she asked, "Are you going to let Jerry and Mandy go to her house?"

"Don't you think it's a good idea? It'll get their minds off your leaving."

"Maybe she can get *your* mind off my leaving, too. She seemed to be doing a pretty job of it when I got here."

"Terri, you *can't* be jealous of Jennifer Larkins."

"What did you tell her about me? *Who* did you say I was?"

They'd reached her car.

"Are we really going to discuss this now?" he asked.

"It happens to be rather important. Did you even hint that you were planning to marry me? That I wasn't just your children's sitter, but their future stepmother?"

"I'm sure Jennifer read between the lines."

In other words, no, he hadn't.

"Don't invent a grievance so that you can go off angry," he said.

"Why on earth would I *want* to go off angry?"

"Finding fault with me might give you some justification for being friendly with Sommers once you get to Little Rock. He'll be inviting you out to the best restaurants every night, offering to squire you here and there, doing everything in his power to get back in your good graces and win you back. Don't you think I realize that? I might be a small-town businessman, but I'm not stupid."

"No, but you certainly are suspicious. This isn't a pleasure trip! I'll be spending most of my time in the hospital with my aunt Evelyn!"

He visibly exercised restraint, relaxing his grip on her arm. "I hope she gets along well," he said soberly. "Is she in good health generally?"

"To my knowledge, she has no problems with her heart. She has boasted about her normal blood pressure."

"Then probably she is a candidate for the surgery Jennifer described."

"I'll know more after I talk to Aunt Evelyn's doctor."

"You'll call me tonight?" he asked, opening her car door.

"Will you be home?"

"Where else would I be?"

"You might be at Jennifer's. Don't look so skeptical," she said. "I can easily imagine her inviting all three of you to stay and have supper when you go to pick up Mandy and Jerry."

"It would be perfectly innocent if she did invite us and I accepted. I'm not interested in Jennifer as a woman, and she's not interested in me as a man."

"So you *would* accept."

He closed his eyes briefly, giving his head a little shake that wasn't a negative answer but a venting of exasperation. "That was theoretical. You're determined to pick a fight with me, but it's not going to work. I'll be home tonight, not with Jennifer. You'll have to use some other rationalization for going out to dinner with Sommers, if you've already made a date with him."

"I refuse to dignify that statement with a reply." Terri turned to get into her car, fighting tears of anger and hurt.

"Don't leave without letting me kiss you goodbye," he pleaded, catching her by both arms.

"Out here? In front of all the world?"

"Out here. In front of all the world."

Terri swallowed the huge lump in her throat and let him turn her around to face him. He kissed her on the mouth and then enveloped her in his arms, hugging her tight.

"Drive carefully," he said, his voice rough with emotion. "Call me tonight."

"I will."

They hugged for a few seconds longer, before he released her and helped her into her car, his touch strong and gentle. Terri tooted her horn and waved when she was out on the street. He waved back, standing in the same spot. From his heartsick expression she might have been going away for a whole year.

Or forever.

"Thank you for coming, dear." The words were spoken drowsily, but Terri's great-aunt held on to her hand tightly.

"I couldn't get here fast enough to make sure you were being given the best treatment." Terri kept her tone light. "When I arrived, I found you in a private room with several beautiful bouquets of flowers." It had been such a shock seeing Evelyn Peters lying asleep in the hospital bed, pale and gaunt.

"Christopher sent the white roses. Wasn't that thoughtful of him?"

"He can be very thoughtful," Terri agreed, visualizing the gift basket in her hotel room with a bottle of wine and fruit and cheese.

"Such a handsome man. The two of you make a striking couple."

"*Made* a striking couple, Aunt Evelyn. We're divorced." The correction was gentle. "How are you feeling?"

Some time during the next few days, when her great-aunt wasn't groggy with painkillers, Terri would tell her about her plans to marry Jeremy. By then, she should be able to talk about him without bursting into tears.

A brisk tapping on the door caused her to turn her head in time to see a stocky bald man in a white doctor's coat entering.

"This won't do at all," he declared in a booming baritone, striding over to the foot of the bed. Hands on his hips, he eyed her, making a *tsk-tsking* sound of disapproval. "Tomorrow we'll take care of that hip, Evelyn, and have you up doing a tap dance in no time."

Terri had surmised that he was her dignified great-aunt's physician.

"Dr. Akers, this is my great-niece, Terri Sommers." Evelyn spoke up weakly to make the proper introduction.

"How do you do, Terri," he boomed, and promptly launched into a highly technical explanation of the surgery that would be performed on Evelyn Peters the next day. He followed up with another explanation in layman's terms. "In other words, we'll give you a new hip joint. After some therapy and rehabilitation, you'll be as good as new."

Jennifer Larkins's diagnosis had been right on target. For all Terri's relief, she was also irked.

At nine o'clock Terri left the hospital and drove to the luxury hotel where Christopher's secretary had reserved her a room. He obviously hadn't given any instructions to pick a moderately priced hotel. Terri hadn't quibbled when she called his office from her cottage after she'd finished packing and spoke with the secretary. She'd figured she could stay one night and locate more economical lodgings for herself.

Entering her room, she saw the message light blinking on the phone and knew that Christopher had probably called. Sure enough, he'd left a voice message: *"Terri, give me a ring at home and update me on your aunt Evelyn's condition. I didn't phone you at the hospital for fear of disturbing her rest. I trust your room is satisfactory. Call me, please."*

After a moment of weary deliberation, she decided to phone him first rather than Jeremy, and get the obligatory call out of the way.

"You sound tired, darling," he said sympathetically after he'd listened to her report on her great-aunt's prognosis.

Too tired to care that the *darling* had slipped out, purely out of habit, Terri reflected. "It's been a long day. Thank you for the gift basket."

"Settle back with a glass of wine and relax."

"I think I'll do that immediately."

After she'd hung up, Terri opened the bottle of red wine with the corkscrew provided by the hotel. Filling one of the two stemmed glasses on a small tray, she fantasized briefly about pouring wine into the second one, for Jeremy. How she wished he were here with her tonight.

Was he at home right now thinking about her? she wondered, crossing over to the bed again.

He answered on the first ring, his somber tone indicating that whatever his thoughts were, they weren't particularly happy.

"Hi. It's me. I just came from the hospital."

"I was hoping it was you. How's your aunt?"

Terri filled him in at some length.

"That's wonderful that the prognosis is good," he said. "What's the time frame?"

"She'll have surgery tomorrow and return to her room for postoperative care through the weekend with some physical therapy. Then she'll be moved to the rehabilitation section of the hospital for anywhere from one to three weeks or longer, depending on how she does."

"Is there a lot of pain involved?"

"I asked Dr. Akers that question, and he said it varies according to the individual. I'm sure there is pain."

"It doesn't sound like an experience for an elderly person to go through alone."

"No, I'm definitely needed here to lend my moral support to Aunt Evelyn. She was so glad to see me." Terri took a sip of her wine, making a mental transition. "So how did Mandy and Jerry like their visit at Jennifer's house?"

"They seemed to have enjoyed themselves. She volunteered to keep them tomorrow and help me out, but I refused her offer. I had already arranged for Mandy to stay at Tommy's house and Jerry to spend the day with his friend Archie, who lives in your neighborhood. What's the name of the hotel where you're staying?''

He'd changed subjects without a pause. Terri had taken another sip of wine and had to swallow it before she answered, naming the hotel.

His brief pause before speaking was as eloquent as if he'd said, *Nice accommodations.* "While I'm jotting down information, could you tell me the hospital and your aunt's room number? Also her last name. I would like to send her some flowers, if it's okay with you.''

"That's really sweet, but why don't you wait and send some later? She has several bouquets.''

"Let me make a wild guess. Is one of them a big splashy bouquet from Sommers?''

Terri sighed. "He is acquainted with Aunt Evelyn.''

"The guy doesn't miss a trick.'' His words were quietly bitter. "What color are the roses in the big bouquet he had delivered to your hotel room?''

"The only bouquet in my room is an arrangement of silk flowers that's part of the decor. But there was a gift basket from Christopher when I checked in. His secretary may have ordered it automatically.''

"A gift basket.''

"With wine and fruit and cheese. I'm drinking a glass of the wine, and after I finish talking with you, I may be depressed enough to finish the bottle.''

"I swore to myself I wouldn't bring up Sommers's name when you called tonight. How was the drive to Little Rock?''

"The traffic was light until I got near the city. What did you fix for dinner?''

"I took the kids out to eat at the Front Porch.''

Terri picked up on his note of reluctance. "And?''

"We'd just sat down at a big table with the Petersons and their two kids, when Jennifer walked in by herself. She joined us.''

"How nice for her to have all that company. Did she just happen to squeeze into a spot next to you?"

"Terri, Jennifer has no designs on me."

"Forgive me if I don't have a lot of confidence in your insight into women, Jeremy. Just for the record, I ate my supper alone in the hospital cafeteria."

The silence from his end of the line told her that she'd answered the question in his mind: Had she had dinner with her ex-husband tonight? "I wish I had been there with you," he said.

"I wished the same thing."

"You sound very tired."

"I am. Emotionally and physically. Today was a stressful day, starting off with that terrible scene with Jerry this morning."

"Followed by the key business at lunch." His voice had taken on deep weariness, too.

"Yes. Then the news that Aunt Evelyn was in the hospital. Then having to say goodbye to you and Jerry and Mandy publicly at the station." With Jennifer present.

"I should have come home and gotten them, I suppose." He sighed. "But you saw for yourself that the station was a madhouse. By the way, Pat Tyler—Pat Adams, I should say—came by. It was good to chat with her a few minutes. She said to tell you hi and that she'll definitely invite you and me and the kids out to have fried fish with her and Clint soon."

Terri tried hard to envision the six of them at the Tyler place. The fact that she couldn't brought a dull pain to her chest. "She seemed happy?"

"That's an understatement."

"I'm so glad for her."

"Me, too."

They talked awhile longer, but the dull pain in the region of her heart didn't lessen any.

"I love you and I miss you," Jeremy said when the conversation died away and it was time to say good-night.

"I love you and miss you, too," Terri answered.

The words, sadly, didn't heal the breach of separation.

Chapter Fourteen

"Let's not eat at the table tonight, Dad." Jerry was gathering up place mats as he spoke.

Jeremy continued spooning servings of macaroni and cheese onto three plates, acquiescing to having supper once again seated at the island with his children.

"When's Ms. Sommers coming back?" Mandy asked plaintively as she got forks from a drawer.

"Probably not for several weeks, at least," he replied.

"But that's a long time!"

"Doesn't Ms. Sommers know how long she'll be gone?" Jerry asked, getting milk from the refrigerator.

They'd fallen right back into the old routine.

"It will depend, I'm sure, on how her great-aunt gets along. Today Mrs. Peters had an operation on her hip that was successful. Now she will have to go through a recovery process."

"Ms. Sommers called you at the station and told you

about the operation being successful?'' Jerry inquired, putting two and two together.

"She passed along the news through Kevin. I wasn't there at the time.'' Missing her call had been a huge disappointment in itself, but grilling Kevin had revealed that Terri hadn't passed along a promise to call Jeremy this evening.

"I want to talk to Ms. Sommers, Daddy,'' Mandy said wistfully. She'd climbed up on her regular stool. "Couldn't we phone her after supper?''

Jeremy looked at his son, who met his gaze and shrugged before responding to the unspoken question: *Do you also want to talk to Ms. Sommers?* "I'd kinda like to tell her about that big king snake Archie and I saw behind their woodshed today.'' Jerry's loyalty to his mother still weighed on him, accounting for the hint of reluctance.

"Yuk!'' Mandy shivered, making a face. "Ms. Sommers doesn't want to hear about a snake with a rat in its stomach!''

"I'll bet she would like to hear about it from me!''

As he claimed his stool between his two children, Jeremy knew they both were right. Terri would be horrified by Jerry's boyishly enthusiastic description of a rather grisly example of the workings of nature, but she would listen with fond attention. Jeremy could picture her clearly, and the mental image of her face boosted his morale immensely.

"Before your bedtime, we'll call Ms. Sommers's hotel,'' he said, picking up his fork. In the last minute he'd gotten hungry. "If she's not there, you can each leave a voice-mail message, saying hi to her.''

An explanation of voice mail at a hotel generated discussion while they ate. With a part of his mind, Jeremy was reflecting that he hadn't gotten from Terri the number of her room or the phone number of the hotel, but he could easily obtain the latter.

His children's excitement was contagious. Jeremy was speaking to himself as well as to them when the time came to place the call and he cautioned, "Don't be disappointed if Ms. Sommers doesn't answer. She may still be at the hospital."

He used the cordless phone in the living room, seated on the sofa with Mandy beside him and Jerry on his haunches at Jeremy's feet.

"Would you ring Ms. Terri Sommers's room?" he said to the male hotel employee who answered.

"One moment, please." After a brief pause the desk clerk added, "We have no guest by that name in our hotel, sir."

"I'm quite certain that you do. She called me from your hotel last night."

Another pause. "A Ms. Terri Sommers checked out this morning."

Jeremy hung up, stunned.

"What's wrong, Dad?" Jerry asked.

"Ms. Sommers must have moved to a different hotel." Moved *somewhere.*

"Which hotel, Daddy?" Mandy was on the verge of tears.

"Dad doesn't know," Jerry informed her, his tone glum. He got slowly to his feet. "You think maybe Ms. Sommers decided to stay in that guest house?" His question was addressed to Jeremy.

"She may have."

"Are we still going to call her, Daddy?" Mandy implored.

Again Jeremy's son intervened on his behalf.

"No, we're not going to call her tonight. Maybe another night. Come on, I'll let you play my electronic baseball game."

"You will?" She slid off the sofa and went with him to take advantage of the rare offer.

"Thanks, son," Jeremy said heavily. "I'll be in later to tell you both good-night."

After he'd had a few minutes in which to recover.

Terri hadn't said a word last night about moving elsewhere. What had brought about the move and where had she gone? Why hadn't she passed along the name of her new lodgings via Kevin when she'd called the station at approximately two o'clock that day?

Possibly she'd just forgotten.

Possibly she *hadn't* decided to make use of that key Sommers had left with her two days ago, the key she likewise hadn't mentioned.

Jeremy postponed going to bed until midnight, but Terri didn't call. The next day he stuck close to the telephone at the station, postponing attending to errands and business around town and battling the growing sense that something was terribly wrong. By midafternoon, the waiting had gotten to be too much for him. He placed a long-distance call to the hospital in Little Rock and asked to be connected to Evelyn Peters's room.

A woman answered in a hushed voice and, without identifying herself, informed him that Mrs. Peters was resting. Jeremy guessed that she was a nurse or some other hospital employee.

"I was trying to contact Mrs. Peters's niece, who has been there with her the past couple of days," he explained.

"She isn't here this afternoon."

In the background he heard a much older female voice ask, "Who is it?"

"A gentleman looking for your niece."

"Probably her husband. Tell him she took a break and went shopping."

"I heard," Jeremy said tersely. "Thank you."

He hung up. Something *was* terribly wrong, all right. That something had to do with Sommers, whom Evelyn

Peters hadn't referred to as Terri's *ex*-husband, but her *husband*.

Jeremy knew with a sick certainty that she *had* moved into Sommers's guest house. And now she was out shopping, hardly more than twenty-four hours following her great-aunt's surgery. It hadn't taken long for Jeremy's fears to prove well-founded. Within a couple days of returning to Little Rock, Terri had already succumbed to the attractions of a big-city life-style.

"Damn it! Not *again!*" Jeremy's fist crashed on his desk, and the impact exploded the same combination of anger and pain he'd wrestled with in private for a whole year following Susan's death.

It hit Jeremy that Terri had been partially right when she'd pinpointed his caution as a kind of emotional cowardice. He *hadn't* wanted to expose himself to another devastating loss of a wife.

The insight didn't lessen his anger or his pain.

"Why don't you go shopping this afternoon, dear? Or visit a friend?" Terri's great-aunt had urged during the morning. She had color in her cheeks today and didn't look so gaunt and old. "You were here all day yesterday and came back this morning. I appreciate your company, but you need a break from this dreary hospital."

Terri had decided she did need a break. "Maybe I will do some shopping." For Mandy and Jerry. The thought lifted her spirits.

"Good. Bring your purchases tomorrow and show me."

"I'll be back early in the evening to visit. I'll bring them then."

It would be a way of introducing the subject of becoming a stepmother to Jeremy's children.

The shopping expedition had done wonders for Terri's morale. True to her word, she returned to the hospital, hours later, lugging shopping bags, foot weary but lighthearted

To solve her great-aunt's bafflement, she produced snapshots of Jerry and Mandy and also one of Jeremy.

"A gas station owner," Evelyn Peters mused after Terri had told her about meeting Jeremy and falling for him and his children. Knowing that Evelyn's view of Terri's being a low-paid employee and soiling her hands with menial housework would be the same as Christopher's, she'd glossed over working as Jeremy's attendant and filling in for Mrs. Grambly.

"You'll like him," Terri said. "He's such a fine man."

"I wonder..."

"What?"

"A man called this afternoon, asking for you. An aide answered. I assumed he was Christopher."

"If it was Jeremy, he would surely have left a message had there been an emergency of some kind."

Despite her own words of reassurance to herself, Terri was struck by uneasiness, and soon afterward said goodnight to her great-aunt. Had Jeremy called the hospital trying to locate her? she wondered on the drive to her moderately priced hotel. She wouldn't find a message from him there because he didn't know she'd changed hotels. Somehow she'd failed to mention her intention to do so when she'd phoned him on Tuesday night. Then yesterday she hadn't talked to him. He'd been away from the station when she'd called with a report on Aunt Evelyn's surgery. Last night she'd gone to her room, exhausted, and had lain down on the bed and fallen asleep. It had been eleven-thirty by the time she'd woken up—too late to call his house.

Plus she'd not felt up to another conversation that would leave her feeling as lonely and hopeless as she'd felt the previous night when she'd hung up.

Jerry and Mandy would still be awake tonight, Terri reflected as she rode the elevator up to her floor. The thought of chatting with each one of them as well as with their father roused eagerness. Inside her room, she dropped her shopping bags on the carpet and went directly to the phone.

Jerry answered. His "Hello" seemed subdued, but Terri could hear the TV playing and surmised that he'd picked up the cordless phone in the living room. Probably he'd been engrossed in a program and was merely distracted.

"Hi, how are you?" she said.

"Ms. Sommers." He spoke her name, registering her identity, before he responded to her inquiry. "Oh, I'm okay, I guess. Last night we tried to call you. Dad was going to let Mandy and me say hi. But you weren't staying at the hotel."

Terri's heart sank. "No, I'd moved."

"That's what we figured out. Dad's in Mandy's room helping her pack her suitcase. You want me to get him?"

"Pack her suitcase? Where is she going?"

"We're all going to Memphis tomorrow to visit Grandma and Grandpa Wells. Dad called them this afternoon and told them we were coming. We'll be back Sunday."

Maybe there was more to the sudden trip to Memphis than Jerry knew. Perhaps one of his grandparents was ill, but wouldn't Jeremy have told his children? His policy was parental honesty.

"You don't sound particularly excited about the trip," she remarked.

"It'll probably be fun once we get there." He paused. "Ms. Sommers, could I ask you something?"

"You can ask me anything, Jerry."

"And you'll tell me the truth?"

"I promise I'll tell you the truth."

"If you stay in Little Rock and marry Mr. Sommers again instead of marrying Dad, it won't be because of me, will it?"

"Absolutely not. Whatever the future holds for your father and me, it will be our doing, his and mine."

He sighed. "I hope Dad doesn't blame me."

"I'm certain he won't." There wasn't much else that she was certain about concerning Jeremy at the moment. "Would you get him please?"

A minute crawled past. Terri's nerves were stretched thin by the time Jeremy spoke into the phone with no note of welcome.

"Hi, Terri."

"Jeremy, I apologize for not letting you know I'd moved to a different hotel. Last night I meant to call, but I got to my room and dropped off to sleep. I hadn't slept well on Tuesday night. Jerry tells me you tried to reach me."

"We did." He sounded odd.

"Is something wrong? How did this trip to Memphis suddenly come about?"

"The kids hadn't visited my parents all summer, and I needed to get away. You're at another hotel?"

"One that's not quite so pricey." She named it. Then his question penetrated. "Where did you think I'd gone?"

"I thought—" He broke off.

Terri could finish the sentence for herself. Complete comprehension had dawned, flooding her with a sense of hurt and touching off anger. "You thought I'd taken Christopher up on his offer. You didn't really believe me when I gave you my word on Monday that I wouldn't stay in his guest house. Did you?"

"Not totally," he admitted. "It bothered me that you were secretive about the key."

"I wouldn't have had to be secretive if I could have relied on your having more faith in me. But I've been on trial since the day we met, when you typecast me as a pampered, superficial beauty who in a matter of time would grow bored with small-town life and be drawn back to the big city."

"That's not entirely true! I never considered you superficial." He went on hesitantly, "This afternoon when I called the hospital, I was told you'd gone shopping."

"So that was you who called, looking for me. Yes, I'd gone shopping. Just how did you construe that information? That I'd seized the first opportunity to hit the upscale department stores that were my favorite old haunts? With Christopher's credit cards in hand?"

"There's nothing inherently wrong with liking to shop in upscale department stores. Whatever my faults, I've never been judgmental about you," he offered in his defense.

"No, just *wrong* in assigning me values and understanding who I really am! I'm sick and tired of trying to prove myself to you, Jeremy! Either you want to marry me or you don't! You accused me of trying to invent a grievance so that I could come to Little Rock mad at you. Well you've invented one reason after another that I couldn't possibly make you a good wife!"

"Terri, please calm down—"

"I *won't* calm down! But I'm almost finished with what I have to say. Between now and the time I return to Yellville, I don't want to talk to you on the phone. Our next conversation will be face-to-face, and you'll look me straight in the eye and tell me your decision about *us*, no ifs, ands or buts."

"Okay," he said.

The gentleness in his voice, combined with the fact that he was agreeing not to be in communication, was Terri's total undoing.

"I'm going to hang up," she said.

"Don't, please. I promised Mandy she could say hello to you. Would you hold on while I take the phone to her?"

Tears were running down her face. "Yes."

She struggled for composure while she waited.

"Hi, Ms. Sommers!"

Mandy's childish greeting conveyed her utter delight i

speaking to Terri and released the floodgate of Terri's maternal love for Jeremy's little daughter. "Hi, sweetie. I've missed you a whole bunch. I hear you're going on a trip."

"To Grandma and Grandpa Wells's house. I hope they take us to Mud Island again. It's not really made out of mud, but that's what it's called. You have to ride through the air to get there. What's that called, Daddy?"

Terri heard his reply from nearby. "A monorail."

"Not that blouse. It doesn't go with those pants, Daddy," Mandy admonished before she resumed her chatter.

Obviously Jeremy was continuing to pack her clothes. Terri could visualize him so clearly, and the picture intensified her despair.

He would carry on without her in his life, just as he'd carried on when Susan had died.

"Jerry, time to get up." Jeremy flipped on the light switch and stood in the doorway to make sure his son heeded the wake-up call.

Jerry sat up in bed, blinking sleepily, his blond hair on end. But it was his serene, happy expression that caught Jeremy's attention. "Dad, I dreamed about Mom. She and I had a long talk, and guess what? She thinks you should marry Ms. Sommers. And when I told her about Mandy wanting to call Ms. Sommers 'Mommy,' she didn't mind at all. Get this. She said it would be fine for *me* to call Ms. Sommers 'Mom,' if I wanted to."

Jeremy's throat was tight. He swallowed to free his voice. "I'm not surprised your mother reacted that way in your dream. She was a very special person."

"I don't know yet if I will call Ms. Sommers 'Mom.' But it would be kind of weird if Mandy calls her 'Mommy' and I call her something besides 'Mom.'" He threw back the cover and got out of bed, stretching.

Jeremy didn't miss his son's use of the present tense.

Having dropped the burden of split loyalties from his young soul, Jerry seemed fully optimistic that his father could now marry Terri without further ado, and the four of them could live happily ever after as a family.

I only wish it were that easy, Jeremy thought as he crossed the hall to wake his daughter.

He wanted to be on the road in a half hour. It was going to be a long day of driving.

Terri's heart gave a foolish little leap as she put down her magazine and rose to her feet to answer the telephone in her great-aunt's hospital room. Maybe it was Jeremy calling, ignoring the ground rule she'd laid down.

But it was Christopher's voice, not Jeremy's that came over the line.

"Hi, how's the patient getting along?"

"Her doctor's extremely pleased. She just left in a wheelchair to have some X rays done."

"Is she up to visitors? I thought I'd come by the hospital during visiting hours this evening."

"I'm sure she would enjoy seeing you."

"Are you holding up okay? You sound rather down."

"I'm fine," Terri lied. *Aside from being terribly unhappy.*

"Why don't you let me take you out for a quiet dinner tonight?" he suggested.

"I wouldn't be very good company."

"You *are* feeling down. What's the matter? Problems with Wells? Is absence not making the heart grow fonder, as it were?"

"Problems with Jeremy," she conceded.

"What you need is a broad shoulder to cry on. I'll plan on taking you to dinner. Bye, now, darling. I'm due in court."

With a sigh Terri cradled the phone. She might just have dinner with Christopher rather than eat alone. Tonight she didn't have any reason to hurry back to her hotel room. She couldn't call Jeremy, even if she weakened, because he would be in Memphis visiting his parents. Terri hadn't asked for their telephone number and he hadn't volunteered to give it to her.

Okay, he'd said without any protest when she'd declared she didn't want any further phone conversations with him for the duration of her stay in Little Rock, a period of at least another seven to ten days. How could he have agreed so easily to breaking off all communication? Didn't he yearn to hear her voice, as she yearned to hear his? Wasn't he interested in sharing this time spent away from him, as she was interested in every little detail of his daily routine, and Jerry's and Mandy's, as well?

Apparently not.

"You look pretty," Terri complimented Evelyn Peters.

She'd combed her great-aunt's silver hair and helped her into a pretty bed jacket. Then she'd held a hand mirror while her aunt had applied powder and lipstick, making herself presentable for Christopher's visit.

"Thank you, dear. Why don't you freshen up?"

Terri took her aunt's suggestion, using the mirror in the bathroom to repair the day's damage to her makeup. Before she rejoined Evelyn, she summoned a smile, falling back on her beauty-pageant experience.

A tap sounded on the door approximately fifteen minutes later. Terri went and opened it. Christopher stood outside, holding a beautifully wrapped package.

"Come in," she invited.

"Hi, darling." He paused and kissed her cheek before he entered and presented the package to her great-aunt.

"How lovely!" Evelyn Peters exclaimed when she'd unwrapped it to reveal an expensive gift box of perfume and dusting powder.

She held the box open on her lap, the satin bow carefully

set to one side, while she conversed with Christopher, who questioned her about her accident and subsequent surgery and treatment. Terri sat and mostly observed her ex-husband exerting the full force of his male charm on her elderly great-aunt, primarily for Terri's benefit. She knew he would never have paid her relative a hospital visit out of kindness or fondness.

He'd had no time for Aunt Evelyn when he and Terri were married. On the rare occasion, Terri had talked him into taking her great-aunt out for her birthday with them or inviting her to their home for a holiday, but for the most part Christopher couldn't be bothered with putting himself out for any relative, old or young—any person, for that matter—who didn't engage his interest. That included his own children.

Jeremy was so different, with his rock-solid values, sincerity and decency, not to mention his many other good qualities. He'd spoiled the chance of her being satisfied with any other man as her husband.

And yet if he was to walk in right this moment and find her there with Christopher, he would feel jealous and threatened.

A brisk rap on the door roused Terri from her thoughts. She turned her head as the door was thrust open, and a uniformed aide breezed in.

"Don't mind me," the girl said when Terri and Christopher both stood. "I'll be in and out before you know I'm here. I just need to take Mrs. Peters's temperature and blood pressure."

Christopher glanced at his watch and looked inquiringly at Terri. She nodded and spoke to her great-aunt, "Christopher offered to take me to dinner, Aunt Evelyn. Would you mind if I left now?"

"I would mind," Jeremy stated, his voice coming from the open doorway.

Terri whirled around, not believing her ears. "Jeremy!"

she gasped, staring at him. Was he a mirage, standing there in slacks and shirt and sport jacket, holding a small, potted African violet? ''What are you doing here?'' she asked stupidly.

''I came to meet your aunt Evelyn. And to ask you to be my wife.''

He walked toward her, and she went to meet him, incredulity giving way to joy.

''Hi,'' he said softly, looking into her eyes. He kissed her on the lips and then, with an arm around her shoulders, nodded to Christopher, who'd come up behind her. ''Sommers.''

''Wells.'' Christopher's voice was flat. ''I was just leaving.''

''Don't let me hold you up.''

''Goodbye, Christopher,'' Terri said. ''It was kind of you to visit Aunt Evelyn and bring her a present.''

''Goodbye, Terri. I'll be in touch.'' With those words of sheer bravado, he departed. Terri was quite certain that she wouldn't be hearing from him again. Christopher realized, finally, that he wasn't the man in her future. Jeremy was.

''Where are the kids?' she asked, eager to focus all her attention on Jeremy, on that bright and wonderful future.

''In Memphis with my parents. My mother will drive them back to Yellville on Sunday and stay a week or two. However long you need to be away.''

''You drove to Memphis and then came to Little Rock.'' Terri was still marveling at his presence, which explained why he'd agreed to no phone calls the previous night. He was counting on talking to her in person.

''I didn't want to put off that face-to-face conversation with no *ifs, ands,* or *buts,*'' he stated.

They gazed at each other, silently conducting the conversation that brooked no reservations or conditions.

I want you to be my wife more than anything, his eyes said. *Will you still marry me?*

Oh, yes! Terri answered without words, her heart overflowing with happiness.

"Is that lovely plant for me, by any chance?" inquired Evelyn Peters with an indulgent note. "I certainly hope so, because I do love African violets."

Terri drew Jeremy over closer to her great-aunt's bed to introduce him, noticing that Christopher's expensive gift box with elegant wrapping paper and bow had disappeared in the meanwhile. The aide, who had completed her routine medical procedures, breezed out with a grin on her face and closed the door behind her.

"Put my plant right here on the table next to me, would you, dear?" Evelyn requested of her niece after she'd graciously accepted the plant from Jeremy and admired the exquisite pink blossoms.

Terri did as she was bade and then moved back quickly to stand close to Jeremy and slip her hand in his. He was speaking to her great-aunt.

"How are you getting along?"

"Quite well, thank you. My niece has been right here with me. Her company works better than pain medication." She smiled warmly at Terri. "I think I'll get some rest now, dear. I'm a little tired." Then she asked Jeremy, "Will you come and visit me tomorrow? I'd like to get better acquainted with you."

Terri looked to him for his answer, too. He squeezed her hand as he replied in his sincere way, "I'll be visiting you every day for the next few days. I plan to be in Little Rock through Sunday afternoon."

"You do?" Terri breathed delightedly.

"How nice," Evelyn said. "Now, you two go and have yourselves a nice dinner. Terri, dear, I won't be expecting to see you before ten o'clock in the morning."

Terri kissed her great-aunt on the cheek, letting her smile say, *Thank you for cutting Jeremy's visit short tonight.*

The corridors outside were too busy to allow for privacy

as she and Jeremy headed for the elevator, but Terri's yearning to feel his arms around her slowed her steps as they reached an alcove with coin machines containing drinks and snacks. His steps slowed automatically, too, and he drew her out of the traffic.

"God, I missed you," he said, hugging her tightly.

Terri was hugging him back. "I missed you terribly. Three whole days together. It's too good to be true."

"Excuse me," a woman said.

They moved in tandem so that they weren't blocking her access to the closest machine, neither of them glancing at her.

"You think we could squeeze in some shopping at a jewelry store?" Jeremy asked. "I want to buy your wedding rings."

"Wedding ring, singular. One that matches the ring I buy for you."

They looked into each other's eyes, then kissed tenderly.

"Excuse me," said a man with a touch of impatience. "You're blocking the coffee machine."

"Sorry," they apologized, speaking absently in unison. Jeremy ushered her back into the corridor, and arm in arm they walked along, closely in tune.

"I bought the most adorable dress for Mandy yesterday," Terri confided. "It will be perfect for her to wear to our wedding."

"She'll put up a fuss to do her flower girl performance again," he warned ruefully.

"We'll let her scatter a few petals if it'll make her happy."

"In that case, you'd better plan on having Jerry act as ring bearer."

"Do you think he'll want to?"

"I know so. My son has made peace with the idea of you taking his mother's place in my life and his. His decision now is what to call you. It won't surprise me if he settles on 'Mom.'"

"What happened?"

"He had a dream in which his mother gave her okay. You should have seen him this morning. He looked as though the world had rolled off his shoulders."

Terri visualized the photograph of Susan Wells and felt warm gratitude. *Thank you, Susan, for the vote of confidence.*

"How do you feel about my kids calling you 'Mom'?" Jeremy asked.

"How would I feel? Humble. Thrilled. How do you feel about it?"

"The way I feel about having you in my life—incredibly blessed."

His answer, spoken simply and fervently, brought tears to her eyes.

They'd reached the elevators, where a dozen people stood, waiting. Terri wouldn't have cared if there had been ten times that many. She turned to Jeremy and hugged him around the waist. He hugged her back.

"I love you," she gulped out.

"I love you."

This time the words carried the magic of trust and commitment.

The doors of several elevators opened. Jeremy ushered her into one of them and they rode down to the lobby. In the parking lot he led her toward his van.

"I've been doing a lot of thinking last night and today," he said. "Why don't we give ourselves a year to decide if we want to continue living in Yellville?"

"Jeremy, I wouldn't uproot you and Jerry and Mandy!"

"Hear me out. We could move to a suburb closer to a city, including Little Rock. I could buy another gas station or open up a different business. The children are young enough to make the transition easily."

"I expect to be content and happy in Yellville."

"In a year we'll know if you are. It's an option. We're not locked in."

Terri was all but certain she wouldn't want to move in a year, but she loved him that much more for being willing to sell his business and home and relocate to a more urban environment for her.

Epilogue

Jeremy was whistling a tune as he entered the kitchen. He stopped in the middle of a note and said in surprise, "Sweetheart, I thought we were going to a movie and out to dinner tonight."

Terri finished fitting a taper into a crystal candlestick and set the candlestick in place on the table, which was draped with a tablecloth and set elegantly for two. "I decided I'd rather have a romantic evening at home. Do you mind?" She could hear her own hint of nervousness.

"Mind? That change of plans suits me to a tee. We'll have the house to ourselves, since the kids are staying overnight with friends." He came over and took her into his arms and kissed her. Still holding her, he surveyed the table. "Wineglasses. Fresh flowers. Candles. Our anniversary isn't until next month. Today's not some other significant day, is it?"

"Not a significant day that you were supposed to remember and buy me a present for," she answered, patting him on the cheek. "But it *is* a kind of anniversary. Last year in late August you came to Little Rock when Aunt Evelyn was in the hospital. We spent those three wonderful days together, bought our wedding rings and generally came to an understanding about almost everything of importance."

"Almost everything," he repeated. "Tonight are we going to cover something we missed?"

Terri's throat was dry. "Yes. But in the course of conversation."

"All right."

He released her, his expression thoughtful. She knew he was already going over in his mind the many discussions they'd had a year ago and trying to figure out what had been omitted.

"I'll go shower and change clothes."

When he returned, dressed as though they were going out to dinner in a nice restaurant, the slightly puzzled look was still on his face, but he didn't question her. He opened the bottle of red wine Terri had set out and poured wine into their glasses, while she served their salads. She'd lit the candles.

After he'd seated her and sat down, he picked up his fork and began eating, obviously waiting for her to begin the conversation.

"Speaking of Aunt Evelyn," Terri said, "I received a lovely thank-you card from her today with a note saying how much she'd enjoyed her week's visit with us."

Jeremy seemed to mull over her words. "I know I've said at least a couple of times, sweetheart, that your great-aunt was welcome to come and live with us. We could build an addition onto the house."

"That wasn't a lead-in, Jeremy. It was just dinner conversation."

"Oh."

"Let's just talk normally. Don't look for clues. Did y[ou] learn any interesting news at the station today?"

"Interesting news." He thought. "Oh, I did learn son[e] good news, but you must already know it. Pat Adams can[e] by the station and told me she's pregnant. She'd alrea[dy] seen you at the supermarket earlier, so undoubtedly she to[ld] you, too."

Terri nodded. Her heart was beating fast. "Pat didn[']t mention that she intended to go by the station. That w[as] news I was going to tell you when my turn came."

"She bought a case of motor oil. I sell it to her at n[y] cost, as you're aware. In past years she picked up a ca[se] every couple of weeks, but Clint has their vehicles in to[p] notch running condition so that the engines don't burn [a] lot of oil."

"Apparently he's tickled pink over their having a baby[.]"

"I would expect him to be tickled." He seemed abo[ut] to add something and then didn't.

"What?" she pressed.

"Nothing important."

"I would like to hear it anyway."

"It was just one of those comments that slip out and c[an] be misinterpreted. I almost said, 'I would be tickled, too.[']"

"And you classify that statement as 'nothing imp[or]tant'?" Terri demanded, a hurt note in her voice.

Jeremy blinked in surprise. Suddenly he went still a[nd] then carefully put down his fork. "During our discussi[on] a year ago we didn't ever touch on whether we would h[ave] another child, did we?"

"No, we didn't. And since then, the subject has ne[ver] come up."

"I have from time to time wondered if we would, b[ut] left it to you to bring the subject up. For all I knew, y[ou] might consider two children enough responsibility."

"I left it to *you* to bring the subject up. For all I kn[ew] you might not want to go through having a pregnant w[ife] for a third time. You might not look forward to having an infant in the house again. It would certainly be understandable if you'd had your share of changing diapers and were perfectly happy being a father of two.''

Jeremy reached his hands across the table and Terri gave him her hands. He clasped them tightly. "Terri, were you afraid to bring up having a baby? Afraid I wouldn't be in favor of it?" he asked gently.

"Yes." The admission came out barely louder than a whisper. "I didn't doubt for a moment you would go along with the idea if it was something I wanted that would make me happy."

"And I didn't doubt that you would go along with the idea if you thought it was something that would make me happy. I guess neither of us wanted the other just to 'go along with the idea.' So we didn't say anything. Personally, I would love for us to have a baby."

"So would I." She sighed happily. "We can wait a year or so until you think it's a good time. I'm not pushing to get pregnant immediately."

Jeremy released her hands and stood up. Terri eyed him in bewilderment as he picked up her salad and his and carried them to the refrigerator.

"Have you lost your appetite?" she asked.

"Let's rearrange your romantic evening at home and eat later. You mind?" He closed the refrigerator door after placing the salads on a shelf and came to stand behind her chair.

"Not at all," Terri murmured when he bent and kissed her neck. "I'll blow out the candles and relight them."

"Otherwise they'll be burned down to stubs. Making a baby isn't something that can be hurried."

"Are we making a baby tonight?"

"Why wait? Wouldn't it be nice to give Pat and Clint's little son or daughter a playmate?"

He pulled back her chair. She rose and turned towa
him and went into his arms, heart brimming with love.

"I can't think of anything nicer," she replied deligh
edly.

As she returned his tender, passionate kiss, the thoug
occurred to Terri, *I hope happiness makes a woman ferti.*
Because if that was the case, she couldn't possibly fail
conceive.

* * * * *

COMING THIS OCTOBER 1997 FROM

THREE NEW LOVE STORIES IN ONE VOLUME BY
ONE OF AMERICA'S MOST BELOVED WRITERS

DEBBIE MACOMBER

Three Brides, No Groom

Gretchen, Maddie and Carol—they were three college
friends with plans to become blushing brides. But
even though the caterers were booked, the bouquets
bought and the bridal gowns were ready to wear...the
grooms suddenly got cold feet. And that's when these
three women decided they weren't going to get mad...
they were going to get even!

DON'T MISS THE WARMTH, THE HUMOR...THE
ROMANCE AS ONLY DEBBIE MACOMBER CAN DO!

AVAILABLE WHEREVER SILHOUETTE BOOKS
ARE SOLD.   TBNG-S

SOME TEMPTATIONS CANNOT BE DENIED.

Kate Moran: she's a woman who has everything—a man who wants to spend the rest of his life with her, a job she loves, a home and a family—until she's tempted by the forbidden.

Gareth Blackstone: Solid and dependable, he's ready to lay down foundations for a life with the woman he loves.

Nick Blackstone: He's returned home to Eden, Indiana, to confront the tragedy of his past. But his return would jeopardize all of their futures.

HOME TO EDEN

bestselling author

DALLAS SCHULZE

The homecoming begins in September 1997
at your favorite retail outlet.

MIRA The brightest star in women's fiction

Look us up on-line at: http://www.romance.net

MDSHTE

Silhouette is proud to introduce
the newest compelling miniseries by
award-winning author

SUSAN MALLERY

TRIPLE TROUBLE

Kayla, Elissa and Fallon—three identical triplet sisters are all grown up and ready to take on the world!

****

In August: **THE GIRL OF HIS DREAMS (SE#1118)**

Could it be Prince Charming was right in front of her all along? But how was Kayla going to convince her best friend that she was the girl of his dreams?

In September: **THE SECRET WIFE (SE#1123)**

That Special Woman Elissa wasn't ready to throw in the towel on her marriage, and she set out to show her husband just how good love could be the second time around!

In October: **THE MYSTERIOUS STRANGER (SE#1130)**

When an accident causes her to wash up on shore, the handsome man who finds her has no choice but to take in this mysterious woman without a memory!

Don't miss these exciting novels...only from

Silhouette® SPECIAL EDITION®

Look us up on-line at: http://www.romance.net TRIPLE

Daniel MacGregor is at it again…

New York Times bestselling author

NORA ROBERTS

introduces us to a new generation of MacGregors
as the lovable patriarch of the illustrious MacGregor
clan plays matchmaker again, this time to his three
gorgeous granddaughters in

THE
MACGREGOR
BRIDES

From Silhouette Books

Don't miss this brand-new continuation of Nora Roberts's
enormously popular *MacGregor* miniseries.

Available November 1997 at your favorite retail outlet.

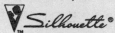

Silhouette®

Look us up on-line at: http://www.romance.net   NRMB-S

**These delightful titles are coming soon to
THAT SPECIAL WOMAN!—only from
Silhouette Special Edition!**

**September 1997   THE SECRET WIFE
                    by Susan Mallery (SE#1123)**

Five years ago Elissa's dreams came true when she married
her true love—but their honeymoon was short-lived. Could
she and Cole Stephenson get a second shot at happiness?

**November 1997   WHITE WOLF
                    by Lindsay McKenna (SE#1135)**

Hard-core cynic Dain Phillips turned to mystical medicine
woman Erin Wolf for a "miracle" cure. But he never suspected
that Erin's spiritual healing would alter him—body and soul!

**January 1998   TENDERLY
                    by Cheryl Reavis (SE#1147)**

Socialite Eden Trevoy was powerfully drawn to Navajo
policeman Ben Toomey when he helped her uncover her half-
Navajo roots. Could her journey of self-discovery lead to full-
fledged love?

**IT TAKES A VERY SPECIAL MAN TO WIN THAT
SPECIAL WOMAN....** Don't miss THAT SPECIAL WOMAN!
every other month from some of your favorite authors!

Look us up on-line at: http://www.romance.net   TSWA-D

National Bestselling Author

MARY LYNN BAXTER

"Ms. Baxter's writing…strikes every chord within the
female spirit."   —Sandra Brown

LONE STAR *Heat*

SHE is Juliana Reed, a prominent broadcast journalist whose
television show is about to be syndicated. Until the murder…

HE is Gates O'Brien, a high-ranking member of the
Texas Rangers, determined to forget about his ex-wife. He's
onto something bad….

Juliana and Gates are ex-spouses, unwillingly involved in an
explosive circle of political corruption, blackmail and murder.

In order to survive, they must overcome the pain of the past…and
the very demons that drove them apart.

Available in September 1997 at your favorite retail outlet.

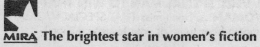

MIRA The brightest star in women's fiction   MMLBLSH

Look us up on-line at:http://www.romance.net

DIANA WHITNEY

Continues the twelve-book
series 36 HOURS in
September 1997
with Book Three

OOH BABY, BABY

In the back of a cab, in the midst of a disastrous storm,
Travis Stockwell delivered Peggy Saxon's two precious babies
and, for a moment, they felt like a family. But Travis was a
wandering cowboy, and a fine woman like Peggy was better off
without him. Still, she and her adorable twins had tugged on
his heartstrings, until now he wasn't so sure that *he* was
better off without *her*.

For Travis and Peggy and *all* the residents of Grand Springs,
Colorado, the storm-induced blackout was just the beginning
of 36 Hours that changed *everything!* You won't want to miss a
single book.

Look us up on-line at: http://www.romance.net   36HRS3

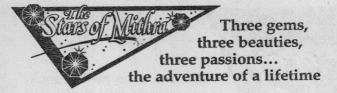

Three gems, three beauties, three passions... the adventure of a lifetime

SILHOUETTE·INTIMATE·MOMENTS®
brings you a thrilling new series by
New York Times bestselling author

Nora Roberts

Three mystical blue diamonds place three close friends in jeopardy...and lead them to romance.

In October
HIDDEN STAR (IM#811)
Bailey James can't remember a thing, but she knows she's in big trouble. And she desperately needs private investigator Cade Parris to help her live long enough to find out just what kind.

In December
CAPTIVE STAR (IM#823)
Cynical bounty hunter Jack Dakota and spitfire M. J. O'Leary are handcuffed together and on the run from a pair of hired killers. And Jack wants to know why—but M.J.'s not talking.

In February
SECRET STAR (IM#835)
Lieutenant Seth Buchanan's murder investigation takes a strange turn when Grace Fontaine turns up alive. But as the mystery unfolds, he soon discovers the notorious heiress is the biggest mystery of all.

Available at your favorite retail outlet.

Look us up on-line at: http://www.romance.net   MITHRA